Imogen, Obviously

Imogen, Obviously

BECKY ALBERTALLI

BALZER + BRAY

An Imprint of HarperCollins*Publishers*

Balzer + Bray is an imprint of HarperCollins Publishers.

Imogen, Obviously
www.epicreads.com

Library of Congress Control Number: 2022952461
ISBN 978-0-06-304587-3 (trade bdg.) — 978-0-06-332526-5 (int.)

Typography by Jenna Stempel-Lobell
23 24 25 26 27 LBC 5 4 3 2 1

First Edition

For Sophie Gonzales, who made space.

DAY ONE
FRIDAY
MARCH 18

1

I haven't quite unclicked my seat belt, but I'm getting there. Obviously. Just waiting for my brain to stop doing the thing where I'm being interviewed on a talk show in front of a vaguely hostile live studio audience.

Imogen, is it true that it's your first time visiting Lili on campus, even though she's one of your two (2) best friends, and she's invited you fifteen billion times, and Blackwell College is so close to your house, you literally drove by it last weekend going to Wegmans?

Gretchen raises her eyebrows at me from the driver's seat. "Want us to hang for a sec?"

"Or more than a sec," adds Edith, and I twist around to look at her. She's buckled in, legs crossed, denim jacket spread over her lap like a blanket. Bright blue eyes and wind-ruffled curls. My hair's two shades darker and a little straighter, but besides that, we're almost identical. Everyone thinks so.

Otávio's back there, too, playing a game on his phone. This

campus isn't much of a novelty for him at this point—he and his parents come up here a lot, even just to take Lili and her friends out to dinner. But this time, he's just along for the ride. I'm the only one who's staying.

For three nights. Approximately sixty-five hours. Not that I'm counting.

"I'm good." I tack on a smile. "I don't want you getting caught in rush hour."

"I don't give a shit about rush hour," says Gretchen.

I know she really means it, too. I didn't tell Gretchen my parents needed both cars this weekend. She just caught me checking the Yates Transit bus schedule and swept in for the rescue. Say what you want about Gretchen Patterson, but she's a drop-everything kind of friend, through and through.

"I can't believe you're meeting Lili's queer college friends." Edith stares out the window, puffs her cheeks out, and sighs. "I want queer friends."

Gretchen blinks. "Um. Hello?"

"See, but you're more of a mentor," says Edith.

I breathe in. "Okay, texting Lili now."

"Are you *sure* you don't want—"

"Yup!"

Edith claps. "Look at you. Lone wolf, living up to your badass reputation."

Right, so now I'm trying to picture the alternate universe where my reputation falls anywhere in the vicinity of badass. Like, let's just put that in bold for a minute. **Imogen Scott:**

4

badass. It barely even makes sense as a concept. I'm the kind of person who has a favorite adverb (*obviously*, obviously).

Edith, on the other hand.

I mean, our baby pictures tell the story. Like the one from the Yates County Fair animal barn, where I'm standing next to an all-caps sign that reads: PLEASE DO NOT PET DONKEY!!!!!

Edith is in the corner of the frame, petting the donkey.

Or the one of me at an easel, carefully painting a blue stripe for a sky. Edith is crouched beside me in a diaper, chest fully covered in her own tiny green handprints. And of course, there's a whole series from my seventh birthday where Edith is literally dressed like Jason from *Friday the 13th*.

To be fair, my birthday is Halloween. But.

It was noon. And she was five.

She springs out of the back seat as soon as I open the passenger door—as if Otávio Cardoso, certified teddy bear, is going to fight her for shotgun. But instead of moving up to the front, she follows me around to the trunk of Gretchen's car.

"Immy, hear me out. As your big sister—"

"That's factually inaccurate—"

"Chronologically? Sure," she says. "But spiritually? Aesthetically?"

In effect, Edith's a modern-day Amy March. Whereas I fall squarely in the category of Wants-to-Be-Jo, Is-Actually-Meg.

"All I'm saying is, the whole point of college—"

"According to you, a junior in high school."

"*The whole point of college,*" she repeats, "is that it's a chance to break out of your comfort zone. I've given this a lot of thought, and—Immy, I really think you should give up flossing for the weekend."

"The point of college . . . is me not flossing."

"Exactly."

I hoist my suitcase out of Gretchen's trunk and pull the door shut. "I'll take it under advisement."

"Also, I think you could use a few spontaneous campus high jinks."

"Mmm."

"This is spring break! At college! With cool queer people!"

"You know we have queer people in Penn Yan, right? A whole club of them?" I tilt my palms up. "You could try—I don't know—actually going to one of the meetings sometime?"

She shakes her head. "Can't do Tuesdays."

Edith has a standing Zoom date with her girlfriend on Tuesdays. And on days that aren't Tuesdays. But even before Zora, she always managed to find a reason to avoid Pride Alliance. Meanwhile, I've been to almost every single meeting since freshman year, as the group's only capital-*A* Ally. Or I *was*, until Otávio joined at the beginning of this school year, after Lili came out. Everyone in the group lost their minds about Otávio. *Woke king, brother of the year,* et cetera. Kind of funny, I guess. People still seem confused about why I'm there.

For a while, I was worried I *shouldn't* be there. I spent weeks reading every blog post and Reddit forum I could find about allies and safe spaces, and whether it was even okay for me to show up at the meetings. Was I just another straight girl invading queer territory? Was I an outsider, sucking all the oxygen from the room? The discourse offered no clear consensus. I hated that—hated the lack of certainty. My mind never really settles in a new space until I know all the rules for engagement. What's encouraged, what's allowed—or even what's not allowed. Because restriction carries its own kind of safety.

Well, I knew I was *technically* allowed to be there. At least according to the official guidelines for extracurricular groups, as outlined in the Penn Yan High School student handbook. And of course I knew how important it was to Gretchen, given everything that happened in the queer club at her old school. Not that she'd ever outright admit this, but I think we both know I'm her emotional support hetero.

I just feel a little unworthy sometimes—too normie, too distinctly unqueer. Like when Gretchen calls Otávio and me "heteropotamuses," or when people can't even ask us our snack preferences without saying they're "conferring with the straights."

My phone buzzes with a text from Lili. *You're here!!!!!! And I'm coming!!! give me like five min!!!!!!*

By now, Gretchen and Otávio have already stepped out of the car to join us. I shake my head. "Seriously, this is already so above and beyond—"

"Hush." Gretchen takes my suitcase and starts rolling it to the edge of the parking lot, the rest of us trailing behind her. When we reach a sidewalk, she stops to survey the space—a small, grassy quad tucked behind a cluster of brick buildings. No sign of Lili yet, which isn't all that surprising. Lili's always running "five minutes" behind, which sometimes means five minutes and sometimes means she just woke up, still needs to get dressed, and she *wishes* that would take five minutes.

A bunch of students spill out of one of the buildings—bright-faced and boisterous, full weekend mode. Gretchen leans in, studying them so intently, I half expect her to scribble down field notes. Maybe that's what I should be doing—observing real college kids in their natural habitat.

After all, in less than six months, I'll be one of them. At this very school, even.

That part doesn't feel real yet—though, in fairness, it's only been a week since I accepted Blackwell's offer. Gretchen thinks I'm playing things too safe, sticking too close to home—but once the scholarship money came through, it wasn't really a question. The location's just a bonus.

"Oh ho ho." Gretchen nudges me sideways, eyes still locked straight ahead. "Found one."

"One of what?"

"College guy."

"They do tend to have those on college campuses—"

She laughs. "I mean a *cute* college guy. Hottie with a body."

"Not a disembodied head. Got it."

Edith leans in, following Gretchen's gaze. "What are we looking at?"

"Gray shirt, white hat. That's Imogen's spring break fling—"

8

"Um. What?"

Edith looks delighted. "Do we know him?"

"Absolutely not."

"Not *yet*—but we will! Let's call him Bruce. Or Bryce?" Gretchen tilts her head. "Bruce. I'm thinking . . . sophomore. And he's from somewhere cool."

Otávio looks up from his phone. "Who's Bruce?"

"MAINE. He's from Maine."

I blink. "Is Maine cool?"

"And he likes lobsters. Because he's from Maine." Gretchen shrugs. "Sorry, that's all I know about Maine."

"Mmm. Are we done?"

"WAIT. No. No. Hold up." Gretchen presses both hands to her cheeks. "New target. Okay. Okay, just stepped out of the second door. Not the facial hair guy. Green hoodie, next to the girl—"

"Even better. Guy with a girlfriend."

"A girlfriend wearing a carabiner and a thumb ring?"

I bite my lip. "Maybe?"

"Hey—sorry! Hi! I'm here!" Lili skids to a stop on the sidewalk, sneakers only halfway on her feet. She hugs me, hugs Edith, ruffles Otávio's hair, and then hugs him, too. Then she turns stiffly to Gretchen. "Hi."

"Hi." Gretchen nods.

Lili claps. "Okay! Should we . . ."

"Yes! Okay, um. See you guys at home?" I say. "Gretch, really, thank you for driving."

"No prob. Hey." Gretchen meets my gaze. "You good?"

"Yeah. Yup! Of course."

Lili rolls her eyes faintly and reaches for my suitcase.

Gretchen hugs me. "Tell Bruce we say hi, okay?"

"And no flossing," Edith adds, her dimple flashing with even the quickest of smiles. Just like mine does.

Texts with Gretchen

GP: Okay we're off!! Have FUN!!!

GP: And take lots of pictures with your man!!!! 🦞 🦞 🦞

GP: Ok but seriously, let me know if you need a rescue

GP: I can swing back and pick you up, for real

GP: I don't leave til tomorrow morning

GP: anyway, I love you, have fun at COLLEGE

2

"Rescue?" Lili's eyes narrow. "From *me*?"

"Oh, no—I think she just means, like. College." I gesture vaguely toward campus.

Lili stops short. "Hey. Are you worried?"

"No! I'm fine. I'm good! Just Gretchen being Gretchen."

"Yeah. She's extremely Gretchen." Lili veers us down a winding concrete path. "Anyway. Hi! This is Blackwell!"

"Hi, Blackwell!"

It's my first real glimpse of campus. My future home.

I mean, I've passed it hundreds of times. Dad even drove me up and down the side streets once. But that was more like peeking into someone's house through a ground floor window. This is like stepping into the foyer.

Lili's already playing tour guide. "That's the central quad, and that brick building is the new performing arts center."

"Wow. It's so . . ." I trail off, gaze landing on a gray stone building, wrapped in vines. "It's like a fairy-tale cottage."

She laughs. "That's the registrar's office."

"It's too pretty!"

"Now you know why I've been on your ass to visit!"

"I know. I know—"

"But, hey—at least you've visited me the exact same number of times as Gretchen!"

My cheeks go warm. "No, I know. Lili, I'm sorry—"

"I'm kidding." Lili shoots me a wry glance. "It's fine, okay?"

"Yeah. No, I'm just." I swallow. "Everything got so crazy, with applications and homework, and the car stuff. And then Nana's wrist—"

"Right. No, Immy, I get it. Seriously."

"I just don't want you to think I didn't—"

"I don't! Really. I'm just glad you're here." She smiles. "It's going to be perfect."

And maybe it will be. Maybe it'll be one big extended sleepover, just like when we were kids. We used to spend entire weekends together—building fairy houses, playing Mario Kart, getting ice cream at Seneca Farms. In the summer, we'd basically just go back and forth between my house and hers, like it was some kind of joint custody arrangement.

I had entire rituals at Lili's house. I was such an early bird when I was little—up and wide awake before six in the morning, even though Lili and Otávio slept until at least nine or ten in the summers and on weekends. But those mornings were some of the best times of all. I'd tiptoe downstairs in my pajama shorts, Lili's beagle mix, Mel, trailing behind me. Lili's parents were almost always up by then, and Lili's dad would say, "Bom dia, querida!" He'd make me milky coffee with lots of sugar before disappearing with a book. Then I'd settle in on the couch with Mel and Lili's mom, and usually we'd get through an entire movie before Lili came down. It's how I found most of my favorites—*But I'm a Cheerleader, Clueless, Reality Bites.* Basically every nineties rom-com ever made. Lili's mom used to watch them on VHS after she moved to New York, when she was trying to master colloquial English.

The point is, Lili and I are really more like cousins than friends, which is why visiting her at college should feel like picking up where we left off. Like unpausing a movie. But now that I'm here, I'm wondering if the pause even happened. Maybe I stopped and everything else just kept going.

"Oh, this is kind of cool," Lili says. "There's, like, this whole network of underground tunnels connecting the buildings on this side of campus."

"Like a storm shelter?"

"You could probably use them for that." She stops at a bench, propping her foot up. "I don't know why they were built. You're not even really supposed to go down there—you have to find someone who knows which specific doors are unlocked."

"So it's like a secret society?"

Lili laughs, tugging the back of her shoe up over her heel. "Totally not. Do you remember my friend Tessa?"

My mind conjures the image of a ponytailed girl in boyish plaid—present in so many of Lili's photos, it's pretty clear they're best friends. I guess she's kind of the new and improved me.

"Her brother's a junior here, and he brought us down there last semester. It's so cool. And creepy. But cool-creepy. The walls are covered in graffiti, but it's all from the eighties and nineties. It's like a time capsule."

Lili smiles back at me so easily, it makes my chest tug. I don't think I've ever seen her this wide-open. I mean, maybe at home, when it's just the four of us—her, me, Edith, and Otávio. But never at school. Even though she had a whole group of friends from her grade, she never seemed to fully relax around them.

Here, though—she's smiling and waving at acquaintances as we pass them, saying, "That's Clara from my philosophy class," or, "Okay, so Mika actually did a TikTok collab with that guy—forgot his name, but it was the one with the little candy house. Did you see that one?"

I did. Three times, and I texted it to Gretchen, too.

Lili's friend Mika is sort of TikTok famous—mostly for creating these really detailed dioramas and using a green screen video app to make it look like they're dancing inside them. I can barely wrap my head around the fact that Lili's friends with an actual celebrity. Though all of Lili's friends are basically celebrities to me, from her stories and pictures alone.

Lili veers off the quad, leading me down one of the residential streets near campus—mostly frat houses with giant Greek letters on display, populated by shirtless guys on lawn chairs.

All of whom seem to have missed the memo that it's March in upstate New York.

She stops in front of a slatted wood house with colorful flags draped from most of the windows. "So . . . this is Rainbow Manor. It's kind of the queer frat house? People live here, but they also do events and community outreach work. Stuff like that." She shoots me the quickest half smile. "And they throw the best parties."

It's like stepping into an alternate universe—sorry, but I've known Lili Cardoso since she was three years old, and parties are her personal hell. This is a girl who carried thick, dog-eared Tamora Pierce books all around camp every summer, just in case there was unexpected free time and someone tried to talk to her.

It must be different with her college friends. Her so-called pack of queers. They found each other at an orientation-week mixer, and they've been a ride-or-die squad ever since. Lili's first real queer friendships.

I'm really happy for her. Obviously.

Even if I feel a little far away from her sometimes.

It's hard to explain, because it's not like she's trying to phase me out. I've lost track of how many times she's invited me to crash in her dorm for a weekend. And when her roommate moved off campus after winter break, it was basically a standing invitation.

I really meant to take her up on it.

But sometimes I get in my head about things like this. I

think it's the way Lili talks about this place—not a trace of snark or cynicism. Pure marshmallow. I know it's a good thing, but it's a little unnerving. It's like her whole life clicked into place as soon as she left.

Which makes me the backstory. A relic of Lili's heteronormative small-town childhood. I even look the part—a cardigan that's almost as long as my skirt, my sandy-brown ponytail bobby-pinned on the sides. Even my purse looks a little too hometown preppy—a miniature crossbody satchel in brown fake leather.

Maybe this would be easier if I looked like Gretchen—cotton-candy pink hair and a wardrobe ripped straight from the set of *Euphoria*.

"For real, are you okay?" Lili asks. "You're eerily quiet."

I blink. "Oh! Sor—"

"Don't apologize—I'm just saying. Also, we're home!" Lili gestures at a trio of brick buildings arranged around a cozy grass courtyard. "The middle one's Rosewood—that's us. But all three are mostly freshmen."

I pause to take it all in. The three structures—mismatched but complementary, connected by a network of intersecting paths. Everywhere I look, there are students on benches, on blankets, roaming in packs of two or three or six, with messenger bags and backpacks. Absolutely none of them look like freshmen. They look years and years older than me.

"Let's drop off your bag," Lili says. "Are you hungry? When do you want to eat?"

"Whenever—"

"Immy, no. Don't do the people-pleasing thing."

"I'm not!"

"You are!"

"Well, I don't mean to!"

"Yeah, I know." She laughs a little, then exhales. "Sorry."

"No, *I'm* sorry—"

"Or not! Let's just not. We're not sorry. We're remorseless. Got it?" She hugs me sideways.

I grin. "Got it."

We've barely taken two steps toward the dorm when a guy sneaks up behind Lili, covering her eyes with his hands. "Guess who!"

Lili doesn't even pause. "Declan, meet—"

"Imogen!" He kisses my cheek. "Finally."

He breaks into a smile, revealing a tiny gap between his front teeth, and for a moment, I'm speechless. I know him from Lili's pictures, of course—this runway model of a boy. He's white, with icy-blond hair and an angular face. Meeting him in person really does feel like a celebrity encounter.

Except for the part where he recognized me, too. I don't know why it didn't occur to me that I might exist to Lili's new friends the same way they exist to me.

Declan grabs my suitcase, brushing off my startled thanks. "Babe, we've been *waiting*. We've heard quite a lot about you."

I glance sideways at Lili. "Oh yeah?"

"I talked some serious shit," she says. "They hate your guts now."

"Not even close." He turns to me, lowering his voice to a stage whisper. "Don't worry, I tune out every time she starts talking—"

Lili shoves him. "Hey, what's the plan for dinner?"

"Funny you should ask! We were just about to head to Winterfield. Hoping to 'beat the rush,' as the young folk say."

"Oh, those young folk. Always beating the rush. What a smoking-hot new slang expression."

Declan laughs, opening his mouth to respond, but he's interrupted by a pair of new arrivals—Mika and Kayla. And it's that same unnerving déjà vu.

I recognize Mika from TikTok, of course. They're Japanese American and nonbinary, styled with their own blend of masculine and feminine aesthetics—soft-glam makeup and hair barrettes, boy-cut jeans, and a bird-printed button-down. I think Lili told me they're from the Minneapolis suburbs. It's still so strange to me that someone in Minnesota would even have upstate New York on their radar. Kayla being from Albany makes a little more sense. She's tall and lanky, with deep brown skin, angular cheekbones, and Sisterlocks pulled into a bun. I know she's an anime geek—Lili said she used to do cosplay. She does a jokey fake gasp when she sees me. "Is this *the* Imogen?"

"Yes. Hi! Kayla, right?" My hand twitches at my side—I don't know if I'm supposed to put it out for a handshake, or what. Is this a hugging situation? Should I go in for the cheek kiss like Declan?

Mika tucks a lock of hair behind their ear and smiles. "Feels like we already know each other."

"You're coming here in the fall, right?" Kayla asks. "Like, officially?"

"Yup! Yeah, I'm excited," I say, nodding really fast—mostly to distract from what Edith calls my Resting Bunny Face: wide-eyed, soft, forever on high alert. I don't think it's as bad as it used to be—now I only really slip into bunny mode when I'm meeting someone new. I can always feel when it's happening, because it's like my mouth unhooks from my brain for a minute. Even if I'm in the middle of talking. It's fun.

I come by it honestly, though, because my dad does it too. He's always been shy, the way I am. My mom loves telling the story of how she thought Dad was a huge film buff for years, since he took her to so many movies when they first started dating. Really, it was just so he wouldn't have to talk. But then Mom got him a vintage popcorn bucket for Christmas, so he had to spend the next few years *pretending* to be into movies, because he didn't want to hurt her feelings. Pure Imogen energy, basically.

But Dad hides it better than I do—either that, or he's better at disappearing to the basement when he needs to. Still, I can always tell when his brain goes offline. It's sort of tucked into the pauses when he talks.

"I think it's going to be amazing," my mouth adds. "I know how much Lili loves it here."

I play it back in my head—okay, good. I sound mostly normal. *Amazing. Lili loves it.* Just some basic Imogenericisms.

"Okay, I love that?" says Kayla. "The *maturity*. Love to see it."

Lili rubs her forehead. "Ha. Okay, so. I don't want to hold you guys up. We still need to drop this bag off, but we can meet you at dinner. Is Tessa coming?"

"Haven't heard from her yet. Probably still with the himbos," says Declan.

"I'll poke my head in just in case." Lili turns to me. "Her room's right next to ours. Actually, you share a wall with her."

The way Lili talks about it, you'd think I was moving in permanently.

What's weird is realizing she's not entirely wrong.

Texts with Gretchen

IS: Awwww, thanks

IS: I'm good though, seriously

IS: Everyone's really nice!!

IS: Gretch it's so beautiful here

GP: Good!!!! Just got back

GP: Wait

GP: Did you meet Mika 🤩

IS: Yes 😊

GP: gsfdgjhsjfj;lk;k';

GP: Tell them I say hiiiiiiiiii

GP: WAIT

GP: don't do that

GP: Play it cool

IS: I'll try haha

IS: I think we're meeting them for dinner later

GP: SHUT UP

GP: IMOGEN YOU'RE HANGING OUT WITH MIKA
        HIYASHI

GP: okay okay we're cool, we're chill

GP: I mean, what are they like in person?!!!! Tell me
        EVERYTHING

3

The halls of Lili's dorm are narrow, with white cinder-block walls, tightly looped gray carpets, and the same rectangular flourescent light fixtures we have at school. But there are homey touches, too—the word *hello* spelled out in washi-tape block letters, taped event flyers, and a giant white sheet of paper tacked up near the bathroom, half-covered with doodles and handwritten quotes. Right away, I spot one attributed to Lili, written with purple marker in someone else's handwriting: *To be or not to be; that is the chest hair.*

I wouldn't call it a gut punch—more like a tiny, sharp poke beneath my rib cage. Other people's inside jokes always hit me like that, but I can never quite pin down the feeling. A variation on loneliness, maybe.

"Okay, brace yourself," Lili says, pulling out her room key. "My room is basically a closet."

There's a dry-erase white board stuck to Lili's door, featuring a chibi-style drawing of two cats with their tails looped into a heart. Taped above it are a pair of cloud-shaped construction-paper signs, just like the ones I've seen on most of the doors we passed.

WELCOME, EMILIA

WELCOME, SYDNEY

I let out a laugh as soon as Lili opens the door. "So when you said it's the size of a closet, you meant Kylie Jenner's closet."

"Okay, it's small for a double!"

"How often does Sydney stay here again?"

She makes a face at me, parking my suitcase next to one of the beds. There are two of them, flush against perpendicular walls, both made with quilts and sheets I recognize from home—Lili's home. Her favorite rainbow-haired unicorn, Puppy, is tucked under the covers of one of them.

I guess it's a *little* on the cozy side—less because the room itself is small, and more because the furniture comes in pairs. Two desks, two dressers, two wardrobes, two short wooden bookshelves. But it's all so covered in Lili's familiar clutter, I feel instantly at home. There's an assortment of Pop-Tarts and granola bar boxes on top of one of the dressers, intermingling with ceramic horse figurines and month-old birthday cards. Her bookshelves are pure chaos—Homer, Virgil, Euripides, and Aristophanes, alongside Madeline Miller, Roxane Gay, and a memoir by someone who used to be on *The Bachelor*. And of course, Lili's postcard collection is on full display, sticky-blobbed to the walls in random clusters. Niagara Falls next to the printed cover of Issue 1 of *Check, Please!* "Tracy Mitrano for

Congress" next to "Bem-vindo a São Paulo."

But above both beds, it's just photos—rows of prints, sloping subtly downward because Lili's never met a straight line in her life. The ones above my bed are mostly from this year—group selfies and sunny snapshots of her friends in various combinations. But the ones above Lili's bed are from home.

I cross her room for a closer look, smiling at the lineup: my family's barn at sunset, Penn Yan's Main Street, a double rainbow over Keuka Lake. Small-town New York state in tiny four-by-six glimpses. And mixed throughout: family portraits, childhood pictures. Naturally, there are at least a dozen pictures of Mel, plus the one from my tenth birthday where Lili's *dressed* as Mel. I'm standing beside her in that one, dressed as my cat Quincy, and we're both wearing glow necklaces and holding up our overstuffed trick-or-treat pillowcases. There's one of Lili and Otávio, ages seven and five, beaming, in matching white Corinthians soccer jerseys—and beside it, taken almost a decade later, Lili literally crying while getting a book signed by Casey McQuiston. She's even got the photo her mom insisted on snapping two summers ago, the year we scooped ice cream at Seneca Farms. Lili was at the height of her moody black eyeliner phase, glaring over the counter. I'm posed dutifully beside her with a metal scoop and a how-can-I-help-you smile.

But my favorite picture of us is the one from last summer's Pride, a week after Lili came out. She's wrapped in a pink, yellow, and turquoise flag, and I'm leaning against her, elbow propped on her shoulder. Edith took the picture, and she must have said something funny right beforehand, because we're clearly both howling with laughter.

"I love everything about this," I say, settling onto Lili's bed.

"Ha—thanks." Lili plops down beside me. Then she stares straight ahead for a moment without speaking. "Okay, we gotta talk," she says finally.

My heart flips. "Oh—"

"Nothing bad! I mean, not, like, catastrophic? I don't know." I nod slowly, and she looks at me. "So. My friends—"

"Seem great! Seriously. They're so nice."

"Yeah, no, definitely, but that's . . ." She trails off, scooping her dark hair off her neck—twisting it up, letting it fall. "I know that was a little weird out there—not because of you," she adds. "Imogen, no. If you apologize right now, I will actually kill you."

I press a muffling hand over my mouth, and she laughs.

But then she sighs. "So here's the thing. My friends here are so *queer.*"

"So are you." I pause, furrowing my brow. "Oh, God—do they think—I don't want anyone to feel unsafe, or—"

"Immy, come on—no one thinks you're a queerphobe." She shakes her head at me, smiling. "And yes, I know I'm queer. I'm valid. All of that. I guess it's just me seeing the way—I don't know. They have their shit together, you know?"

"Okay—"

"Like Kayla?" she adds. "She came out in middle school. She took a girl to the eighth-grade dance and kissed her on the

26

dance floor. Right in the school gym."

"Whoa, nice!" I say, cringing before the words have even left my lips. My voice always pitches higher when people talk about girls kissing—which makes literally no sense, seeing as I'm surrounded by queer people 24/7. I know Gretchen finds it annoying sometimes. Though other times, she says it's adorable, and that I'm an innocent bean with Mommy's-first-day-at-PFLAG energy. But that just makes me even more self-conscious.

Maybe the awkwardness is just one of those small-town things you have to shake off and unlearn. Apart from Pride Alliance meetings, it's not like Penn Yan is some sort of queer haven. I can't even fathom two girls kissing on the dance floor of my middle-school gym. The image doesn't compute. I know there were one or two gay couples in my grade back then, but it was kind of a quieter thing. Not a secret, but definitely not front and center.

And everyone in Pride Alliance talks about how hard it is to date people from our school. Gretchen says it's because everyone knows everyone in Penn Yan. And you can't exactly hold hands with a girl in the cafeteria when your teachers are friends with your homophobic parents. Hypothetically speaking, that is, since Mama Patterson isn't homophobic, and neither are my parents or Lili's. But I guess homophobia managed to leak into the atmosphere somehow. Even Edith, who's basically never *not* been out, hadn't dated anyone before Zora.

I really wish I could be more casual about this stuff.

"So that's Kayla," says Lili. "Tessa and Mika both had girlfriends in high school. Actually, middle school too, for Mika—they were with their ex for, like, five years. And Dec's from Manhattan, so who even knows? He's on a whole other level. It's hard not to feel inadequate, you know?"

"Because you haven't dated anyone?"

Lili and I used to joke about that a lot. We were the Forever Alone Club. No boyfriends. No random hookups. Just a pair of perpetually single besties who spent way more time hanging around animals than boys.

It's not that I didn't want a boyfriend. I did. I *do*. I fall in and out of crushes all the time. It's just not something I talk about much—I don't even get into the specifics with Gretchen and Lili. Crushes have always felt viscerally private to me. I know that's weird. It's definitely sort of lonely. But I don't think being single ever made me feel inadequate.

"It's not that." Lili frowns. "Not exactly? I just feel like such a baby queer sometimes. I'd only been out for three months when I got here."

"They shouldn't judge you for that."

"They didn't." Lili pauses. "I kind of told them I came out in high school."

I feel so out of my depth. "Do people really care when you came out?"

"I mean, my friends don't." Lili covers her face with both hands. "I don't know, I was being a dumbass, and—okay." She gives a short, muffled moan before pulling her hands away. "I have to tell you something."

Suddenly, it's summer again—that Sunday evening in June. Lili had been roped into stopping by this girl Brianna's graduation party, which was exactly as boring and awkward as we'd expected. So we left early. She drove me home. I remember it was raining, just barely, and I was a little hypnotized by the droplets streaking down the passenger window. And then Lili stopped at a red light on Main Street and said my name out of nowhere.

"So I think—I'm probably pan. Like pansexual?"

She was staring straight ahead when she said it, didn't even miss a beat when the light turned green. But she was biting her lip just like she is now, and I almost wonder—

"Um." She laughs nervously, and I'm jolted straight back. Lili's dorm room. Something she needs to tell me. "Promise you won't hate me," she says.

I laugh. "I promise I won't hate you."

"Uh. You might." She blinks, presses her lips together, then starts talking really quickly. "Okay, it was orientation week. Everyone's hanging out in my room, and I guess somehow the topic of dating came up. So I was sitting there, just—not saying anything, feeling like such an imposter—"

"You're not—"

"I know! I know it's ridiculous. Not even sure what was in my head at that point, but I just wanted to be more—legit, I guess? So I was like, 'Yeah, totally, I totally had a girlfriend,' except—Immy, I was *not* selling it. Like, at all."

"You don't need to sell anything! You're already completely legit."

"I was being a dumbass, remember? So, at the same time, I'm just panicking, because clearly, they were going to see right through me, and it's like, *cool, cool.* Everyone's gonna think I'm a straight girl faking the whole thing, right?"

"You're—did they?"

"Not at all! Like, they didn't even question it! They were just like, 'Oh, nice, how did you two meet?' So of course now I'm scrambling a little—like, well fucking done, Emilia, have fun making up a fake ex-girlfriend on the spot." She shuts her eyes briefly. "But then Tessa—she was sitting right where you are, and all of a sudden, she's like, 'Oh, is this her?' And she points to this picture." Lili scoots sideways, tapping the edge of one photo.

It's the one where we're laughing, from Pride.

"Oh!" I blush. "She thought—"

"Yeah."

"I mean, it's funny," I say.

"I told her you were," she says softly.

I laugh a little. "That I'm . . . your girlfriend?"

The word feels weird on my tongue, almost alien.

"Ex-girlfriend. We amicably broke up last summer. I'm so sorry. Ugh. It's so shitty and creepy, I know."

I blink. "No! No, it's—"

"It just—it seemed like such an easy answer at the time. Which is no excuse. I just didn't think it through. Any of it." She lets out a panicked laugh. "Like the fact that my quote-unquote 'ex-girlfriend Imogen' is a real person they'd be meeting one day."

I try to wrap my head around it. "So they know I'm me. They just think we dated?"

Lili presses both hands to her cheeks. "We got together on

New Year's, broke up in July, but that's it. You're you, we're best friends, we grew up together, all of it. Everything else is true. Oh—but you're queer. They think you're bi." She winces a little. "Sorry."

"No, it makes sense. Of course I am. Would be. If we dated. Obviously." I nod, really fast.

"Okay, you're being *too* cool about this. Immy, I lied! I erased your identity."

"My straight identity? I don't think that's a thing."

"Stop saying what you think I want to hear! You're allowed to feel a certain way about this."

"But it's not a big deal."

"The fact that all my friends think you're queer? And that we dated? You're cool with that?"

"I mean, why wouldn't I be?"

Lili shakes her head. "How are you not freaked out? Like, you have to be wondering if I'm secretly in love with you, right?"

"What? No—Lili—I didn't—"

"I promise I'm not. I'm just saying, you have a right to be kind of unsettled by this. I don't even mind if you blow my cover. I mean, I *mind*. But if you want to set the record straight, we totally can. I get it."

I open my mouth and shut it, head still spinning. I'm a little stuck on the part where Lili thinks *I* think she's in love with me.

Which she's not. And I don't.

But the fact that she thinks I'm wondering that? Like I'm that special kind of straight person who assumes all queer people can barely keep their pants on around her?

I mean, admittedly, I do wonder sometimes what queer girls think of me. But it's just the occasional fleeting thought. Definitely not a you-love-me kind of thing.

Not that I'd mind if a queer girl was into me. I'd honestly find it super flattering.

I hug Puppy the unicorn close to my chest. "So it's just . . . I'm bisexual? And we used to date, but we're friends now. And other than that—"

"Just that. Everything else is real, I promise. No fake dates or memories or anything. Just stuff we actually did. Like the ice-cream crawl and all the barn stuff and when we took Mel and Eloise to Watkins Glen. I didn't change any of that. They just probably think we went home and made out afterward. But we don't have to talk about that part," she adds quickly. "I really don't want to make you uncomfortable—"

There's a knock. Lili looks at me.

"I'm not uncomfortable. Seriously."

"Okay, well. I fucking owe you one," she murmurs, before calling out, "Come in!"

The door opens, and a girl in a bathrobe walks in—white, with short, shower-damp, dark hair, holding a plastic toiletry bucket. Obviously Tessa—though her hair was longer in most of Lili's pictures. There's something unforgettably open about her face—her big brown Winona Ryder eyes, her Clea DuVall freckles.

"Hey, are we meeting everyone at Winterfield? I can be

ready in five. I just—" She stops short. "Oh my God—Imogen, hi! I'm Tessa. Sorry—I usually wear clothes."

"Hi! Yup. Imogen," I say. "I wear clothes, too."

She does this quick, bubbling laugh—like a low-pitched giggle, really—and her smile reminds me of getting your braces off. Not that I've ever seen Tessa with braces. No idea if she even had them. I just mean there's an element of surprise to her smile. A little flash of *oh wait*.

Then she runs a hand through her hair, and there's something so boyish about the gesture, it leaves me a little off-balance.

"I feel so underdressed next to you," Lili says, stepping into the stairwell.

I peek down at my skirt. "Do you think I should—"

"No, you look perfect. I'm the one who looks like a zombie camp counselor." She pauses mid-staircase to pull the backs of her sneakers over her heels. "Hey. You sure you're okay with everything?"

"You mean the ex-girlfriend thing?"

"I just don't want you to feel like you can't be yourself, you know?" She glances back over her shoulder. "Almost there—one more floor."

We reach the bottom, and Lili leads me into a hallway that looks just like hers—cinder-block walls and wooden doors, some propped open, bursting with laughter or music or video game noises. Everything smells like a movie theater.

"Popcorn dinner. What a lifestyle," says Lili.

Tessa steps out of the elevator as soon as we pass it. "Fancy meeting you here."

Lili arches her brows. "Too good for the stairs?"

"The himbos wore me out." Tessa's gaze flicks to me, cheeks going red. "Not. You know. Sexually. I'm not—I'm a lesbian. Who can't stop talking. Apparently." She swipes at her bangs, nudging them sideways. Now that her hair's a little drier, it's settled into the sort of perfectly disheveled tomboy bob I could never pull off in a million years. Not quite chin-length. I've always loved hair like that, though, especially when it wings out at the ends a bit, like Tessa's does. I mean, if I were really bi, I bet I'd fall for her based on hair alone.

"Okay, Declan says he's now a—direct quote—'gaping wound of hunger.'" Lili looks up from her phone. "Bro, you are *literally* in a dining hall surrounded by food. Does he think he's not allowed to eat until we get there?"

"We better go save him." Tessa bumps her own fisted hands together. "Imogen, are you ready to experience culinary perfection?"

"Oh," Lili says. "This is not that."

5

We set off down one of the paths that loops behind the dorms, and Tessa fills us in on her game of capture the flag. With the so-called himbos, who wore her out, but not sexually. "So the flag's supposed to be visible," she says, "but since Callum literally can't go five seconds without cheating—"

"Callum's her brother's friend," Lili explains.

"Yeah, Cal's, like, the king of the himbos. Or he thinks he is. He's an asshole, though. Like, his entire personality is just . . . anus."

"I didn't even know himbos had a monarchy," I say.

Lili and Tessa both burst out laughing, and I have to bow my head so I don't look too blatantly pleased with myself.

My stomach feels like the first day of school. Butterflies and panic. Tessa's pivoted to talking about how someone named Dan may or may not have a secret girlfriend, but I keep losing the plot. Because secrets and girlfriends are pretty much my whole entire problem right now—a problem that's looming larger and larger the closer we get to the dining hall.

It just feels like such a minefield all of a sudden. One wrong detail, and the whole story crumbles. I don't think Lili even gets how precarious this is. Sure, I can trot out a few greatest hits from our friendship, but what if someone asks about our first date? Our first kiss? There's no truth there for me to lean on. What if my version of the story doesn't line up with whatever she's already told them?

Also, what if I'm not believable as a queer girl?

Because that's the thing. I'm not just straight—I'm hopelessly, blindingly, *obviously* straight. Gretchen says queer people have a sense for this kind of thing, a sort of unspoken recognition. It's just something you know in your gut.

"Like gaydar?" I'd asked, which made her laugh.

"Kind of? It's like—you can just tell. I think it's evolutionary. It's a safety mechanism, right? You're like, okay, this person's probably not going to hate-crime me."

I got this twinge in my chest when she said that. Queerness recognizing queerness. It's kind of beautiful when you think about it.

I really do wish it was mine sometimes.

I remember the first Tuesday of ninth grade, my first ever Pride Alliance meeting. Gretchen made us get there ten minutes before the meeting even started—which meant ten minutes spent hovering near the door of Ms. Dugan's classroom like we were on a stakeout mission. Gretchen was so excited, she was practically slaphappy, but I was getting more and more nervous by the minute.

I couldn't shake the feeling that the group would kick me out on sight. I kept picturing the conversation grinding to a halt the minute I stepped into the room. There'd be a few moments of chilly silence. "Can we . . . help you?" someone would finally ask.

Of course, that first meeting ended up being so totally chill, I couldn't believe I was worried in the first place. The group was smaller than I'd expected—not sure why I'd basically pictured the NYC Pride march in the middle of Penn Yan High School, but there were just about a dozen people there that day. Gretchen and I were the only freshmen, but even that was kind of a cool dynamic. Like being the beloved youngest cousins at a family reunion. Everyone seemed sincerely happy to have us there. And when I got tongue-tied in the welcome circle, no one rushed me—which made it easier to push through the shyness.

"I'm Imogen. She/her," I'd said. "And I have a queer sister."

6

The dining hall's so much bigger than I expected. Definitely bigger than my school's cafeteria and probably twice as loud, even though only about half the tables are full. With its domed, windowed ceiling, it looks like a giant circular greenhouse.

Lili and Tessa lead me to a partitioned-off serving area near the back windows, with all these little counters and food stations to pick from. There's a grill called the Burger Joint, in between a sandwich counter and a vegetarian stir-fry station. There's a pizza corner with gluten-free *and* vegan options, and I haven't even looked at the salad and pasta bars yet. I can hardly wrap my mind around the array of choices.

Tessa takes one look at my face and laughs. "Yeah, it's a lot. But I've got you." She grips her tray with one hand, patting my arm with the other. "Let's narrow it down. What's your stance on pizza?"

"Deeply pro."

"Hey." Lili nudges me with the edge of her tray. "Buttery

grilled cheese at two o'clock."

"Ooh, paintbrush?" asks Tessa.

"Paintbrush."

Which turns out to be a grilled-cheese technique involving a pastry brush and a giant bowl of melted butter. "It's joy in food form," Lili says. "Better than chocolate. Better than puppies."

"You shouldn't eat puppies," I say.

We finish loading our trays and head to the registers, where Lili pays for everything with a swipe of her student ID card. Tessa's right behind us—we pause at the edge of the dining space to wait for her.

"You ready?" Lili's voice is perfectly casual. But there's something sewn into the folds of the question. *It's showtime, Imogen. Lights, camera, action.*

By the time we settle in at the table, Declan, Kayla, and Mika are almost entirely done eating. But no one seems to be in any hurry to leave. Lili slides in next to Declan. "All good on the gaping-wound front?"

Kayla raises her eyebrows. "Do I want to know?"

"Fully healed, thank you," Declan says, patting his stomach and yawning. "Also, you literally just missed security escorting two Chi Phi bros out the back."

"Um, you're really going to bury the lede like that? Tell them why they were escorted out." Kayla shakes her head. "These dudes were *on a table* performing a striptease—"

"Half a striptease," says Declan.

Mika leans in. "They're both missing the point. The striptease was just misdirection. They're up there baiting the security officers, and meanwhile, their accomplices are strolling out of here with a vat of ice cream. And you know who it was?" They turn to Lili. "The sex carnival guy."

Lili gasps. "It was *not*."

"No joke."

"Who's the sex carnival guy?" I ask, and everyone laughs. Which makes my cheeks go warm, even though I know—I *know* they're not laughing at me. But I feel so out of the loop. Two steps behind. Like I'm visiting another country and I only know half the language.

"Yeahhhhhh," Lili says, pressing the heel of her hand to her forehead. She turns to me. "Did I ever tell you about Sydney's party?"

"Sydney, your roommate?"

She nods. "Yup. So this was, like, October, I think? Sometime in the fall—Sydney was still there, obviously. And I was out somewhere that night—"

"It was the Halloween party!" Kayla interjects.

The Halloween party. My heart tugs sharply at the memory. Waking up to pictures of Lili and her friends grinning in their coordinated costumes, piled onto someone's extra-long twin bed. I'd gone to a house party with Gretchen, but it was boring and weird, and no one understood our costumes. We were home and in pajamas by ten.

"Right, right," Lili says. "So it's—I don't know—two in the morning. I'm just getting home—Tess is there, too. And it turns out, in our absence, Sydney's decided to have an orgy."

I feel my eyes go wide. "Oh—"

Lili pats my shoulder. "Not a literal orgy. But yeah, my room looks like a bomb went off. The whole place reeks of beer. Sydney's *nowhere*. Meanwhile, you could hear people throwing up in the bathroom. The retching noises." She shudders. "And I'm here totally sober, totally speechless. Tess is standing there with her jaw on the floor—"

"It's true." Tessa nods solemnly.

"And then I realize"—Lili claps her hands together—"there's a pair of total strangers hooking up in my bed."

"Oh no . . ."

Lili hangs her head. "Right in front of Puppy."

"Okay, tell her the next part," says Kayla, eyes dancing.

Lili mutters something under her breath.

"What was that, babe?"

Lili sighs. "I said, 'The sex carnival is over.'"

"Said?" Tessa bites back a smile. "I think it was more of a bellow."

"And then I washed my sheets eight times."

"And the world gained an iconic new concept," Kayla concludes. "Sex carnival."

Lili grimaces. "What a legacy."

"Well, that and Jean-Claude," I point out.

42

Lili buries her face, but I can tell that she's smiling.

Kayla waggles her eyebrows. "Uh-oh. Who's Jean-Claude?"

"Her fake Twitter persona. Jean-Claude LePoisson, age twenty-four, he/him. Spoke only Google-Translated French."

"A certified sexy bichon," Lili adds.

"*Was* he sexy?" I ask, "or was he just holding five baguettes?"

Declan props his phone between two trays. "We have a bio. I repeat, we have a bio." He clears his throat. "Je suis Jean-Claude et j'habite en France. Very convincing. Especially with the geotag underneath for Rochester, New York."

"Also fake! Just less fake. Jean-Claude forgot to change the location when he stole the account."

"So, to be clear—your French catfish persona is an account thief," says Mika.

"Yup! He stole the handle from a twenty-nine-year-old lesbian in Rochester named Melissa. Who was also me." Lili taps her chest. "Age eleven. No idea I was queer."

"A repressed queen!" Kayla grins. "See, this is incredible. Now we know who to call for dirt on Lili."

"I have dirt," I confirm.

Lili holds up her middle finger and kisses its tip. Tessa turns to me, grinning. "Yeah, we're keeping you."

I grin back, feeling almost heady with my own lack of restraint. I'm never this unlocked around new people. But maybe college is really that different from everything that came before it. Maybe I'll make this place mine.

I can actually picture it. Me, a year from now, fully absorbed into this group. By then, we'd have our own language—layers of inside jokes and references, incomprehensible to everyone but us. Entire conversations tucked into the quickest exchanged glances.

I think about Lili, and how her face lights up every time she talks about Blackwell. It's like she's fallen in love with this whole entire place.

So maybe I'll fall in love with it, too.

The sun's just starting to set as we make our way back to the dorms—the group's disbanding, but only temporarily. We're meeting in about an hour for a trivia night in the student center.

"It's super chill," Lili assures me.

"The most chill," Tessa adds. "And you can win money."

"Except we don't, because we're really bad," Lili says.

"Okay, but hear me out." Tessa points at her. "I think tonight's our night."

Lili smiles a little. "Oh yeah?"

"I'm just saying. We've got Imogen now."

I let out a startled laugh. "What?"

"True." Lili grins.

"*And* Jean-Claude," Tessa adds. "He'll definitely come through on all the French questions."

"There has never, ever been a French question."

"We just have to be strategic! Play to our strengths." Tessa pokes my arm, and my heart does the quickest half flip. "What's your area of expertise?"

We reach the dorm, and Lili swipes her keycard to open the door.

"Um." I pause. "Overthinking?"

"Ooh, nice. Yup. Always need one of those on the team," Tessa says.

"She's being modest," Lili says, glancing back at me. "Immy, you're a literal award-winning chef. You're just not going to mention that?"

Tessa stops short. "You're an *award-winning chef*?"

"Yeah . . . I don't want to brag, but"—I bite back a smile—"I kind of swept the ten-and-under category in the Li'l Cookies Library Fundraiser Bake-Off."

"Yeah you did." Tessa high-fives me.

"Best Rice Krispie Treat of my life," Lili says.

"Thanks! It's the recipe from the back of the Rice Krispies box."

"Still counts!" Lili presses the elevator call button. "And— let's see. She makes the absolute best vision boards."

"Like at the eye doctor?" Tessa tilts her head. "Read this line of letters and numbers? Which way is the E pointing?"

I laugh. "No. It's like a visual aesthetic collage, kind of?"

"Wait, let me pull up my Notes app and write these down," Tessa says, tugging her phone from her pocket. "Okay, Imogen's . . . areas . . . of expertise. Rice Krispie Treat making, vision boards—"

"And typing with a cat in her lap," Lili adds as we step inside the elevator. "She's great at that. Oh, and emoji precision."

"What?" I smile.

"Like, you're really good at finding the exact right emoji."

"Thank you?"

"Most people get lazy about it. But not you." Lili presses the third-floor button, turning back to Tessa. "Ooh, put down that she's good at looking like she's not paying attention when she's actually paying *perfect* attention. Like, it's actually kind of creepy."

I nod. "These all sound like very normal trivia categories."

"Yeah, we've got it in the bag," Tessa says, tapping her toe against mine with a grin.

7

Lili shuts the door, plopping beside me on the edge of my bed. "How are you holding up? This is a lot, I know—"

"No, it's great! I'm good."

She stares me down.

I laugh. "Really!"

"You're not overwhelmed?"

"Why would I be overwhelmed?"

"Um. I don't know." Lili leans back on her palms. "Being here? Meeting everyone? Having to play along with my big dumbass lie—"

"But it was fine! It wasn't even a thing."

I mean, it's just backstory, right? The past is *always* just backstory.

I think about that sometimes—how the only way to let someone into your reality is to retell it. Even true things come out filtered, imperfect, and muddled. So what's the harm in Lili taking it a step or two further?

"Okay, but it's stressful! And Immy, I know you! I know your little hamster-wheel brain was already freaking out about whether my friends were going to like you—which, for the record, Kayla's already texted me to say you're awesome, and Mika said you're—and I quote—'transcendently sweet.'"

My cheeks go warm. "That's so nice—"

"And don't even get me started on little miss flirty-pants Tessa—"

"She's—what?" I look up with a start.

"Oh, don't worry! It's Tessa. She does that."

"No! Yeah, no—I wasn't worried." I pause. "Did I seem worried?"

"Not at all. I'm just saying—"

"Because it wouldn't bother me. You know? Like, I'm not freaked out by it."

"By Tessa being a flirt?" Lili looks slightly bewildered.

I blush. "By, you know. Girls in general. Sorry." I cover my face with both hands. "I'm acting really straight right now, huh?"

Lili laughs. "What?"

"I just don't want to make anyone uncomfortable. And I don't want to blow your cover." I peek through my fingers. "I know I'm not the most believable queer girl."

"That's—sorry, but *what*? Immy, I don't even know what that means. 'Believable queer girl?'" Lili blinks. "What makes a queer girl believable?"

"I don't know," I say softly.

48

The truth is, I've never quite been able to pin it down. The way queerness announces itself. And how it seems so intuitive for people. How people just seem to *know*.

I mean, there's Gretchen's whole unspoken-recognition gaydar thing. But it's more than that. There's a certain aesthetic to queer girlhood. Or maybe it's several aesthetics, but I don't fit any of them. I don't have Tessa's tomboy energy or Gretchen's pink hair, or a jean jacket like the one Edith wears every day. Even Lili, in her ringer T-shirt and gym shorts, looks potentially queer. Like she *could* be queer.

I wouldn't even know where to begin. Bulk order of enamel pins? Some kind of hair transformation? I've never dyed my hair, and it's never been shorter than shoulder-length. And I probably wear dresses and skirts more than pants. I'm pretty sure there were a few years in elementary school where I *only* wore dresses. All my socks had to have either lace or ruffles.

I'm not explaining this well.

I try to put it into words, and it just sounds like a list of surface details and stereotypes. I bet I'd be laughed off campus if I said any of this out loud. Or canceled. Probably both. But there's got to be some kernel of truth buried in there, right? There have to be some sort of visible markers of queerness. Otherwise, how could so many people know at a glance that I'm straight?

Maybe it comes down to vibes. Or that particular sort of awkwardness straight girls sometimes get around queer girls. Gretchen called me out for that over the summer.

The entire conversation is burned into my brain, beat by beat.

We were cross-legged on the floor of her bedroom, analyzing a bunch of DMs and texts she'd gotten from this girl named Ella. They'd met a few weeks earlier at one of those summer STEM enrichment programs. Gretchen couldn't decide if the texts were flirtatious, and she kept talking herself in circles about it. And since I don't have a clue what flirting looks like, I was basically just nodding along.

Until Gretchen stopped mid-sentence. "Hey, can you try not to do that?"

When I looked up from her phone, she was blinking back tears. She wiped her eyes with the heels of her hands.

"I—I'm not sure what I should stop doing," I'd stammered.

"You seriously don't see it."

I shook my head.

"Well, just so you know, it's been pretty hard to talk with you about girls I like. And I've been feeling that way for a while now."

I remember it felt like my lungs had stopped working. "About—girls?"

"You're, like, palpably uncomfortable! You don't even make eye contact when I talk about Ella. And it's *every time*. Whereas with Caden—anytime it's a guy, you're all in." She lets out a breath. "And I get it. I get that you can relate more when it's a guy. But my crushes on girls are real too! And they're important to me! And yeah, it's funny that you get so flustered about it, but it also kind of makes me not want to share them."

Her voice cracked a little when she said that, and I sat there, half-frozen, half-frantic. I cast my thoughts back to all the other times Gretchen had talked about Ella, about Caden, about anyone. *Had* I felt uncomfortable?

I didn't think so—but then again, would I even have realized it if I was? Unconscious queerphobia does exist, after all.

I was so flooded with guilt and shame, I could barely wrangle the words. "Gretch, I'm so sorry. I don't even know what to say."

"It's fine. You didn't know," she'd said. "I appreciate you apologizing, though."

"I can't believe I made you feel like that."

"Yeah . . . it's kind of one of those things. Like, we live in a queerphobic society, you know? It's almost impossible not to internalize at least some of that. But it's good, because once you're aware of your biases, you can actually start to work on them," she'd said. "And I'm always happy to help with that stuff. Always."

Texts with Gretchen

IS: Okay so

IS: Just got back from dinner, heading to trivia in a sec

IS: But M is totally cool; and down-to-earth, zero influencer vibes

GP: AHHHH that's so great

IS: They're pretty quiet in person! Like waaaay more introverted than they are online

IS: You know how there's always that one person in the group who doesn't talk a lot, but they're always super engaged

IS: Like they're clearly taking EVERYTHING in?

GP: Uh, Immybean, that's you 😂

GP: you're the Mika of pride alliance!!!

IS: HAHAHAHA

IS: Wow

IS: That is extremely flattering

IS: So like the thing about Mika is they're completely not awkward

IS: Quiet but not awkward

GP: The rarest combination!!!!

GP: Ahhh this makes me so happy

GP: Look at you, all grown up

GP: Your first night out on campus!!!

8

My first night out on campus.

I know it's just trivia, not an orgy. Not even orgy-adjacent. But there's no stopping the rush of butterflies in my stomach as I follow Lili and Tessa up the central staircase of the student center. There's a lounge area tucked into one of the back corners of the space—bland and functional, like a waiting room, or one of those seating areas at the mall. Other than a few square tables in the center, it's mostly just chairs and couches arranged into clusters.

"So, there are usually, like, five teams," Lili says. "Three or four people per. We're always the biggest group."

I spot Declan and Kayla in a pair of blue-gray armchairs on either end of a short, rectangular table. In between them, Mika's perched on the edge of a couch, leaning forward to write on a white board. Just enough room for Lili, me, and Tessa to scoot in beside them.

A moment later, a Black girl in a beanie steps into the center of the space, trailed by a white girl holding a miniature dry-erase board. "Hello, hello! Where are my trivia fiends?"

A loud *woooooo* erupts from a trio of girls in bodycon dresses and heels.

"All right! Let's do this. For those who don't know me, I'm Sasha, and this is Erin." Sasha pauses, peering around the space. "Okay, cool, lots of familiar faces, a couple new people. Let's run through the rules really quickly. So, we've got twelve questions. Erin's going to read each one out loud, and then we'll start the clocks. You've got three minutes to confer with your group and write your answer on the white board."

Erin holds up her white board, beaming like a TV presenter.

"When time's up, drop your markers, and we'll see what you've got. One point for every right answer—wrong or incomplete answers get nada. No partial credit. Um. And then there's the wild card round at the end, where you can wager your points. The team with the highest point total at the end gets the jackpot."

Erin rubs her thumb and forefinger together and mouths the word *ooh*.

Sasha continues. "And I know you wouldn't dream of it, but just a reminder! No googling, no texting your space-engineer auntie or whatever. Honor system, okay?" She gives an exaggerated thumbs-up. "Okay! Let's lock in those team names."

Mika holds up the dry-erase board, displaying the words *l'equipe: Jean-Claude LePoisson* in elegant cursive.

Lili does finger guns. "Funny."

Minutes later, Sasha claps a few times to get everyone's attention. "Okay! Diving in. Erin, take it away!"

Erin glances down at her paper. "All right! Question number one! What is the body's largest organ?"

Skin. I think?

Mika's already uncapping the dry-erase marker.

"Skin. Definitely," says Lili.

"Definitely," agrees Kayla.

"Markers down, boards up!" Sasha declares. "And the answer we're looking for is . . . skin!"

I shoot Lili a grin. "Aren't we supposed to be bad at this?"

"Oh, they'll get harder."

"Okay, let's see . . ." Erin scans her page of questions. "The 1999 film *10 Things I Hate About You* was inspired by which Shakespeare play?"

The Taming of the Shrew, I think.

"*Much Ado About Nothing*?" says Kayla.

I stop short, all my certainty gone in an instant.

Could it be *Much Ado*? Did *Taming* just burrow its way into my head somehow?

Maybe I've been wrong about this for *years.*

Although.

It kind of has to be *Taming*, right? The plot tracks pretty closely—even the character names line up. Does that mean Kayla's wrong?

I rub my cheek, feeling weirdly unsettled.

Gretchen told me about this experiment once, where a psychologist asked groups of people to compare the lengths of different lines. Solomon Asch—that was the psychologist's name. I love when the syllables of someone's name match with mine.

Asch was studying conformity, but he was sneaky about it. He'd always put one clueless subject in a group of people who were secretly in on the plan. Then, sometimes the undercover people would all say the same wrong answer on purpose—just to see if the real test subject would go along with it.

"Most of the time, they did," Gretchen had told me. "Even when the right answer was completely obvious. But these people actually convinced themselves they were wrong. They overruled their own visual perception."

Gretchen had been dumbfounded by this, but to me, it made sense.

Perfect sense. Too much sense.

It's definitely *The Taming of the Shrew*, right? One hundred percent. So.

I draw in a deep breath and say it.

Kayla smacks her forehead. "Yes! Thank you. No, you're totally right."

"Two for two!" Tessa high-fives me. "What did I tell you? Tonight's our night."

And by the time we hit the halfway point, I'm starting to think she may be right. We haven't missed a single question yet.

Erin clears her throat. "Next up! What animal is featured on California's state flag?"

"Oh, come on. State flags?" Declan says.

"Not California!" Tessa shakes her head. "Look at us. A Philadelphian, a Minnesotan, a New York City kid, and three upstate New Yorkers."

"I literally don't know what my own state flag looks like," says Mika.

I pause. "Is it a bear?"

"Oh?" Declan asks.

"I don't know! It might not be—"

But I'm right. And then the next question's practically made for me. "What actress starred alongside Noah Centineo and Madelaine Petsch in the 2020 Netflix romantic comedy *Shop Talk*?"

"Kara Clapstone," I say.

Lili grins. "Your sister would actually disown both of us if we missed this one."

She's not even joking—*Shop Talk* has basically been Edith's religion since the trailer dropped. Even though Gretchen says it's assimilative, unrealistic garbage made for straight people. Not just Gretchen, I guess—lots of people online seem to feel the same way about it, especially because Kara Clapstone is straight in real life. But Edith doesn't care about the *Shop Talk* discourse—I'm not sure she even knows about it. She doesn't seek that stuff out the way I do.

Like the first time I watched *But I'm a Cheerleader*. Before I'd even left Lili's house, I was already scouring the internet for other people's reactions. But that just made me more confused.

Every think piece felt like the definitive final word—and then I'd be fully convinced by the exact opposite points in the next one. I was a human sailboat, blown in every direction by a storm of decades-old media discourse.

Am I allowed to love this? That was always the question. When Sasha confirms our answer, the whole group lets out a cheer and high-fives me.

"Killing it!" Lili says.

"Wait." Kayla's hands fly to her mouth. "Lex Appeal missed that one. Are we actually—"

"Next question," says Erin. "What singer was born with the name Robert Allen Zimmerman?"

"Uh," Kayla says.

Declan shakes his head.

Mika and Lili both tilt their palms up.

"Don't know, but he sounds Jewish!" says Tessa.

Five pairs of hopeful eyes turn to me.

I wince. "I'm sorry. No idea."

Lili elbows me. "Stop feeling bad."

"I know, but—"

"Nope. Not on you. This is an act of collective dumbassery."

We end up guessing Robbie Williams. It's our first wrong answer of the night.

Then Erin asks what breed of cat has no tail, and we miss that one, too. Every single one of us thought the word was *minx*. But it's *manx*.

"No sad faces," says Kayla, tucking an errant loc behind her ear. "Let's rally. We've got this, okay?" She coaxes us in for a big group fist bump—and I get this happy jolt in my chest when our hands come together.

"Okay, folks!" says Sasha, once we've scored the last question. "The current standings are . . . tied for fourth place, each with nine points—Lex Appeal and the Meaty Ogres! In third, with ten points—Team Jean-Claude LePoisson!"

"We're not last?" Kayla's jaw drops. "We're not last!"

"In second place, with eleven points—Team Panda! And in the lead, with a perfect twelve points, Team Down Low Too Slow!" Sasha concludes, and the three girls in bodycon dresses let out the world's loudest *WOOOOOOO.*

Tessa shakes her head. "Every week. They're totally drunk, too, but man. They know their shit."

"All right! Now it's time to decide how many points you want to wager for the wild card," says Sasha, while Erin fishes a messenger bag out from under a table.

Kayla exhales. "We've got to do this, yeah? We've gotta go all in."

Mika, nodding solemnly, draws a giant stylized *10* on the white board.

"So for tonight's wild card," Sasha says, "we present: *Where's Waldo?*—speed edition."

Lili turns to me with huge eyes, both hands over her mouth.

"We'll set the clock, give you a page number, and then

you've got thirty seconds to find Waldo. You find him, you get your points!"

When Erin hands Mika our team's Waldo book, Lili doesn't miss a beat. "Give it to Imogen."

Mika looks from Lili to me, eyebrows raised. "Have you memorized it?"

I laugh a little. "No."

"So you're just really good at this?" asks Tessa.

"A little bit." My chest floods with warmth.

Sasha opens her phone timer. "And . . . go!"

It takes me all of twelve seconds to find him. "There." I tap the corner of the page.

"Holy shit," Tessa says.

The timer goes off before anyone else finds Waldo, and Team Jean-Claude LePoisson just *erupts.*

"WE WON! WE FUCKING WON!" Kayla's jumping up and down. Suddenly, we're all out of our seats, a tangle of hugs and high fives.

"Immy! You did THAT!" declares Lili.

"*We* did—"

"Uh-uh. You're the MVP," Kayla says. "Own it."

It takes a full five minutes to calm down enough to take a picture with our "trophy"—a wrinkled ten-dollar bill. It's the most beautiful ten-dollar bill I've ever seen in my life.

"New favorite picture. Texting it to all of you!" Tessa turns to me. "Imogen, let me add you to the group chat."

The group chat. I'm joining the group chat.

It's so thrillingly official.

And a moment later, there it is: the six of us in full color, beneath the fluorescent lights of the student center lounge. Lili and me, and her four best friends from college.

Maybe they're my friends now, too.

9

The walk back to the dorms feels otherworldly. Like a movie montage—nothing but vibes and soft edges.

Kayla smiles up at the stars. "We really beat the Down Lows."

"A miracle," says Mika. "They were very graceful losers, though."

"Yeah, they're super nice." Kayla turns to me. "They just show up with their thermoses of booze every month and completely annihilate us. It's like their pregame. They're probably at a frat party now."

"Literal hottest girls on earth," Declan says.

Even in the darkness, Kayla's eye roll is unmissable. "You have the most basic goddamn taste, I swear to God."

"Babe! Are you jealous?"

She shakes her head. "His ego after getting one question right. Incredible."

"Okay, Albany—you take the New York City questions next time."

"Anyone else have no idea Tribeca was an abbreviation?" Lili says, glancing up from her phone.

Tessa points to her. "Me! I just thought it was a name. Like Rebecca."

"Three Rebeccas," I say. "Tribeca."

There's a sudden chorus of beeps and vibrations—my phone buzzes against my leg through the side of my bag. When I tap the screen, a notification informs me I've been tagged in one of Lili's pictures—our victory photo, of course.

Kayla smiles down at her phone. "Cuuuuute."

"Our little family," says Mika.

I study the photo—the group of us in a staggered line, Lili and Mika holding either end of the ten-dollar bill like it's the world's smallest banner. The lighting's atrocious, but every single one of our expressions is pure, unfiltered joy. It's the kind of picture you have to smile back at.

My phone buzzes again. *Tessa Minsky started following you.*

I shoot her a quick smile—she's walking right beside me, sipping on some kind of snack pouch. When I follow her back, she grins and starts typing.

A DM pops up a moment later. **Noticing your bio says nothing about Waldo skills??**

I don't even pause to glance at her. Instead, I exit my DMs, tap the Edit Profile button, and type "Skills: Waldo" right after my pronouns.

A few seconds later, Tessa laughs under her breath. Then: *touché, Scott, touché*

I get this flutter in my chest when I read that. *Scott.*

No one's ever called me by my last name so casually before, and I think—

I really like it.

She takes another sip of her snack pouch, eyes glinting.

I lean in for a closer look. "Is that—baby food?"

"No. Kind of? It's just applesauce. But the pouch is its most delicious form. Like, you can taste the difference." She holds it up for me to study. "How come no one ever talks about how much better it tastes from the pouch?"

"Because babies can't talk?"

"I'm just saying." She pats the side of it fondly. "It's an objectively superior applesauce distribution system."

"Objectively! Wow."

"Think about it—it's portable, easy to eat, doesn't require a spoon."

By now, the group has drifted a few yards ahead of us, even Lili. But it feels so cozy somehow. Is this what my life looks like in a year? Walking alongside new friends through a grassy courtyard under the stars? When I see the sign for Rosewood Hall, will I think: *home?*

"Okay, but sometimes you just want applesauce with a spoon." I shrug. "The world needs both."

Tessa grins. "The bisexuals have spoken."

I smile nervously back.

She really, truly thinks I'm bi. Didn't even question it for a minute. No one did.

I was so sure Lili's friends would see through me. They'd feel the heterosexuality radiating off me in waves.

"But I feel like it's slightly more fluid," Tessa adds, and I almost lose my footing for a second.

Applesauce. Right.

People always say sexuality is fluid. Or it can be.

But I've never quite been able to figure out what that means.

Like, what changes, exactly? Is it just a shift in terminology? Does attraction really, truly change over time? Is it different for every person?

Can you just . . . become queer?

I'm not even talking about dating. Obviously. Seeing as I've never dated anyone. Or kissed anyone.

I've had crushes. On boys. That's always been pretty straight-forward.

But when I try to imagine dating girls, the concept's so unwieldy. Even the idea of having dated one makes my head spin. *My ex-girlfriend, Lili.*

I picture her face—her long-lashed brown eyes, full lips, expressive dark brows. There's no question Lili's pretty, but the idea of kissing her is as weird as the thought of kissing my sister. My brain can't take it seriously.

But with girls in general?

I mean, it would depend on the situation. Let's say a

hypothetical girl needed me to kiss her to make her crush jealous. Or to discourage some guy from hitting on her. Or if we were at a party on campus and her ex walked in with another girl. If the hypothetical girl in question asked me to, I'd *definitely* hypothetically kiss her. It wouldn't be a big deal at all.

Except—it would be my first kiss. So maybe it's a slightly big deal in that sense. I'm not necessarily dying for my first kiss to be a favor for an acquaintance.

It just wouldn't be the absolute end of the world, is all. Favor or no favor.

Of course, it would have to be a favor—otherwise it would be problematic, for sure. I don't want to be that straight girl who kisses queer girls and discards them like it's not even real. Or it doesn't count. Or they should be grateful I bothered.

Gretchen had to school me on the issue once when we were freshmen. I'll never forget the flatness of her voice when she said, "Hey. Uh. Imogen, can I talk to you about something?"

It was the last full day of school before fall break, so we were all extra goofy in Pride Alliance. I remember a bunch of people were confessing their queer celebrity crushes, and I guess I thought I was supposed to weigh in. So I said I'd kiss Clea DuVall as Graham in *But I'm a Cheerleader*.

If Clea wanted to. Obviously.

It was such a stupid thing to say, in retrospect. Maybe I thought I sounded open-minded.

"I know you weren't trying to be problematic," Gretchen had said, and at first, I'd thought she meant the movie itself.

Or maybe the issue was me—loving a movie that wasn't mine to love.

She settled into a chair across the circle from me, even though everyone else had gone home at that point. It freaked me out a little bit—the small stretch of extra distance between us. I remember straining to read her expression.

"It's just that there's this whole history with the way straight women treat queer women," Gretchen said. "Straight women will joke about being queer, or how they wish they were lesbians—that kind of thing. I guess they think we'll be flattered? But the reality is, no, we'd literally rather you just understand and acknowledge your own privilege as a cishet woman. You don't have to appropriate our attraction. And I know you were kidding with the whole Clea DuVall thing, but like . . . queer women are real? It's not a joke for us. It just really hurt to hear that."

"I'm so sorry." The air spilled from my lungs like they were untied balloons. "I totally get it. I'm just. I'm so sorry."

"No, it's fine! Now you know," Gretchen had said, softening like she always does. Apologies disarm her so quickly. She always seems to expect people to put up a fight. But I'd never shout down an actual queer person about queer stuff. How could I?

Sometimes I think about what that moment must have felt like for Gretchen—how it must feel every time a straight girl casually tries on queer attraction for clout.

Or for fun.

Or because everyone else in the room is discussing it.

I know the bi thing hasn't always been super easy for Gretchen. Her mom's amazing, but the town they moved from is even smaller than Penn Yan. And Gretchen doesn't really pass as straight most of the time in the way Lili does. Or even Edith, who usually only gets clocked as queer on sight by fellow queer people. But with Gretchen, even before the pink hair, it was the cut of her jeans, or her bangs, or her eye makeup.

I remember once we were in the bathroom at the little movie theater in town. A girl—white skin, dark hair, at least twenty pounds of eyelashes—stepped out of a stall with her skirt tucked into her very sheer tights. Underwear fully visible. Definitely a see something, say something situation. Even though I hate talking to strangers, I was rehearsing an intervention in my head.

But luckily Gretchen swept in before I had to—so I stood at one of the sinks, watching the whole thing play out in the mirror.

"Hey," Gretchen had said, but the eyelash girl was fully absorbed in her phone. So she tapped the girl's arm, and the girl looked up with a glare that made the air feel ten degrees colder. Gretchen seemed taken aback. "Um, I just wanted—"

"I'm not interested."

"Wait, what?"

"I *said*." The girl set her phone down on the ledge of a sink, leaning in to study her reflection while she washed her hands. "I'm. Not. Interested."

Gretchen laughed shortly. "In what?"

Eyelash girl shut off the sink. "I don't know how to make this any clearer." She turned to face Gretchen, enunciating every single word. "I date men."

My mouth fell open. "She wasn't—"

Gretchen cut in. "Cool! Want to know what I'm not interested in? Your ass. You know how I know that? Because I can see the whole fucking thing."

Then Gretchen turned on her heel and walked straight out of the bathroom. Not a single glance back. Orpheus, take notes. It was—and I mean this completely sincerely—absolute legend behavior.

Of course, I followed her—stopping for just a second in the doorway, because my dumbass bunny brain needed to make sure the mean homophobic girl had sorted out her skirt situation. She had.

Gretchen, for her part, seemed almost chillingly calm about the whole interaction. We left the theater, found her car, and buckled in.

She didn't say a word.

But instead of leaving the shopping center, she just drove across the strip and reparked in front of CVS. For a moment, she gripped the steering wheel, practically frozen.

Then her whole body deflated.

She turned to me, stupefied. "Did she really fucking say that? Seriously? Do straight girls even hear themselves? Do they have, like, any self-awareness at all?"

"Self-awareness from the girl with her skirt in her tights?"

Gretchen let out a choked laugh. "Immy, I'm *tired.*"

"I know."

"Like, it's so pervasive. This girl doesn't know shit about me. Oh, I have dyed hair? I'm wearing overalls? Hey, I must want to fuck you in a movie theater bathroom." Gretchen exhales. "The sheer *arrogance.*"

"You might say . . . she showed her ass." I glanced slyly at Gretchen, who laughed and shoved a hand over my face.

"You fucking nerd. I love you so goddamn much."

And I felt the way I always feel when I manage to cheer someone up. Like I just made the rain stop with a wave of my hand.

DAY TWO
SATURDAY
MARCH 19

Texts with Gretchen

GP: Good morning, sunshine!!!!! How was your first night of college?

GP: Did you sleep?

GP: Did you floss??

IS: Good, yes, yes

IS: (of course)

IS: What about you? Are you on the road yet??

GP: Not yet

GP: Soon though

GP: Waiting for SOMEONE to get off the phone

GP: She's talking to Grandma

GP: I keep giving her puppy eyes

GP: She's not budging

IS: Aww, okay

IS: Tell Mama AND Grandma P I say hi though

GP: Will do!

GP: So what's the college life agenda for today

IS: Haha I don't know

IS: Lili's still sleeping

GP: Oh no wait

GP: That's so awkward??

GP: What do you do if you get hungry

IS: No, it's fine!

IS: She has pop tarts and stuff

IS: And she left me her swipe card in case I want to go
        to the dining hall

IS: I may text the group chat in a bit to see if anyone's
        up

GP: The group chat huh

GP: Look at youuuu

IS: ☺

10

One quick text to the group chat. Easy breezy, no pressure—right?

But I can't seem to bring myself to type the words. Or even open the text thread. What's the texting equivalent of tongue-tied?

It just feels too—I don't know. Presumptuous? A little too uh-hi-why-is-this-townie-high-school-child-texting-us-at-eight-a.m.-on-a-Saturday?

If I were home right now, I'd have been up for at least an hour already, spring break notwithstanding. All three dogs would be walked, the cats would be fed, and I'd be on the couch, attempting to read *Evelyn Hugo* amid a steady stream of Mom questions. *Now, is that the one Edie loves, about the actress? How is it? Oh, sweetie, what was the name of that singer you like? Not Lorde. The one whose relatives were on the* Titanic. *Immy, what does* sus *mean?*

I squeeze my eyes shut, breathing past the lump in my throat.

I just feel so far from home right now.

And so far from last night, from that glittering walk back to the dorms. How do I find my way back to that feeling?

I check my phone again.

They're probably all still sleeping, anyway. Even Tessa, who claims to be an early bird. She told me to text her if I get hungry before Lili wakes up—which seemed like such a sensible plan in the haze of last night. Now I can't imagine following through with it. In a way, it's even more intimidating than the thought of texting the whole group.

I keep thinking about what Lili said. How she thought Tessa was flirting with me. If I invite Tessa to breakfast, does that count as flirting back? Would I be leading her on? Would I be queerbaiting?

What if I already am, just by going along with Lili's whole story? Pretending to be bisexual. Even if it's not technically queerbaiting, it's definitely appropriation.

I set my phone facedown on my chest, right over my skittering heart.

I should just forget about breakfast. May as well get my shower out of the way while the bathroom's still quiet.

I've been dreading that—my first dorm shower. But I think I've finally figured out a nudity avoidance system. It's a whole tedious production involving the bathroom cubbies, a full extra outfit, and a hanging waterproof bag. I can't imagine walking down the hall in just a towel—even though no one else seems to mind it. One guy sauntered out last night with just a strategically placed washcloth. I was brushing my teeth at the time, and I almost choked on toothpaste.

Am I too big of a prude for college?

I tiptoe past Lili, slipping into the wide, empty hallway—so quiet, it's almost unnerving. Even waking at three in the morning to pee, I could still hear chatter and music spilling from a couple of rooms.

The bathroom's overhead lights are still off, but the glow from a night-light is enough to see the shower knobs. I pull the curtain closed, and for a moment, I just stand there. Eyes squeezed shut. Still in my pajamas.

It's the first time I've really been alone since I got here.

Maybe that's what scares me most about college. It all feels so public. How do people live so casually with strangers? With roommates? When do you ever get the chance to wind your heart back to normal?

The moment I step into the hallway, there's Tessa—in sweatpants, a T-shirt, and a tiny Star of David necklace. She stops short. "Scott! I was just about to text you. Any interest in breakfast? Have you eaten?"

"Oh—yes! I mean, I haven't."

"Okay, awesome. My treat."

I shake my head. "You don't have to do that! I can grab Lili's card—"

"Nope. I've got meal points to burn." Tessa pats her back pocket.

Lili's still passed out, so I dump my toiletries and pajamas on the end of my bed. Then I swipe my phone off the nightstand, popping off a quick text so she knows where I am.

Tessa looks up from her phone. "You ready?"

"Ready." I smooth the sides of my cardigan down over my shorts. Knowing I got dressed in a shower stall this morning makes me slightly paranoid that I've missed some critical buttons or zippers. Just a fun little stress cherry on top of this morning's anxiety sundae.

I'm getting breakfast with Tessa.

Which means I'll have to carry on a breakfast-length conversation with Tessa.

Tessa, who isn't a stranger—but I don't know if I'm allowed to call her a friend yet either. That's what makes it so hard, though. No one expects you to go beyond surface level when it's an actual stranger, so you can step outside your own brain if you need to. Flip the switch into bunny mode. It gets tricky with the in-between people.

I wish Gretchen were here. She'd know just how to play it. She has this way of turning small talk inside out, finding all the real parts underneath.

I follow Tessa out through a side door, and the morning chill prickles my legs with goose bumps. "Okay," she says, "what are we in the mood for? Dining hall? Student center?"

"Oh! Um. Whichever one has the best spoon applesauce," I say.

"Wow, who raised you?"

"Cory and Kelly Scott."

Tessa stops short. "Your mom's name is Kelly? *My* mom's name is Kelly!"

"Are you saying . . . there's more than one Kelly?"

"Okay, Scott—you know what?" She shakes her head at me smiling, and my heart does this stumble.

"What?"

She bites her lip, but it still tugs up at the corners. "Nothing."

"What?" I smile back.

"Nothing!" She laughs and turns to face me, walking backward like a tour guide. "I just have you figured out—that's all."

"Oh, really?"

"Yup. You're a closeted goofball."

I laugh, startled. "What?"

"And a troll. But in a subtle way. And you're very sweet about it. Here, I'm taking you through the quad," she says, veering us down a short, tree-lined path.

Suddenly I'm staring at the view from every campus brochure, every postcard, even the website's landing page—the stone clock tower, flanked by old lecture halls and columned administrative buildings. My gaze lands on the vine-draped registrar's office, and I realize with a start that it's the same quad Lili showed me yesterday—just a different vantage point. I can barely take it all in, it's so beautiful.

The part that really gets me, though, is the lawn that surrounds it. It's intersected by sun-dappled paths, lined with quaint wooden benches, and a few of the trees have started to sprout tiny red blossoms. It's not even ten in the morning, but students are already everywhere—jogging or talking or sprawled out, reading, on blankets. Movement and stillness. The whole space feels alive.

"Pretty, huh?" says Tessa.

Before I can even respond, a puppy stumble-runs toward us, almost tripping over her ears. "Oh God. *Hi.*" I kneel to pet her, my ponytail slipping over my shoulder. "Hi, cutie. Where'd you come from? Are you a basset hound?"

"New friend?" Tessa crouches beside me.

I check the bone-shaped tag on her collar. "Aww. Hi, Daisy. That was my goat's name."

"A goat, like, a *goat?*"

"Mmm. Yeah, she was the goat kind of goat." I scratch Daisy's ears, sighing happily. "Is this what college is like? Puppies materializing out of nowhere?"

I press my nose to Daisy's snout, and it's like pressing pause on the entire world.

I read somewhere that animals have some kind of hormonal calming power, and I really do think it must be true. At the very least, it's true for me. Like when I was too shy to talk for my whole first week of kindergarten, until my mom talked my teacher into letting me hold the class guinea pig during circle time. I still remember the twitch of his heartbeat under his fur, the way it seemed to put me under a spell.

Daisy's owner jogs over to reclaim her, and I watch her wagging tail recede into the distance. A moment later, Tessa hugs me. "You good?"

I look up, startled. "Yeah, why?"

"That just looked like a tough goodbye." She presses her heart. "No judgment, Scott. Breakups are hard."

I elbow her, and she laughs—and I try not to grin at the sound of it.

Texts with Gretchen

GP: Imogen, can you explain to me

GP: Why twenty billion people all just decided to take I-86

GP: Right now

GP: At 11 am on a Saturday

IS: Twenty billion people 🫠

GP: AT LEAST

GP: We're not even past Binghamton yet!!!!!!!

GP: Coming up on 3 hours dfghjklkjhg

GP: Vassar you better be worth it

IS: I mean if 20 billion people are heading there, that's probably a good sign?

GP: Hahahaha I love you

GP: Okay I have approached Mama Patterson for comment

GP: She says "sweetie, please, let me just" and then a horn honk and then "oh come the fuck on"

GP: Fourth f-bomb in 20 minutes 🫣

GP: College tours are FUN

IS: I'm sorry!!

GP: Ehhhh

GP: It's fine

GP: It'll be fine

GP: Anyway, how are you???

GP: Still liking your future?

11

My future.

Gretchen's not wrong, but it hasn't sunk in yet. My brain's so zoomed in on this visit, I keep forgetting it's just a preview.

But maybe that's how it should be. No pressure to build this weekend into something it's not. No need to shove each moment under a microscope, just to pin down how I feel.

"I'm taking you back the long way," Tessa says, as we leave the dining hall. "Have you seen the scissors yet?"

"The sculpture?" I shake my head. "Just in pictures."

I remember Lili's sheer delight when she first saw it on the website—giant metal scissors made to look like they're plunged into the ground. At the time, she was still deciding between Blackwell and Ithaca College, but the scissors sealed the deal.

"It's a *sign*." She turned to me, wide-eyed. "From the town with the world's largest griddle to the school with the world's largest scissors."

I wasn't entirely sure they *were* the world's largest. And I definitely didn't see the point of basing huge decisions on the presence or absence of large metal objects.

What I did know was that Blackwell College was much closer to Penn Yan than Ithaca was.

"Definitely a sign," I said, nodding.

Tessa cuts sharply left, leading me past one building and behind another—and there it is. We're practically in its shadow.

"Hi, scissors." I peer up at the wide-open V of its handles.

"What do you think?" Tessa asks. "Everything you dreamed of?"

"Eleven out of ten." I pull my phone out—and even though I've got a pile of unread texts, I tap straight into my photo app.

"Want to be in it? I can—wait, actually—" Tessa cups her hands around her mouth, jogging toward a guy in a baseball cap. "Andrew!" He stops, circling back to give her a fist bump. Tessa points vaguely at the scissors before handing him her phone.

The next thing I know, I'm crouched beside her, beaming side by side in the triangular space between the scissor blades. "It's all about the vibes," Tessa says.

"Is the vibe decapitation?"

She laughs. "Pre-decapitation."

Andrew snaps a few more pictures and returns Tessa's phone, giving her hair a quick ruffle before he leaves.

"So, how do you know Andrew?"

"Oh, he's one of the himbos. Friends with my brother." Tessa smiles down at the screen for a minute, swiping and tapping. "Okay, texting these now!"

"Right! I forgot your brother goes here."

"Yup!" We set off down one of the paths. "Dan—he's a junior. He's the best."

"So he's a himbo?"

"He wishes." Tessa laughs. "No. His friends are himbos—he's how I *know* the himbos. But he's kind of, like, you know. Scrawny Jewish guy. Loves sports. Knows all the stats. Emphatically not a jock."

"Do you have to be a jock to qualify as a himbo?"

"You know, it's actually been a while since I've reviewed the himbo qualifications."

I grin, and she grins back, and it's almost unnerving how easy this is. We've spent the whole morning together, but I don't think there's been a single awkward silence. It's unprecedented.

I mean, it's unprecedented for *me*.

We're almost at the edge of the courtyard. "So, Dan's twenty," she says, "I'm eighteen, and our sister, Rachael, is sixteen. All June birthdays, almost exactly two years apart. But they're both Geminis, and I'm a Cancer." She nods significantly. "What about you?"

"Siblings or zodiac?"

"Mmm. Both."

"Okay, well." I smile a little. "I turned eighteen on Halloween."

"A Scorpio. In-te-rest-ing." She tilts her head.

I pause, raising my eyebrows for a moment. "And I have a sixteen-year-old sister. Edith."

"She's queer, too, right? Lili told me you have a little baby gay sister."

"Definitely. Super queer, really funny. Kind of chaotic?" I nod. "You guys would get along."

Tessa bursts out laughing. "Because she's queer and chaotic?"

"And funny!"

"Well, I *am* a middle-child Jewish lesbian with ADHD." She waves her hands in a flourish, and I laugh. "Okay, but I'm actually so jealous you have a queer sister. Like. What a win."

"Aww. So Dan and Rachael aren't queer?"

"Nope. I'm the token gay. I mean, as far as I know." She tilts her palms up. "They were pretty cute when I came out, though. They kidnapped me and brought me to the Big Gay Ice Cream shop in the Gayborhood."

"The what in the what?"

"In Philly! That's where I'm from. Well, I'm from the Main Line. The Big Gay Ice Cream shop closed, though. I actually cried. I think it still exists in New York? The city, I mean."

My brain sprints to catch up. "I had no idea ice cream could be gay."

"It can," Tessa says. "It even tasted gay. I actually think Dan and Rachael got gayer from eating it."

"Is that how it works?"

"Yup," she says, as we pass a bank of benches at the edge of the quad. "Dan especially—instantly fifty percent gayer. He literally drives a Subaru Outback now."

I laugh. "That's what my parents drive."

"Of course they do. They created two queer kids."

My chest goes tight. It's so easy to forget I've been lying through my teeth this whole time. I wonder what Tessa thinks I was like as a kid.

Probably like Edith, I guess.

Edith, who announced on the first day of preschool that she was going to marry a girl. When she played house, there were always two mommies. Sometimes she'd get distracted in the grocery store, staring at pretty women—once she even plucked a sunflower out of a cut flower display and gave it to one of them in the checkout line. She couldn't have been older than five at the time. I don't even think she'd met an out lesbian in real life at that point.

Queerness was just something Edith implicitly understood—like how babies pick up languages without even trying.

"Oop," Tessa says, glancing up from her phone. "Lili needs confirmation that you're alive. She says you're not answering your texts."

"Oh! God. Sorry. I haven't checked in a minute."

"Your texts or your pulse?"

I smile a little. "Neither."

She presses two fingers to my wrist. And there's a tiny, soft thump in my chest.

"Okay," she declares after a moment. "Pulse is good. You're definitely alive."

I blink. "I should text her, huh?"

Tessa's already typing. "Nah—I'm on it. Anyway, we're home."

I text Lili a quick apology anyway, with some extra emojis to drive the point home. Then Tessa lets us into the dorm with her keycard.

I swipe through our scissor photos while we wait for the elevator, and Tessa grins down at my screen. "Look how totally unfazed we are by our impending decapitation."

"Honestly, we seem pretty fine with it."

"Good for us!"

I zoom in a bit to do a closer crop on my favorite of the bunch. It really is cuter than it has any right to be—nothing but easy smiles and sunlit faces.

I post it to Instagram with a scissor emoji for the caption, right as the elevator doors slide open.

Texts with Gretchen

GP: IMOGEN

GP: WHO ARE YOU SCISSORING

GP: WHAT'S HAPPENING

IS: Wait

IS: What?????

GP: 📎

GP: Don't get me wrong, I'm happy for you 😂

IS: OMG

IS: I would NEVER

IS: Post that online I mean!!!!

GP: 👀

IS: GRETCHEN NO

IS: Hahaha omg

IS: I just meant like

IS: I don't want you to think I'm saying OMG I WOULD NEVER, like I'm grossed out or scandalized

IS: By a very natural and beautiful expression of intimacy

GP: This

GP: Wow

GP: This is my favorite conversation

IS: Should I edit the caption

IS: Like would other people read it like that? 💀

GP: Haha depends

GP: Are they gay

GP: You know, this could actually be the test

GP: What do u think of when you see ✂️

GP: Gay Rorschach!!!!!

IS: Please say you're joking

IS: I tagged Tessa in this

GP: Aww is Tessa gay??

GP: Then I guess it's a grand gesture!!!!!!

GP: Promposal walked so public scissoring invitation could run

IS: GRETCHEN PLEASE

GP: 💀 💀 💀

GP: Immybean it's fine

GP: You're YOU

GP: No one thinks you're dropping sexmojis on the main

IS: :-|

GP: Okay also can we just acknowledge TESSA
GP: She's actually so hot??
GP: She used to have longer hair, right?
GP: I recognize her
GP: From Lili's page
GP: Kind of a soft butch vibe now, huh. I like it

IS: I don't know what soft butch means, but she did
        have longer hair

GP: Sweet heteropotamus
GP: ✄

12

When we reach Lili's room, Kayla's leaning in the doorway like a catalog model—legs crossed, hand grazing the doorframe, locs swept into a ponytail. But she steps into the room when she sees us, leaving space for us to follow.

"Oh, hey!" Lili looks up from her desk chair. "How was the scissor?"

My cheeks flood with heat. "Good. Yes! It was great."

I sneak a quick glance at Tessa, who seems completely unfazed. Then again, Tessa's not the one dropping coded sex solicitations into her Instagram captions.

God, I don't even one hundred percent know what scissoring *is*. All I can picture are naked Barbies with interlocked legs mashing up against each other. Which, clearly—

It occurs to me, suddenly, that Kayla just asked me a question.

"Oh! Sorry—I zoned out."

"You're good!" Kayla says. "Just gauging your opinion on

the issue of small German sausages."

I stare at her. Has it always been like this? Has everyone been constantly talking about sex this whole time, and I've just never picked up on the code?

I clear my throat. "You mean—as a euphemism?"

"Oh, she means a literal sausage," Lili assures me.

"Well, technically, it's liverwurst pate in a sausage casing. But it's smaller than you're thinking." Tessa raises both pointer fingers, inching them closer together to demonstrate. Which turns out to be unnecessary because, a moment later, Kayla whips out the actual sausage. Right here in Lili's dorm room, with only a single clear sandwich bag for protection.

She holds it up by the ziplock, eyeing it with begrudging respect. "The beast itself."

It's about the size of my thumb, sealed in orange plastic—the label reads *BRAUNSCHWEIGER Liverwurst* in Oktoberfest font.

I almost drop my phone. "Oh, I hate it."

"It's an abomination. Literal violence wrapped in plastic." Kayla nudges aside my clothes and toiletries from this morning, sinking onto the edge of my bed. "Apparently, it was in a company gift basket Declan's mom got for Christmas? And for some demonic reason, Dec decided to bring it back with him after break."

"Scott, you should definitely touch it," says Tessa. "I don't think you can really *understand* the sausage until you feel how warm and squishy it is—"

"I'm fine!"

Lili laughs. "You'd probably die if you opened it at this point. Like, I actually think just cracking the seal would release toxic death fumes into the air. Mika won't go near it."

"And he just brought it here?" I ask. "Like . . . as a souvenir from home?"

"God only knows what goes through that white boy's head."

I pause. "And how do you have it?"

"Because," Tessa says, "they've turned it into a diabolical back-and-forth revenge game."

"Like hot potato," chimes Lili.

Tessa beams. "Exactly. Like a fucked-up game of hot potato."

Kayla nods. "So I'm in class yesterday, digging around my bag for my minty Life Savers—"

"They keep her from falling asleep in class," Lili explains.

"That, and they're delicious," says Kayla. "Anyway, I find the roll and eat one, but I'm still really tired, so I grab a second one. Then, right before class ends, I go for a third—and what do I find?" Kayla holds up the sandwich bag. "This fucker, rolled into the Life Savers wrapping with a couple of mints on either end. I actually threw up in my mouth when I saw it."

"Which completely defeats the purpose of the breath mint!" adds Tessa.

Kayla dangles the corner of the bag between two fingers.

97

"So now? Payback. I know my girl Tess is in." She looks from Lili to me, her face deadly serious. "The only question is: Are you?"

Lili translates. "Imogen, would you like to hide a tiny sausage in Declan's room?"

Suddenly, Kayla launches off the bed, drops to one knee, and holds the sausage aloft like a diamond ring.

What could I possibly say but yes?

Texts with Gretchen

GP: Detour!!! Getting lunch in Woodstock

GP: Have you been here? It's cute!

IS: I have not, but that's where my grandparents met!

GP: WHAT

GP: Like the actual festival??

IS: Yup!

GP: NO WAY

GP: WHY HAVE YOU NEVER MENTIONED THIS

GP: WHY HAVE I HEARD THE PANCAKE STORY
NINETY MILLION TIMES

GP: BUT NOT THIS

IS: Haha idk!

GP: I can't even process this info!!!!!!

GP: Wow

GP: Like what other secrets are you hiding??

GP: Other than ✂

IS: See, now I don't even want to tell you what I'm
about to do with a tiny German sausage

GP: IMOGEN

GP: What are you about to do

GP: With a tiny German sausage

GP: ????

13

Kayla lays out the mission in urgent, hushed tones. "He just left for the painting studios," she says, "and Lili's friend Clara lives on his hall—she's gonna let us in, so we don't have to try to figure out the tunnels. Which is great, because I don't fuck around underground."

"That's actually my favorite Dr. Seuss book," says Tessa. "*I Don't Fuck Around Underground.*"

"*I Don't Fuck Around Underground, Said the Hound,*" I add.

Lili looks up from her phone and blinks, shaking her head.

"Page one," Tessa says. "'I know this might astound, but I'm kind of tightly wound, and thus I don't fuck around in the depths of underground,' said the hound."

"'Because fucking around underground,' the hound expounded, 'is bound to make a sound,'" I say, without hesitation.

"So . . . whenever y'all are done with whatever the fuck that was," Kayla says.

Lili taps her phone screen. "Okay! Clara just confirmed that Dec's room is unlocked and open for business."

"She picked the lock?" I ask. I don't know if I should be scandalized or impressed.

Lili shrugs. "He probably left it open."

"Can I just say that our timing is *perfect*? It's supposed to rain tomorrow and then get chilly, and"—Kayla smiles fondly down at the sausage—"that's right, little man. Guess who's going straight into Declan's winter gloves."

"Right down into one of the fingers," adds Tessa, "for a squishy surprise."

I press my palm to my cheek. "This is a whole other level of gross."

We step outside and barely make it ten feet into the courtyard before Kayla stops short, tugging Lili back by her sleeve. They both stand, frozen, for a moment, staring at one of the dorms—presumably Declan's. A moment later, Lili raises her phone up to her mouth like it's a walkie-talkie.

"Two professional spies in the making," Tessa murmurs. "Such finesse."

I laugh. "So how did you decide to align with Kayla over Declan?"

Tessa pauses, glancing briefly at Kayla and Lili, before leaning in closer. "I'm not aligned with Kayla," she says quietly. "I'm aligned with chaos."

I raise my eyebrows.

"I'm playing both sides. Neither of them has any idea. I'm actually the one who thought of the Life Savers thing."

I shake my head, awestruck. "You are—"

"Absolutely!" Tessa interjects suddenly. Her eyes flick sideways as Kayla and Lili sidle back up. "Of course I can take a picture of you with the sausage!"

"You want a picture with the sausage?" Kayla looks at me strangely. "This sausage?"

"She does!" Tessa pats my shoulder, grins, and steps back a few feet, phone aloft.

"She *definitely* does," Lili adds.

"If you say so." Kayla shakes her head, takes the sausage bag out of her purse, and then peels the sides back, letting the sausage poke out like a banana.

I shoot Tessa a quick grimace—she smiles innocently back. Then, I carefully pluck the sausage out of the bag, pinching its plastic wrapping between my fingers like a claw machine.

I have never, ever seen Lili open her camera app this quickly.

"This is incredible," says Tessa, voice threaded with laughter. She grins down at Lili's phone screen while I pass the sausage back to Kayla. "Scott, oh man. Your expression in these."

Lili holds her phone up. "I'm framing this."

The photo's zoomed close on my face, which I'm sure would make me self-conscious under any other circumstance. But everything about the expression is just so undeniably, hilariously *me*. Cheerful smile and panicked eyes, in brazen contradiction. I laugh. "Oh God."

"A masterpiece," says Tessa, meeting my gaze with a grin.

In the sunlight, her eyes are the exact color of acorns.

14

Clara ushers us in through the dorm's front door with the sub-tlety of a Disney villain, before creeping back down the hall on her tiptoes. Kayla turns to face us. "We ready?"

Lili and I nod.

Tessa flashes a thumbs-up.

It's eerily quiet for a Saturday—I guess everyone's either grabbing lunch or still sleeping. Declan's room is on the first floor, around the corner from the front entrance.

Kayla points at the 114 above his door. "Here we go."

I nod without speaking—my heart's beating so fast. The door creaks a little when Kayla opens it, and I almost jump out of my skin. She freezes in the doorway, peering around the dark space. "Coast is clear."

Once we're all inside, Kayla pulls the door shut behind us and flicks on the lights. "So here's what we're looking for." She pulls her phone out, taps the screen a few times, and tilts it up to show us a photo.

Lili smiles. "I know her."

In the picture, Lili and Declan are posed on either side of a snowman, and Declan's waving at the camera. Kayla zooms in on his gloved hand. "Dark gray, kind of a thick material, and it bunches in at the wrist."

"It'll be the one that looks . . . like a glove," Tessa adds.

"I mean, yeah." Kayla lets out a quick laugh. "Okay! I'm gonna start checking coat pockets."

I scan the room, suddenly struck by a pang of déjà vu—which makes no sense. Maybe it's just that this whole room looks like a movie set. It's a single, so it's a little smaller than Lili's, but there's something so bright and open about the space. There's a fake brick accent wall and an actual closet in back. All the art above his desk is framed and perfectly centered. And the books on his shelf are stripped down to their spines—all white hardcovers. Even the clutter on top of his dresser feels intentional: a pink paper peony, a short stack of moleskine notebooks, and—

A shoebox-sized, made-to-scale, painstakingly detailed replica of this bedroom.

"Wait—oh! I've seen this on TikTok." I press a hand to my cheek. "This is, like—wow. *Unbelievable* in person."

"Right? Dec and Mika did this one together. They're both so sickeningly talented." Lili settles onto the floor near his dresser, while Kayla repositions Declan's peacoat over the back of his desk chair.

"Should we check the closet? I kind of just want to see

Declan's closet." Tessa opens it slowly, glancing back over her shoulder at me. "Okay, Waldo queen. Work your magic."

I nod slowly, taking in the space—small, but crisply organized with a bunch of stacked plastic drawer units. "Oh my God, it's so neat," Tessa says, shaking her head. "Okay, sorry, this level of cleanliness, but he's holding on to that nasty rotten sausage? I don't know, man. It's giving serial killer."

Kayla and Lili both laugh from across the room.

"I mean, if he's palming it off on Kayla," I point out, "he's not *technically* holding on to it. Oh!"

Tessa's eyes widen. "Did you find something?"

I crouch next to the drawers. "Look—tassels. Could be the end of a scarf?" I reach for my phone, snapping a quick picture.

"Ooh, good call. Never forget this moment," says Tessa.

I laugh. "No, I mean, I want to be able to put it back exactly the same as we left it, right? With the drawer cracked a little like this, tassel hanging out . . ."

"Oh. Shit. You're good—"

"FUCK," Lili hisses, scrambling to her feet. "Clara just texted. He's coming back. I don't know why—fuck."

"Get the light!" Kayla whispers.

"No time. Just hide!"

Tessa yanks the closet door shut, sinking to the floor beside me. For a moment, all I hear is frantic rustling and a few muttered curse words. But then, sure enough—

The door creaks open.

I quickly silence my phone—and Tessa mouths *oh* and does

the same. She's sitting so close, the act of slipping her phone back into her jeans makes our arms brush together.

My heart's going a little bit haywire.

Outside: A few short footsteps. Then a pause. Then the creak of Declan's bedframe.

Tessa turns to me incredulously. *Is he gonna nap?* she mouths, pantomiming sleep with prayer hands pressed to her cheek.

I shrug, palms tipped up.

Another low creak.

She shoots me a panic face, but it quickly breaks into a smile. I can barely catch my breath for a moment.

This closet

Is just

So small. She pokes my knee, and I let out a fake, noiseless gasp.

I poke her back.

She scrunches her nose at me.

A bubble of laughter rises up from my chest for no reason. But then Tessa clamps a hand over my mouth, and it makes something twist inside me.

The skin of her palm on my lips.

I keep hearing Gretchen's voice in my head.

She's actually so hot??

Is Tessa hot? I never know how hotness gets decided. Or where it stands in relation to cuteness. Or sexiness. Or beauty in general.

A door opens and shuts, and Tessa pulls her hand back with a start. For a few interminable moments, we sit frozen in silence, ears cocked toward the door.

Then, at last, there's more rustling and a single dull thud. "Hey," Kayla says under her breath. "All clear."

Tessa opens the door a crack—then opens it all the way to find Kayla, shaking her head and looking vaguely shell-shocked. Lili army-crawls out from under the bed, settling in beside her.

"Were you both under there?" Tessa asks.

"Oh yes. And our boy's hand?" Kayla exhales. "Two inches from my face."

"Needed his phone charger, apparently," adds Lili. She shoots me a wry smile. "Exciting first mission?"

Declan's gloves are, in fact, in the scarf drawer, which makes Kayla sigh in relief. Lili shoves the sausage into the glove's middle finger, and we try to match my photo when we put everything back. But once the sausage is in, we don't linger—I think we're all still a little flustered.

Kayla splits off, heading to her own dorm, and I end up sort of drifting behind Tessa and Lili. They're talking about some party they went to at Rainbow Manor. Or a future party they're planning to go to. I can't focus long enough to figure out which.

I guess my brain's still in Declan's closet.

How do I explain the part where Tessa's smile made my chest hurt?

Or when she covered my mouth with her hand and I sort of wanted to kiss it.

It's like scrolling through someone else's pictures, catching a glimpse of yourself in the background. That sudden jolt of *hold on, wait, go back!*

Was that me?

Texts with Gretchen

GP: Hello hi I would like an update on the 🌭 situation

GP: Was it fun

GP: Was it wrapped

IS: Definitely wrapped

IS: 📎

GP: Oh my god, your face

GP: 💀

GP: This is my new favorite Imogen picture

GP: You and your tiny German sausage

IS: Thank you, it was very tiny

IS: Have you guys made it to Vassar yet?!

GP: Pulling in now!!!

GP: Slightly freaking out bc they just emailed me that the girl who was supposed to host me had to leave campus suddenly for a family emergency

GP: (Per her tiktok, the "emergency" appears to be the Wallows performing in Albany)

IS: Oh no! Wait—what are you going to do?

GP: I mean tonight I have to stay in the hotel with Mama
P 👻

GP: They're going to try to find someone else for
tomorrow though

GP: It just sucks because I can't really go out if I'm
staying with my mom, and then there probably
won't even be any parties tomorrow because Sunday

IS: I'm sorry ☹️

GP: Tbh I'm concerned about the integrity of my pros/
cons lists when I'm not even getting the full dorm
experience

IS: Yeah but what if you went to a party and it was the
worst, and then you just assumed parties at Vassar
suck in general

GP: True true good point
GP: Haha imagine the Worst Party
GP: We have to plan it

IS: Oh definitely
IS: Okay
IS: The menu: fish and only fish
IS: The guest list: literally only those guys from men's
rights forums who talk about getting cucked

GP: YES!!!!

GP: Just a bunch of incels from the manosphere, hangin'
        around the fish table, rating hott girlz on a scale
        from one to ten

IS: The music: Kid Rock deep cuts

IS: Dental office lighting

GP: And creepy baby dolls on display

GP: With human teeth

IS: I hate this party so much

GP: I could check no on a billion RSVP cards

GP: and it wouldn't be enough

15

By sunset, we've all claimed prime spots on Lili's floor—Declan, Mika, and Kayla with their backs against one bed; Lili, me, and Tessa against the other. Lili turned the overhead lights off, leaving only the hazy glow from a trio of lamps. In the background, we've got Mitski's new album streaming faintly through Declan's fancy mini Bluetooth speakers. It's as cozy as a slumber party, down to the not-quite-empty pizza box in the center of the room. Turns out, you can buy whole pizzas downstairs—Lili's dorm has a late-night snack bar.

I'm working my way through the pair of crusts I've saved for last, while Tessa leans closer, holding her phone out in front of me. "Full-paragraph comment. Every single TikTok." She pauses to grin up at Mika. "I love your parents so much."

Mika smiles a little. "I went home for break, and they'd printed a bunch of screen grabs to display on the fridge. Right next to the Christmas cards. *And* they printed out Jade's top nine Instagram collage post. How do they even find this stuff?"

"Is Jade your sister?" I ask.

"Ex-girlfriend. My parents are slightly obsessed with her."

I press a fist to my mouth. "Oh no . . ."

"No, it's fine! We're best friends. We grew up together—like, we still talk literally every day. And she's at Cornell, so we get to visit a lot. I'm pretty sure my parents think we're still secretly dating?"

Kayla laughs. "Mika, *everyone* thinks you're secretly dating."

"And you all have beautiful imaginations." Mika scoots forward to grab another pizza slice.

"Okay, for real," Tessa says, "it's pretty amazing that you and Jade still get along that well. Same with you two." She looks from Lili to me. "Just the fact that an overnight trip with your ex was even on the table."

"I have sleepovers with my exes," says Declan.

Kayla rolls her eyes. "Not that kind of sleepover, Don Juan."

I hug my knees to my chest, feeling the tips of my cheeks go warm. "Yeah, it's—you know. It's been totally fine."

Lili shoots me a quick, awkward smile. "Right. Definitely."

"Oh man," says Tessa. "I tried the friendship thing with Jillian, and it worked for a little while. But it got weird when she started dating someone."

"I get that," I say.

"Not because I was jealous," Tessa adds quickly. "It was just awkward. Like, she'd mention her new girlfriend all the time, but she did it in this back-off-Tess kind of way. Like I'm about to make a move? Come on."

Lili laughs. "Didn't she slide into your DMs, too, the first time she saw another girl on your Instagram?"

"Oh, *immediately*. And I'm like, 'Um, so that's my cousin Annie.'"

I hug my legs tighter, trying to ignore the nervous kick in my chest. "She must have freaked out the next time you started dating someone."

"Every time. Every girl. All zero of them." Tessa shoots me a quick, sideways smile.

I smile back, not entirely sure if she's kidding. She has to be, right? There must be thousands of girls with crushes on Tessa. I mean, I'd be losing my mind over Tessa if I were queer.

I keep thinking about Declan's closet—and how we sat so close, our knees overlapped.

"Oh!" Mika yawns and stretches. "Did we figure out the deal for tomorrow yet?"

"What's tomorrow?" asks Lili.

"Costumes! For Friday. The dark academia party."

Kayla claps. "Yes! I want to do a thrift store run. Remember that store in Waterloo I went to with Audra and that guy Dilf? Audra's my roommate," she adds, glancing at me.

"His name was Dilf?" Tessa laughs, short and incredulous. "Like . . . a DILF?"

"*Is* he a DILF?" Lili asks.

"No idea. I think it's just a nickname?" Kayla shrugs. "I *hope* it's a nickname. He's that white guy with the eyebrow ring and the really light blue eyes, who kind of looks like a cult leader? And he has a bong named Creature?"

"Of course he does." Tessa looks sincerely delighted.

"Anyway, the point is, it was a very cheap store, and I want to go back," Kayla says. "Anyone interested?"

Lili shoots me a querying glance, and I nod and shrug.

"I'm in if these two are," Tessa says, bopping my head, and then Lili's. And I'm pretty sure I've slipped into someone else's life.

DAY THREE
SUNDAY
MARCH 20

Texts with Gretchen

GP: I'm supposed to have my tour today and it's raining 🙈🙈🙈

GP: Are you guys getting this hell weather too?

GP: It's not even the romantic kind of rain, I wouldn't even want to kiss in it

GP: Maaaaaaybe if it was hot Tessa ✂️ 😌

16

Either my phone's gotten brighter or the room's gotten darker. I squint at Gretchen's texts, rub my eyes, and flip it over, screen down.

It's barely past seven, and Lili's still sleeping. I'm so tired, even yawning feels like too much effort. But every time I try to close my eyes, they spring open, so I just peer through the inky black until I can make out where the walls end. It takes a full minute for me to realize the drumroll of pounding raindrops isn't just Lili's white-noise app.

I tug my phone off the charger, staring again at Gretchen's short stream of texts.

I could write back to the part about hell weather, right? Add a couple of emojis and press send. It doesn't have to be that deep.

I can't explain why that scissor emoji makes me so jumpy. I know that Gretchen's just teasing. Obviously. But I feel so weird about it.

Why do I feel so weird about it?

It couldn't be lesbophobia, right? That wouldn't even make sense. My two best friends are queer women. I have a gay little sister. Other than Otávio, I literally don't have any close friends who *aren't* queer.

Though that's what every bigot says, right? *Queerphobic??? Me??? BUT I HAVE A QUEER FRIEND!!*

I reread Gretchen's texts, feeling strangely out of orbit. The thought of her and Tessa kissing makes my brain short-circuit.

And in the rain? Sorry, but what kind of rain *would* be romantic to kiss in? I get that it looks cool in movies. But in real life, you'd be clammy and cold and your socks would soak through, and you'd probably just be worried the whole time about your phone getting wet. Unless you're so desperate to kiss this particular person, you don't even notice the discomfort. Or you do, but it's worth it.

I guess that's the whole point.

"Hey! You're dressed." Lili sits up in bed, yawning. "Morning."

"Morning! Guess what I made."

She rubs her eyes, blinking. "You . . . what?"

"A dark academia vision board!" I hold my phone up.

"Ohhhh. Nice." She nods dazedly.

"For the thrift store. Just to use as a reference. If people want to, I mean."

"That's amazing," she says, another yawn breaking through. "They're gonna love it."

"You haven't even seen—"

"I know, but Immy, your boards are always perfect." She clasps her hands and stretches them up, then back, then side to side. "Because you're very, very intense about them."

"Rude but accurate." I smile into my own fisted hand.

I know I can get a little overly invested in this stuff, but a proper vision board is serious business. Because it has to work as a cohesive whole—which means being intentional about color palette and positioning. But, of course, the real magic is in the details. And it's not just about matching plaids with tweeds.

A good vision board knows its audience. Which, in this case, means masculine, feminine, *and* androgynous aesthetics, sized to fit everything from Kayla's height to Lili's curves to my own pear-shaped, corn-fed squishiness. At the end of the day, an outfit only works if you can imagine a real person wearing it.

For example, Tessa. Dressed like Timothée Chalamet in *Little Women*.

Specifically, the vest and the little necktie bow he wears in that scene with Florence Pugh, when Amy explains to Laurie how marriage is an economic proposition.

That, but on Tessa. I can picture it perfectly.

Hours later, I'm huddled next to Lili under the awning behind her dorm, holding her umbrella while she texts. "Okay! They're pulling up in a sec."

I glance back over my shoulder. "Should we wait for Tessa?"

"No, she's not coming. The himbos are dragging her to Wegmans."

It hits me like a punch for some reason.

"Oh," I say.

Lili opens her umbrella, positioning it over our heads. "Ready to make a run for it?"

We barrel toward Kayla's parked minivan—a big, clunky Honda Odyssey that looks like it came straight from the carpool line, covered in animal-rescue bumper stickers, with a few little dents in the back. I'm shivering and half-soaked by the time we reach it, and I scramble in behind Lili when the back doors slide open. It's one of those minivans with three rows— Mika's riding shotgun and Declan's in the back, so we take the middle. "It's like a school bus, I know," Kayla says. "Tell me you come from a big family without telling me you come from a big family."

I buckle my seat belt, trying to smile normally. "How big's your family?" I ask.

Kayla starts backing out of the space. "Well, I'm the youngest of four. So when I graduated, my parents went out, bought a Mustang, and gave me this beaut." She pats the steering wheel. "How do you like those ass dimples? Courtesy of my brother, who dents the car every time he backs out of the driveway."

"As an only child New Yorker, this is highly unrelatable content," Declan chimes from the back.

"I'm sorry—were you not the center of attention for five seconds?"

I make myself laugh along with the group, but I feel a little droopy inside. Almost wistful.

Tessa's not coming. And I don't know why I care.

Texts with Gretchen

IS: Hell weather has landed in Geneva as well 🙁

IS: We're going shopping though

IS: Getting costumes for the dark academic party

IS: *academia

GP: DARK ACADEMIA YES

GP: So fucking jealous

IS: No don't be!!!

IS: It's next weekend, I won't even be there 🫣

IS: I'm just the fashion consultant

GP: Uh oh, I see ellipses!!

GP: Vision board landing in 3 . . . 2 . . . 1 . . .

IS: 📎

GP: atta girl

17

Hand-Me-Down Closet is about fifteen minutes from campus, in a dreary shopping center tucked behind the outlet mall. "We're really here," Lili says, one hand pressed to her heart. "Dilf's favorite thrift store."

"The one and only," says Kayla.

The parking lot's practically empty—probably par for the course on a rainy Sunday. Lili nudges me as Kayla pulls into a spot. "Immy, text them your vision board!"

"You made a vision board?" asks Kayla.

"It's just a thing I threw together—"

"She woke up at the crack of dawn. Scoured the internet for *hours*—"

"One hour! Not even." I press send, my cheeks going warm.

"Heyyyy," Declan says. "Nice."

"Yeah, you nailed it," Kayla murmurs, zooming in on her screen while she unbuckles. "Look at all those brooding white people."

She laughs, and I smile. "Yeah, no. They are."

We dash inside, wiping our feet on the mat in a damp huddle. I peer around the space—this definitely isn't one of those curated vintage boutiques on Linden Street. It's fluorescently lit chaos: bar mitzvah T-shirts and shoulder-padded suit jackets, interspersed with stretchy short dresses and every possible iteration of denim. But I can already spot a few intriguing tartans and blazers, half-hidden among the racks. I love treasure hunting in stores like this. It's the ultimate hidden-object game.

Almost makes me wish I could stay for the party.

I think I'd want to wear a dress or a skirt. Something vaguely Victorian, but not too on-the-nose. Jo March vibes, but not like I raided her closet. Old-timey collegiate.

"What the fuck even is this?" asks Lili, holding up what appears to be the skeleton of a lace-up bodice. "Are you just supposed to put the stringy part over your nipple and hope for the best?"

"Maybe you wear it over a real shirt?"

Mika drifts over. "Have you seen any suspenders?"

Lili points out a display of accessories in the back corner, before circling back to a rack of dresses. "Okay, some of these dresses are actually cute. Immy, you should try stuff on!" She runs her fingertip down one of the zippers. "What's the optimal skirt length? Are we talking Christian mommy blogger? Spicy Christian mommy blogger?"

"Emilia Cardoso. Ma'am. What kind of porn are you watching?" asks Kayla.

"Wouldn't you like to know—ooh!" Lili hands me a deep green shirtdress. "Here—this is very you!"

"Really cute," I admit, though I can already tell it's going to be tight over my hips.

Of course, having one dress to try on makes me want to round up a few more—and by the time I reach the fitting rooms, I've managed to gather an armload. The rooms turn out to be surprisingly luxurious. Maybe not Anthropologie level, but they're well-lit, with plenty of space for the half dozen or so pieces of clothing I've gathered. I spread everything out as much as possible—dresses on hooks, pinafore over the back of a chair, skirt hanging from the doorknob. I don't love trying on clothes, but I love the part that comes right before it, when every dress seems like it just might change the whole game. Must be the Halloween baby in me. I've always loved a good low-stakes transformation.

Unless it's not a transformation at all. Maybe it's recognition. It's that little click of *hi, me, nice to meet you!*

As expected, the bottom half of the shirtdress is tight enough to make even the spiciest Christian mommy blogger blush. Definitely not wearable if I plan on bending or sitting. Or even breathing, really. But just as I'm about to peel it off, my phone buzzes—Tessa responding to the inspiration board in the group chat.

This is so extra, I love it

And then: Also guys wtf is this rain

There's a grumpy-faced selfie attached—wet bangs and rain-spattered cheeks, the entrance to Wegmans visible in the background.

I smile down at my phone.

It occurs to me that the top half of this dress fits perfectly. And half of a perfectly fitting dress is all you really need for a selfie. Now I just have to rein in the bunny eyes, tuck those weird hanks of hair behind my ears, and—

"Hi, hello! Reporting for outfit feedback duty."

Lili's voice, just outside the fitting room. I shove my phone into my bag so forcefully, I half expect it to split a hole through the bottom. "Almost done—sorry!"

"Immy, if you make me quote a Rachel Hollis book title at you, I swear to God."

I nod quickly, even though she can't see me. I'm pretty sure only half the lights are on in my brain.

But I manage to pull on a gray plaid pinafore over my *Upstate of Mind* T-shirt, and it's actually pretty perfect. Super cheap, for one thing—probably because there's a fairly big hole in the waistband. But it's in the back, and it's right at the seam, so I bet I could sew it closed. I could even duct-tape it. Anyway, I really like it, even paired with my random fake-retro T-shirt. Honestly, the longer I stare at the mirror, the more I love the whole weird combination. It makes me look . . . kind of queer? Like the kind of girl you'd meet at a gay coffeeshop or something?

Or, you know. Literally every straight, white girl after two days on an American college campus.

I step out, and my heart's in my throat. I don't know why this feels like a test.

"Um, okay, I *love* the pleats." Lili taps her chin. "Let's see a spin."

"So, there's kind of a hole in the butt—"

"The spiciest Christian mommy blogger! I love it!"

"Let me see!" Kayla slips out of the stall next door, wearing what appears to be an ivory lace wedding dress.

Declan glances over. "Miss Havisham. Nice."

Kayla flips him off without missing a beat.

Then she grins at me. "Look who's serving up the biggest bi energy."

"Me?" I blink.

"Bi vibes? Through the roof," Declan says.

Lili's eyes meet mine for the barest split second, and she bites back a smile.

"As much as I hate to agree with this asshole," says Kayla.

Declan side-hugs her. "Look at this girl pretending she didn't stop the clocks when I left her at the altar."

Kayla wrinkles her nose, and Lili laughs—I'm pretty sure I'm laughing too. But my brain's on another planet entirely. It's in a completely different solar system.

Biggest bi energy. Bi vibes through the roof.

It's clearly a compliment—or a solidarity thing, since Kayla and Declan themselves are both bi. So it's not that I mind it. Of course not. It just doesn't entirely compute.

I'm straight. So how are my bi vibes through the roof?

Is it really just the aesthetic? Am I two lemon squares and a haircut away from making out with girls at a Clairo show?

Or does it all come down to confirmation bias?

Kayla and Declan think I give off bi vibes. Because Kayla and Declan think I'm bi.

Kayla pulls around to the back side of Rosewood and twists in her seat to face me, brown eyes gleaming. "Imogen, we gotta talk."

I look up, startled. "Oh! Okay—"

"Did you or did you not just purchase a plaid pinafore?"

"I . . . did?"

"Mm-hmm. And would you say said pinafore would fall under the aesthetic umbrella of what we might refer to as 'dark academia'?"

I smile a little. "Probably."

"Probably?" Kayla taps her phone and hands it back to Lili. "Ms. Cardoso, will you please direct the defendant's attention to exhibit A?"

"My vision board?"

"And will the defendant please describe the attire of the brooding white person in the bottom left corner?"

"It's . . . a gray plaid pinafore."

"Precisely." Kayla bangs her fist on her palm like a gavel. "You have a costume. Therefore, the court of Kayla Richardson hereby summons you to return to campus this Friday and attend one party at Rainbow Manor."

"Hereby seconded," says Declan.

"Thirded," says Mika.

"It's not a vote," Kayla says. "It's a decree."

"You guys." I'm smiling so hard it makes my cheeks ache. I glance at Lili. "I probably shouldn't . . ."

"Right. I forgot you're on the avoid-campus-for-another-six-months visitation schedule," Lili says, and I know—I *know* she's just teasing.

But the sharp edge to her tone wipes the grin clean off my face. And judging by the ripple of awkward forced laughter, I'm not the only one who hears it.

Texts with Gretchen

IS: Okay that looks like a castle!!

IS: BEAUTIFUL

GP: RIGHT?

GP: You should have seen it last night

GP: Vassar at sunset 💯

GP: Remember when the sun existed 🏰 🏰

IS: I kind of like it with the gray sky background though

IS: Like, it's spooky

IS: But cozy

GP: If you say so lol

GP: BUT HEY GUESS WHAT

GP: I think they found someone to host me tonight ✌️

IS: Oh! Wait

IS: That's awesome

IS: So you'll get to stay in the dorms?

GP: I mean I'm lowkey scared to get my hopes up

GP: And then end up back in the hotel with my mom lol

IS: Okay, but Mama P is in fact amazing

GP: That is true

GP: Oh, she says hiiiiiii

GP: And she hopes you're having so much fun!!!!

GP: So much!!!!!

IS: Thanks 🖤

IS: Driving back from thrift store now

IS: But I think we're all meeting back up for dinner at
        Lili's favorite diner?

IS: Which is apparently called Diner

IS: It's off campus, I hear the pancakes are the BIGGEST

IS: Well

IS: Second biggest 😊

18

But by the time dinner rolls around, no one seems to care much about pancakes.

Or the fact that I'm leaving tomorrow.

Declan's the first to reply. So . . . you might want to take a quick peek out the window lol

"Has it gotten really bad out there?"

Lili reaches back to tug the blinds up, peering through the glass for a moment. "Wimp. It was way worse this morning."

"You think he's trying to bail?"

Our phones both buzz again—Mika. Ooh, yeah. I don't know if it's a diner night. May just heat up soup and make some tiny furniture.

Declan writes back with a full array of chair and couch emojis.

I stare at my screen, feeling strangely out of breath for a second.

"Really?" Lili scowls. "On your last night?"

"It's fine. I totally get it."

"It's not even raining that hard!"

I peek out the window again. "I mean, it's not great."

Another buzz—this time it's Kayla. haha i guess we should take a literal rain check

"Okay, I guarantee these losers forgot it's your last night," Lili says, tapping into the text box. "Watch, they're gonna—"

"Don't!" My heart jumps. "Please."

Lili shoots me a perplexed smile. "I wasn't going to, like, *bully* them. I was just going to remind them you're leaving—"

"I know. Yeah. I just—that just feels so weird. I don't want to pressure them into hanging out with me."

"Immy, they just forgot. It's not personal."

"I know." I stare at my knees, feeling so weird in my skin all of a sudden. Like I'm being pinpricked from the inside.

I guess it's just a little embarrassing, right? The way I thought it was real. My college friends. The group chat. Just one of the pack, right? Like I wasn't just some random high school kid they met literally two days ago.

Like I'd carved out some kind of home with these people.

By now, it's almost seven, and Tessa still hasn't replied to the group chat. Lili stands and stretches. "All right, I'm giving up on her. Do you want to just grab stuff from the snack bar? We can bring it up here and watch a movie if you want."

"Sure."

"Okay . . ." Lili grips the doorframe. "What do you *want* to do?"

"I'm fine with whatever! Really."

She sighs. "Immy, come on. Don't do this."

"Don't do what?"

"Your people-pleasing schtick! I'm tired of it. Save that shit for strangers, and just be real with me!"

And with that, she takes off down the empty dorm hallway. I chase after her, stung. "I am real with you!"

She stabs the elevator call button with her finger. For a moment, neither of us speaks.

"I'm not trying to people-please," I say, finally. "I'm just—"

"No, I know. Immy, I know—"

"I just honestly don't care if we watch a movie, okay? That's all."

"I *know.*" She bites her lip. "Sorry. It just sucks that it's raining, and now everyone's bailing on the diner, and I really wanted your last dinner to be special."

"It is special!"

"The snack bar is the actual antithesis of special. It's like the food version of a white sock."

The elevator chimes, doors sliding open to reveal a soaking wet Tessa carrying a soggy paper grocery bag. "Hi! Wait— are you guys heading to the diner? Let me just drop this stuff off and change into something a little less, uh"—she glances

139

down—"wet T-shirt contest."

"Diner's off—everyone bailed. Have you been getting our texts?"

Tessa shakes her head. "Phone died. Not, like, water damage. Just forgot to charge it. They really bailed?"

Lili nods and I shrug.

"Okay, well. Their loss." She shifts the grocery bag in her arms. "I got those vanilla scones—Scott, you would *love* them. Okay, wait, this bag is definitely about to disintegrate. Give me a sec to get situated."

"And plug your phone in," Lili adds, already halfway to her room.

"Yes! That. Also, hold up—I have the *best* dinner idea."

"Oh yeah?" Lili's back in her room by now, with the door left wide-open. But I hang back with Tessa, while she fumbles for her keys. "I can take the bag—"

"Nooo, ma'am. That is my gross bag, thank you very much. You're too dry and too pure."

"Like toilet paper."

"Exactly." Tessa grins. "Okay, here. Can you grab my keys, maybe?" She lifts the grocery bag higher, revealing a carabiner attached to one of her belt loops.

"Oh. Yeah! Should I . . . like. Just take the key off?" My cheeks go warm.

"Or just take the whole thing off the loop—probably easier, right?" Tessa watches me, beaming. "I love how hard you're concentrating right now. You should probably be a surgeon."

"Or a locksmith."

"Why not both?" Tessa says.

I unlock the door and push it open, and Tessa bumps it with her hip to hold it for me. But I linger in the doorway. "I like your room," I say, suddenly shy.

It's smaller than Lili's, and there's only one bed—hastily made with white sheets, patterned with tiny gnomes. There's a shaggy gray rug on the floor, currently covered with short stacks of books and scattered index cards. Just like Lili's room, the walls are one big gallery of photos and posters—a Bowie lightning bolt, a vintage map of Hershey Park, and the words *this must be the place* in stylized yellow and green.

"Talking Heads," I say. "I love that song."

"It's my favorite." She shoots me a quick smile, setting her bag down on top of her desk.

"Well, if it isn't the on-call surgeon." Lili smiles up at me from her laptop when I enter the room. "Who's gonna tell Tess you fainted watching that birth video in Girl Scouts?"

"That video was a nightmare. I stand by it."

"Oh, you definitely weren't standing."

I laugh, cheeks going warm. "Irrelevant. That birth was extremely vaginal—"

"Are you guys talking about extreme vaginas without me again?" Tessa asks. She leans against Lili's doorframe, already fully transformed—fresh gray hoodie, dry pair of gym shorts, and a very cute attempt at a ponytail. Slung over one shoulder is a lumpy Blackwell College duffel bag. "Who's ready for a picnic?"

19

It's like being in *Willy Wonka*—like I'm about to step out into the candy garden. But instead of chocolate and sunshine, it's just a dimly lit, graffiti-covered hallway. And, of course, we aren't outside at all.

We're beneath.

"So these are the tunnels," Tessa says, gesturing loosely. "It's mostly just hallways like this, but there are a few bigger rooms as you walk through."

I peer around. "It's so empty."

"I think Sunday night's pretty quiet. People come down here on the weekends, though."

"Thus the decor," Lili adds, stepping around a few flattened beer cans and a tired-looking disposable vape.

The tunnel widens into what's clearly an abandoned laundry room, judging by the dilapidated washers and dryers. The only other furniture in sight is a single tattered green sofa. Tessa tugs on a string hanging from the ceiling, flooding the space with sharp, fluorescent light. "This," she declares, "is the spot."

"This is where we're eating?" Lili squints down at the sofa.

"Ooh, don't sit there. That's a sex couch." Tessa unzips her duffel and takes out an actual red gingham picnic blanket.

"You know this is, like, a *really* creepy place for a picnic, right?" Lili nods slowly.

I settle in cross-legged on the blanket. "I like it. It kind of reminds me of the barn."

"Immy, it is absolutely zero percent like your barn."

"You have *a barn*?"

Lili laughs. "She has two!"

"I do not!" I turn to Tessa. "The second one's just a shed."

She scoots in beside me. "So do you just straight-up live on a farm?"

"Kind of? It's not a farm farm. But—I don't know—it's a little farmier than a big backyard? Like, my parents grow their own vegetables and we have eleven pets—that kind of thing."

"Eleven?"

I count them off on my fingers. "Three dogs, six cats—seven, if you count the feral one we leave food out for. And then my sister has a rabbit—"

"Flossie Bunny!" says Lili.

"And I have a hamster named Elizabeth."

Tessa raises her eyebrows. "That is a *very* pretty name for a hamster."

"Thank you! I got her during my *Pride and Prejudice* era."

Tessa laughs, and my chest goes taut. Shifting to face me,

she asks, "Where did Daisy live?"

I just look at her.

"Daisy the goat?" Lili asks.

"I can't believe you remember my childhood goat's name."

"Your childhood goat." Tessa smiles. "How many goat names do you think I'm keeping track of?"

"God, I don't even know. Millions, probably." I bite back a grin. "And she lived in the barn."

"Of course she did."

"But we really just use it for storage at this point."

"Well, it's also a performance venue," adds Lili.

"Right!" I nod. "There's a whole stage area in the back for concerts."

"There were *concerts*?"

Lili nods. "Sold-out shows every weekend. We had an extremely devoted fandom of stuffed animals."

"This is downright majestic," says Tessa.

"It was a golden age," confirms Lili. "We used to have sleepovers out there in the summer."

"And we turned it into a haunted house one year for my birthday," I say.

"I officially want your life. Hamster named Elizabeth, barn sleepovers, Halloween birthday." Tessa shakes her head at me. "How does that even work?"

"The barn sleepovers?" asks Lili.

"The Halloween birthday! Do you get double candy?"

"Oh, I wish!"

"Great wardrobe options, though," Lili says.

Tessa looks at me. "I bet I can guess all your costumes."

"All eighteen?"

"Well, the first one's easy," she says. "It's that little pink-and-blue-striped hat from the hospital."

"Nope! Home birth."

"*Wow.* Bet that was interesting for the trick-or-treaters."

"We love a good vaginal birth," Lili says.

Tessa laughs. "Okay, wait, I'm not done guessing! Mmm. I'm getting strong cat vibes. Headband ears, face paint . . ." She streaks her fingers over her cheeks, like she's giving herself whiskers.

"Just figured that out from the vibes, huh?" asks Lili. "Nothing to do with my wall collage?"

"As a matter of fact, that's where the vibes came from."

"As a matter of fact." I shoot Tessa a quick smile. "Let me guess—you were one of those cardboard-box-costume kids."

"That's really what you think of me, Scott?"

"Do I think you've worn a cardboard box in public? Yes."

"Absolutely," says Lili.

Tessa raises a finger. "Okay, you're not wrong—"

"Knew it!"

"—but it wasn't, like, an intact box by the time I was wearing it. Not usually," she adds.

"So it was multiple Halloweens."

"Purim too sometimes." Her eyes crinkle. "Once, my siblings and I won the costume contest at temple, because everyone else was Esther or Mordecai. We were a Nintendo Switch."

"You were not," Lili says.

"For real! Dan was the screen, and he drew this pixelated Purim scene on the chest part. And then me and Rachael were the blue and red controllers. It was pretty cute, since we used to be basically identical. My hair was longer then," she adds, turning to me.

My heart flips. "You cut it pretty recently, right?"

"Over break. My mom was a little weird about it at first. I think she saw it as this big declaration of lesbianism."

"But she's not . . ." I pause. "Would she see that as a bad thing?"

"Oh, no—I mean, I was already out. And they're fine. My parents, I mean. Like, they're liberal Jews, donate to the Human Rights Campaign, love *Schitt's Creek*, all of that. They just get a little weird sometimes about the fact that it's *me*."

"I don't like that," says Lili.

"Yeah . . . I think they just needed time to get used to the fact that, no, I will not in fact be marrying a nice Jewish boy. I mean, you'd think my elementary school tie collection might have clued them in, but." She shrugs. "Like, there's literally a video of me at age *three* singing along to 'Fast Car.' Tracy Chapman. Come on, Mom."

"Baby gay Tessa," says Lili. "What a legend."

Tessa turns to me. "What about you? Are your parents cool?"

"Like objectively cool?" I start to ask, but then my cheeks

go warm. "You mean are they cool with me being—queer? Yeah, absolutely."

"Elizabeth took it well?"

"She was actually pretty quiet about it. Though to be fair, she had, like, an entire corncob in her cheeks at the time."

"Blaming her biphobia on the corn," Lili says. "Tale as old as time."

I laugh, feeling slightly light-headed. "But my parents are cool. Yeah. I, um. Technically came out when I was Lesbian Elsa for Halloween. I was seven."

I can feel Lili looking at me.

I look pointedly away. "But they totally already knew," I say quickly. "They were just waiting for me to say it. I remember all these books started showing up on our shelves, though, about parenting queer kids. And they'd always make this big show of not implying the genders of our future partners."

I feel sick. Like, actually sick.

I just stole my sister's entire coming-out story.

And for what? To add fake texture to the other fake things Tessa already believes about me? Did *Frozen* even exist when I was seven?

But Tessa just smiles. "Hey—three down!"

"Three down?"

"Gory home-birth baby, cat, and Lesbian Elsa!" she says, counting them off on three fingers. Two truths and a lie.

Texts with Gretchen

GP: Leaving art center now, am about to meet my hostess with the mostess!! WISH ME LUCK

GP: But first, here's a selfie where I look translucent 📎

GP: Art center lighting confirming Mom and I are indeed both very white

GP: Hope you're having fun at the diner!

20

I can't sleep. Maybe I've forgotten how. Every time I close my eyes, my foot starts itching, or my pillow feels lumpy, or there's a random burst of laughter in the hallway. Even Lili's white-noise app feels unsettlingly loud.

Almost as loud as my brain.

I can't seem to keep my thoughts from going off-leash.

Like right now. I'm in bed.

But I'm also on a balcony wearing my prom dress. Not my actual prom dress, though. It's the prom dress I *almost* bought, before deciding it was too ruffled and girly and born to hand jive. But when I lean back against the stone balustrades, that's what I'm wearing. Then Tessa steps out in a half-buttoned black shirt, like Graham wears in *But I'm a Cheerleader* when they sneak out to the bar. *Hey, can I ask you something?* she says, eyes as bright as the moon. So I panic a little, scrambling for the perfect words to diffuse the awkwardness. But then she leans in—

No—wait.

She doesn't lean in. She bites her lip nervously and clears her throat. *Do you want to go out sometime? Like—a date?*

Oh! I say. *Tessa. I'm—so sorry.* My voice cracks. *I'm actually straight.* And she laughs sadly. *Yeah, I know. Just had to try. You'll let me know if you're ever . . . not straight, though, right?* And then we exchange wistful smiles, and I say, *Definitely,* and I bury my head in her shoulder—

Actually, no. There's no balcony, no formalwear. We're back in the tunnels, like earlier, only this time we're alone. *So I need you to be my fake girlfriend,* she says, and I laugh and ask why. *Because my ex is in town. She thinks I'm still in love with her, and I've got to show her I've moved on.*

Oh! Okay—

I promise I'm not secretly in love with you, she adds.

No, I wasn't. Ha—

Unless you want me to be.

Want you to be what?

Secretly in love with you. Her gaze meets mine, wide and nervous.

I stare back, and then—

Maybe my eyes spill over with tears.

Hey. Oh. I didn't mean to upset you.

I let out a choked little laugh. *You're not. No. I just. I'm—I thought I was straight.*

Imogen. She wipes away one of my tears, cupping my cheek in her hand.

And I think. *Oh. Maybe—*

DAY FOUR
MONDAY
MARCH 21

Texts with Gretchen

GP: Yeahhh I have to tell you about this girl I'm staying with

GP: Immylou Immybean

GP: Are you still sleeping??

GP: Who are you and what have you done with Imogen???!!

21

My eyes jolt open, heart skittering in my chest.

I'm in a sea of white noise. Completely untethered. Across the room, Lili's chest rises and falls, slow as water.

Unless you want me to be. Secretly in love. With you.

Unless.

I think I might be a horrible person.

Because this Tessa thing? This is worse than normal lying. It's queerbaiting.

Or at the very least, I'm appropriating queerness. Not even just the aesthetics, either. Apparently, my brain thinks *queerness itself* is some kind of thought exercise.

Me: a certified asshole straight girl who sees a lesbian existing and thinks it's a love declaration. Tuck my skirt into my tights, and I'm literally the eyelash girl from the movie theater.

But the worst part is, this isn't the first time it's happened.

I used to get a little hung up on certain girls when I was

younger. Not always. Just sometimes. Especially if I found out they were queer.

It's hard to explain, and it definitely wasn't something I talked about. I guess I could never find a way to describe the feeling without it sounding like a crush. But it wasn't anything like my actual crushes. On boys. It wasn't that thunderstorm of feeling—electric, all-consuming, blaringly loud in my head.

With girls, it was more like that feeling you get when you finish a book and your brain can't quite shake it.

Like when this girl Nisha Khatoon from the track team started coming to Pride Alliance meetings. She sat next to me in the welcome circle her first day, and I remember how weirdly suspenseful it was, wondering if she'd say her labels when she introduced herself.

But that was it. It's not that I wanted to *date* her. She just had the sort of tomboyish confidence and easy laugh that made me want to be her friend. And—

I guess I kind of understood that if I *were* queer, I'd probably be attracted to her.

Just like with Tessa.

There was this one girl who used to come into Seneca Farms when Lili and I worked there. She was white with a curly bleached pixie cut, and I never learned her name, but she always ordered a butterscotch waffle cone. I knew she liked girls, too, because she showed up once wearing a shirt that said *le dollar bean*. I used to count the number of people ahead of her in line, trying to figure out if I'd end up scooping her order. Sometimes I even wondered if butterscotch girl was secretly making the same calculations. Not that she had any reason to like me. Or even notice me.

It was just a thought I liked to carry around sometimes.

But it always felt like someone else's daydream—something I walked out of the store with and forgot to pay for.

Texts with Gretchen

IS: I'm up I'm up, sorry!

IS: Tell me about this girl!! 👀

IS: I take it that means you got to stay in the dorms

GP: Oh I most certainly did

GP: Immy this girl

GP: Piper

GP: I want you to imagine

GP: The straightest girl of all time

GP: A straight girl! At Vassar!!!!

GP: And not a cool straight like you

IS: How can you tell she's straight??

GP: hahahahahahahahhha

IS: No, for real!

GP: How do I know thee girl is straight? Let me count the ways

GP: She has mass produced canvas wall art

GP: On her dorm room wall

GP: "Live Laugh Love"

GP: Put on 3 inch heels for brunch

GP: Also woke up two hours early to make beach waves

in her hair and then PONYTAILED IT

GP: PIPER, WHY

IS: So it's just that she's girly?

GP: I mean yeah, but it's also a certain vibe
GP: You kinda know it when you see it
GP: Oh god, okay so
GP: All her photos are like ten girls in bikinis posing as a
        group on the beach

IS: Photos of girls in bikinis
IS: But in a straight way

GP: Exactly, you get it
GP: Anyway I have officially reunited with Mama P, and
        we are heading to Sarah Lawrence!!!
GP: In Bronxville
GP: I believe you're familiar with it 😌

IS: Yeahhhh hahaha
IS: Well, safe travels to Bronxville, which I now know is
        not a nickname for the Bronx!!
IS: Much like Prussia was not, in fact, an alternate name
        for Russia
IS: The more you know 🫶

22

I don't say goodbye to Tessa.

I mean, her door's closed, so she's probably sleeping. Or in class. Either way, it's for the best, since I don't really trust my face right now. *Hey, Tessa, guess who just had some extremely normal lucid dreams about you being in love with me! Bet you love hearing that from straight girls.*

"You've got your charger, right?" Lili presses the elevator button, still gripping my suitcase. "Toiletries?"

"Think so?" I rub my eyes.

"Aww—looks like someone's ready to get a good night's sleep in her own bed."

I yawn through a laugh. "Do I look awful?"

"No, you just look like those sleepy angel figurines from the Windmill."

I look at her. "You mean the dead angels?"

"Whoa! They're not *dead*—"

"Lili. The bases literally say, 'In Loving Memory.'"

"Well, maybe it's just a souvenir?" She presses her forehead, stifling a laugh. "From a fun memory with an angelic person? An angelic *alive* person!"

"Oh, okay—"

"Like—for example—you." She pokes me with her car keys.

I try to smile, but it falters. "Yeah. I'm not an angel."

I'm a culturally appropriating piece of trash, in fact. Just your run-of-the-mill hetero egomaniac, dabbling in some good old-fashioned telepathic queerbaiting.

It's like I'm incapable of being normal around queer women.

"I'm problematic," I say, hardly louder than a whisper.

She laughs. "Why are you problematic?"

"I don't know." I pause, hand stalling on the door handle of Lili's Toyota Camry. She presses the button to open it, and I take the passenger seat. "I just feel like I maybe overstepped a little this weekend."

She tilts her head toward me. "How so?"

"Maybe *overstepped* isn't the word. I just . . . feel like I was centering myself in queer spaces. Under false pretenses. I don't know if that makes sense."

"Imogen." Lili grips the steering wheel, staring for a second at the dashboard. Then she blinks, buckles her seat belt, and turns the car on. "That's—okay, so I know—I *know* you're being sincere. Not trying to invalidate your feelings. But."

I smile a little. "But . . ."

"Centering yourself in queer spaces? Like, what, my room?"

I shake my head. "*Metaphorical* spaces—"

"Also! In what universe are you responsible for the false pretenses here? I literally roped you into this! Except not actually literally, because there were no literal ropes involved!" She glances up at the rearview and out the back windshield, pulling out of the parking space at a snail's pace.

"It's complicated, though."

"But it's really not. I have a dorm room, and I invited you to stay there." She shrugs, shifting out of reverse. "And guess what! I'd do it again!"

"Okay then." I laugh.

Lili's quiet for a moment. But just as we're about to exit the student lot, she shoots me a quick sideways glance. "Hey. You know you're always welcome here, right? Anytime. Open invitation. I don't give a single shit how problematic you think you are."

My throat goes tight. "Thanks."

"And you should seriously come back Friday for the party."

"You guys and this party." I smile.

"I'm just saying! It's going to be *amazing*."

"Evidently!"

I sneak a glance at Lili's profile, still a little stunned by her enthusiasm. Back home, every party we ever went to was my idea—and even that was just because I felt like I had to. Usually because I'd promised Gretchen. Or because I'd panicked and told someone random that I'd be there. And since my brain likes to turn every off-the-cuff verbal commitment into a blood vow, it was really just a matter of talking Lili into coming with me.

So we'd end up shuffling awkwardly around the edges of some house party for an hour. But we'd always leave early, giddy with the relief of our recovered freedom. Then we'd spend the whole night talking about how much parties suck, even the Pride Alliance ones.

So, when did parties stop sucking for Lili? Was it when I stopped being the person she went with?

"So . . . that's a yes?"

"Lili, no. You should get to experience that with your actual queer friends—"

"—all of whom want you there, too."

"Because they think I'm queer."

"Okay." She shoots me a look I can't quite decipher. "But they also just like you."

Through the window, I watch a Mennonite wagon pull up a dirt driveway, into one of the farms—such a common sight here, my eyes would normally skim right over it. But now I can't stop thinking about that used disposable vape in the Blackwell tunnels. A whole different planet, twenty minutes and a staircase away. It's like stepping out of a noir film into the afternoon sunshine.

Lili turns left onto my street, and I take in all the houses and yards as we pass. Pebbled paths leading up to wooden front doors. The Johnsons' giant fenced-in garden. Metal patio chairs and covered firepits. Everything's just the same as I left it.

Which makes sense, given that I've only been gone for three days. Why does it feel like so much longer?

My parents' car is in the carport, so Lili veers right to park near the barn, turning to face me. "I can't tell if you just don't want to come to this party—or if you *do* want to come but feel like you shouldn't."

"It's not that," I say quickly. "I just think I should probably stick around Penn Yan. I still need to finish some stuff up before next Monday."

"Ah, yes." Lili cuts her eyes upward. "Stuff."

"Just like—homework. And my dad wants us to go through some of the boxes in the shed. Stupid stuff."

Lili lets out a short laugh. "You can just say you don't want to come. It's fine! I don't need a list of excuses."

"They're not excuses!"

"Fine." She exhales. "It's just—it seemed like you had a good time this weekend. You know?"

"I did!" I turn in my seat, my throat suddenly thick. "Lili, I *did*. It was perfect. It was *everything*."

Her expression softens. "Okay. Good. I just—really wanted you to feel at home there. Since it *is* your home. Will be, anyway."

"Five months." I exhale.

"Fastest five months of your life," she says, smiling. "You'll see."

Texts with Gretchen

GP: OMFG I'm at a meet and greet thing and guess who's here

GP: 📎

IS: No way!!!!!
IS: At Sarah Lawrence?

GP: Yes!! She's a student ambassador now
GP: She's even CUTER how is that possible???
GP: That's it, I'm turning in my deposit

IS: Olivia . . . why am I blanking on her last name

GP: Olivia Fields!!!!
GP: Wait no, Olivia FIELD
GP: Singular

IS: Oh no . . . bad news
IS: Not singular
IS: (I'm looking at her Instagram)
IS: I think she has a boyfriend

GP: Yes! She's bi!

IS: Oh, I mean she's taken

GP: Oh right

GP: Maybe she's poly?

GP: Okay nvm I just walked up and she said hi and she
       absolutely didn't recognize me, like not even a
       glimmer of recognition

GP: Ripping up the SL deposit now

GP: Submitting a late application to Blackwell, saving
       myself for hot Tessa, lol

23

Home really has its own soundscape. Rustling leaves and birdsongs and Mom's wind chimes on the side of the house, near the garden. All these beats and ticks and clanks I've never noticed until now. My feline welcoming committee swoops in before I even reach the front door—Adrian and Demi, weaving in and out of my legs, meowing like the world's ending. I keep letting go of my suitcase to scratch their heads and pet their tails down. As I get closer to the door, I can hear faint TV noises. Edith, in full spring break mode.

It's all so completely mundane. I could cry with relief.

I let myself in through the front, and all three dogs rocket toward me. "Hi, babies. Oh, hi!" Eloise leaps up, setting her paws on my shoulders, and I press my nose to her snout.

"Do I hear an Imogen?" my mom calls up from the basement. The school she works at is on spring break this week, too, which means she's probably already elbow-deep in home projects. I leave my suitcase by the door, plopping beside Edith on the couch. She pauses *The Owl House* and stretches. "Hey! How was it?"

"Really fun. Hi, Flossie-bun." Flossie looks up from Edith's lap, twitching her nose at me.

"That's it? Really fun? That's all you've got?"

"It was fun!"

"Yeah, duh. It's college." Edith shakes her head. "But was it life-altering? Transformational? Are you forever changed?"

"Hi, hi, hi! I'm here!" Mom says, coming up the short basement stairs in her overalls. "Oh, I want to hug your little face, but I'm covered in primer. Just finished the base coat inside the shed." She holds both arms up, showing off several big streaks of white paint.

The shed is my parents' current obsession. It looks like a little wooden house, for the most part—smaller than the barn, but closer to the house. We've always just used it for storage— off-season clothes, garden tools, extra rolls of toilet paper, that sort of thing. But my mom got this idea to clear it out and turn it into an extra room off the back of our house. Apparently, my dad's even going to build a little covered walkway to connect them.

"What'd you do with the boxes?"

Edith bites back a smile. "You should see the basement."

"We'll get it all put away by the end of break," Mom says. "I was thinking we could move the futon in there and get some Christmas lights up. Nice and cozy. We'll get good Wi-Fi out there, too." She leans down to pet Smokey and Eloise, who both have just burst in from somewhere behind me. "Anyway, I'm hopping in the shower, and then I'll run to town and grab groceries for tonight. Wish it would warm up a little! Saturday was so nice, wasn't it? Oh, but I'm so glad you're home, Immy. We missed you!"

I smile up at her. "Me too."

Texts with Tessa

TM: Scott you are NOT going to believe who I just saw

TM: You're going to be so jealous!!!

IS: Who??

IS: Is it someone famous 🦉

TM: Better 📎

IS: Daisy!!!!!!!!!!!!

IS: Oh my god

IS: Her EARS

IS: And her little tongue

IS: Was she licking your eye??

TM: SHE WAS AND I LOVED IT

TM: I literally can't believe I just ran into her again

TM: I think she misses you though

IS: Aww, I miss her too!

IS: Tell her me and Eloise say hi 📎

TM: Eloise!!!

TM: Haha I love when their ears flip back like that, she looks like George Washington

TM: What a distinguished lady!!!!

TM: Eloise, you look nice too 😊

24

Edith cranes her neck toward my phone. "Ooh. Who's that?"

"Oh! Just—some of Lili's people."

"Hold UP. College people?" She scoops Flossie off her lap, leaning closer. "Oh my God—are you texting Dylan?"

"Who's Dylan?"

"Lili's friend! The guy who looks like an ice prince?"

"You mean Declan?"

Her hands fly to her mouth. "Did you hook up with him?"

"*What?*" I shake my head, smiling bewilderedly. "No!"

"Then why are you sitting here smiling at your phone like a smitten kitten?"

"I'm not!" I lean back into the couch cushions, rolling my eyes to the ceiling. "Oh my God. No! I didn't hook up with Declan. Or anyone."

"You're just texting him."

"No!" I swipe Mom's dragonfly throw pillow off the couch and throw it at Edith. "I've literally never texted Declan, ever.

Other than the group chat."

Edith grips her head with both hands. "You're in the *group chat*?"

"I'm in *a* group chat." I laugh a little, heartbeat finally inching back to normal. The group chat is definitely safer territory than certain other topics. Like Edith's clown car of a theory that I hooked up with Declan, for example. At least my college group chat is a thing that exists.

And by that, I mean it *existed*. Seeing as there hasn't been a single new message since Kayla requested a rain check last night.

They've probably reverted to their original group chat, without me.

Of course they've reverted to their original group chat without me. I'm Lili's friend from home who visited for three days. That doesn't exactly confer lifelong best friend privileges. And yeah, they talked a good game about wanting me to come back this weekend—but when push came to shove, no one even seemed to care that I was leaving.

Except Tessa, I guess.

Does that make us real friends?

It sort of feels like it. Or at least we're getting there. That would explain the weird dreams from yesterday, right? Maybe that was just my mind trying to pin down our friendship status. Better that than the mortifyingly problematic alternative: I met a lesbian and immediately assumed she was in love with me. *Oh ur a lesbian?? Do u like have a crush on me or something??? Sorry, sweaty, I date guyssss.*

Edith flops backward and sighs. "I can't believe you're just sitting here texting your little queer college group chat. Are you guys just bouncing around hilarious inside jokes? Are you spilling all your secrets, Immy?"

"Secrets?" Heat floods my cheeks. I guess I've always kept certain thoughts private, but I've never really thought of it like that.

Tessa sort of feels like a secret, though. Probably because I just straight-up lied when Edith asked me who I was texting. Well—technically, Edith assumed I was talking to the group chat, and I just went along with it.

Kind of like how I went along with Lili's fabricated relationship backstory. And how I let everyone believe I'm bisexual.

It really begs the question: When, exactly, did I get so comfortable with lying?

Texts with Gretchen

GP: IMOGEN GUESS WHAT

GP: 😱

GP: SOMETHING LGBT JUST HAPPENED

IS: What?!!

IS: Omg did you make out with someone??? Gretchen, it's the middle of the afternoon

IS: How?!

GP: lol cool your jets Immylou

GP: No 😙

GP: YET

GP: But the vibes are full force

GP: And I'm in her room right now 😊

IS: WHAT

IS: !!!!!!

GP: To be fair, she's my host 😄

GP: BUT LOOK AT HER 📎

GP: She's so cute, her name is Brielle

GP: Don't you think she looks like Barbie Ferreira??

IS: I see it!!!

GP: AND WE FOLLOW EACH OTHER NOW

GP: What's my move, do I post a thirst trap??

IS: Maybe just talk to her?

GP: Lol she's in class

GP: Just trying to keep things moving in the right direction

IS: Ohhh okay

GP: WHAT DO I DO

GP: I don't want to look too eager!!!

IS: Hmmm

IS: Would she know the thirst trap is for her specifically?

IS: Can it be a general thirst trap?

IS: Sorry, I'm a little out of my depth here

IS: I don't know how any of this works, I'm sorry 🫠

GP: My sweet virgin queen

GP: All thirst traps are targeted

GP: And general

GP: They are both

IS: Can you clarify in the caption

IS: "This thirst trap is intended for all audiences"

GP: Hahaha ilu

GP: Okay new plan

GP: Doing a throwback to Silk Chiffon

GP: A SUBTLE thirst trap

IS: I love that picture!

GP: I'll tag you 😊

GP: Oop wait

GP: I hear footsteps

GP: NEVER MIND, THIRST TRAP CAN WAIT

GP: It's ONNNN

Texts with Tessa

TM: No, for real!!!

TM: This is like

TM: Actual tradition at this point

TM: On Rosh Hashanah it is decided, and on Yom Kippur it is revealed 😎

IS: I mean that does sound very official

IS: So how do you pick

IS: Can it be any famous person?

TM: Yup!

TM: But it can't be anyone we've done before

TM: And we all have to agree

TM: Full consensus

TM: Which btw is not easy with Dan and Rachael!!!

TM: And I guess you kind of have to pick someone with a lot of iconic fashion moments

IS: Ah okay that makes sense

TM: Also parental assistance is strictly forbidden!!!!

TM: And you CAN'T show anyone your costume until Yom Kippur

IS: So you wear the costumes to temple?

TM: Omg I wish!!!

TM: No, we do the reveal right after

TM: It's a good distraction from fasting though

TM: Like yeah, okay, we're starving, but at least we look like Harry Styles

TM: I mean 📎

TM: Literally the only time I've worn pearls 😄

IS: The green pants!!!!!

TM: I KNOW

TM: They're actually sweatpants, I still sleep in them sometimes and dream about Harry

TM: (Platonically!!!)

IS: This is

IS: Sheer chaos

TM: Why thank you 😊

25

Naturally, dinner's a huge production. Cornell chicken, carrots, and salt potatoes, because my parents felt the need to welcome me home with the most comically upstate New York meal imaginable.

"You guys get that I was, like, twenty-five minutes up Route 14, right?"

"Well, it felt far," Mom says.

"They were kind of pining for you, Immy," says Edith. "These two are definitely not ready for you to graduate."

"Oh, come on, now. We're totally cool! Back me up, Cor."

"Cool as Keuka," Dad says.

The funny thing is, a few hours ago, college seemed entirely sealed off from real life. A universe inside a universe, like a snow globe. Or like one of those dreams you forget as soon as you open your eyes.

But it all feels jumbled together right now. The buttery grilled cheese, the tunnels, the walk home from trivia night.

All these brand-new moments, slipping into every corner and crevice of home. The piles of clutter on the counter. The horrific framed tableau of middle-school pictures. The painting of cherries I made in first grade that came out looking like a giant, bright red penis. Future and past, sharing space.

And then there's Tessa.

We've been texting pretty much continuously all day.

"When are you two getting together?" my mom asks, and I almost jump out of my chair.

"What—do you mean?"

"You said she's coming back tomorrow, right? Just Vassar and Sarah Lawrence this time?"

Gretchen. Right.

"Oh—yeah. We haven't made any definite plans yet." I nod quickly. "We'll just play it by ear, I guess."

Mom picks up her fork. "I'm excited to see where she ends up. I'll tell you, that kid is a trip. Smart cookie, though. Always has been. Oh my goodness—remember her little business cards?"

Edith looks amused. "Gretchen had business cards?"

"You don't remember that, sweetie? It was right when she moved here. I don't even think she was advertising anything. Just, you know. Letting us know she was here."

"Oh, she lets us know," my dad says, and Edith startles all the cats just from laughing.

Texts with Gretchen

IS: Sure is quiet in this text thread

IS: 😊😊 ???

IS: Patiently awaiting updates 👀

Texts with Tessa

IS: Oh I mean

IS: It's party central here

IS: Got my main dude here with me

IS: 📎

IS: This is Quincy 🖤

TM: Shut up

TM: Is that a cat

TM: Like a regular cat

IS: Kind of 😄

IS: He's a ragdoll

TM: Quincy, you are the biggest cat I've ever seen

TM: Hands down

IS: He's thirty pounds 🐱

IS: You should hear him talk! He has a really low voice

IS: And kind of a vocal fry

IS: It's like MOAWWWWWW

IS: And he's almost 15, I think he might be immortal

TM: I'm obsessed with him

TM: Fuck parties

TM: Wait okay not like Fuck Parties as in parties where you fuck

TM: Fuck parties as in

TM: "Parties can fuck off now, I'm hanging out with my immortal cat"

TM: *Your immortal cat 😆

IS: We can share him

IS: Fifteen pounds each

TM: Oh thank god

TM: Brb, canceling karaoke night to devote myself to half a Quincy

IS: Karaoke night!! Omg

IS: That actually sounds really fun 🎤

TM: I've never done it!

IS: Me either 🫣

IS: 95 percent chance I'd wimp out at the last second

TM: No way!!

IS: No like

IS: I'd probably go kind of mute

IS: Happens to me sometimes when I'm nervous

TM: Aww Scott

TM: Really?

IS: Yeahhhh 😁

IS: It's fun

TM: Okay but you're actually so brave though??

IS: 😂 😂 😂

TM: YOU ARE

TM: Look at last weekend!

TM: Like you just showed up to this whole new environment

TM: Won the fuck out of trivia, engaged in criminal sausage behavior, made puppies appear

TM: Like that's brave!! Idk man

TM: College visits are so intimidating

TM: The first time I visited, I basically stayed in Dan's room the whole time

IS: That's so sweet though?? 🥺

IS: Oh my god speaking of college trips

185

IS: So my friend is at Sarah Lawrence tonight

IS: And I think she might be hooking up with her student host?

IS: Like right now??

TM: Whoa!! Nicely done

IS: A very informative college visit haha

TM: Oh definitely

TM: Listen, Scott, if you need an info session of that nature, let me know

TM: Could probably be arranged 😉

IS: Haha, noted 😂

26

I can't find my off switch tonight. Every time I try to close my eyes, they spring right back open.

Which makes no sense. Nothing's incomplete or out of place. I'm in my bed, in my room, in the house I was literally born in. Same posters, same books, same grayish-blue walls. Same white sock flopping out of the laundry basket, same toilet paper roll in the corner of Elizabeth's tank, same empty water glass on my nightstand.

But I feel so unzipped for some reason. Like someone left me wide-open.

I sit up in bed, staring at the seams of my quilt.

Then I sigh and pull my phone from its charger.

It's like pressing a bruise. That stupidly predictable jolt of pain.

People always talk about FOMO, but this doesn't feel like fear at all. It's an ache. Staring at a tiny handheld screen, watching someone else's memories coalesce in real time.

Blackwell College is less than thirty minutes away, and it might as well be the moon.

It's a story told in snippets. A group selfie, tongues out. Declan rolling his eyes so hard, only the whites show. A dimly lit TikTok of four people walking, filmed from behind. Lime-green text superimposed over a photo of Mika holding a microphone. *Adele is QUAKING*

A random Monday night out. It's the most ridiculous thing to care about.

As if the group was supposed to cancel all joy when I left. As if I was ever a part of the group to begin with. I'm a high school kid who got to try on college for a weekend, but that's not my real life. Not yet.

But will this tight-knit group of queer kids even want to hang out with me once they find out I'm straight? The truth has to come out eventually, right? It's not like I can fake being bi forever.

A text from Tessa pops through, and I'm so startled, my phone almost slips from my hands. There's a video attached, plus the caption: *Our girl can SING!!??*

I turn the sound on and press play—and it's really just a ten-second clip of the back of some guy's head. But Lili's easy vibrato is unmistakable—even the high notes always sound so effortless.

I know just which decade-old picture to send in reply.

I swipe back in time through my "throwbacks" album until I find it—a quick shot taken from the side of the barn. Lili onstage, with two short rows of stuffed animals, propped up against hay bales. **Can confirm,** I write.

Tessa writes back immediately. **Omg YES**

And then: **Wait is that Puppy??** 🦄

Of course, I reply. **He's her biggest fan!**

Tessa starts typing, and the world shrinks to fit into three tiny dots.

In my stomach: a shooting-star feeling, out of nowhere.

Something's glitching.

The way my heart's pounding straight through my chest.

The way my brain's completely stuck on Tessa. If I didn't know better, I'd almost think this was an actual crush.

But how do I know if it's real?

How do I know I'm not just being a pick-me? Or a people pleaser. What, Lili needs me to pretend I'm bi? I'll be so bi, I'll forget I'm pretending.

Unless.

I don't know, maybe I'm overthinking this.

Do I just . . . have a crush on her?

It seems so far-fetched, though. It would be one thing if I'd never met a queer person before. But my sister's queer. My best friends are queer. If it weren't spring break, I'd be spending tomorrow afternoon at a Pride Alliance meeting.

My mind spools back again to that first day, my first welcome circle. "I have a queer sister," I'd said.

It didn't even occur to me to say I was straight. I guess Edith being queer felt like a complete story already. Her queerness implied my straightness. Because one queer kid made sense, but two in one family? Overkill.

And I know that's ridiculous. Factually inaccurate. Disproven in an instant by the Wachowski sisters, by Tegan and Sara. There was literally a pair of nonbinary siblings at the meeting that day. But I think the idea got lodged in my brain somehow anyway.

Maybe it's just that I know what being a queer kid looks like, and it looks nothing like me. I've never stolen a sunflower for a woman in the supermarket. I've never trick-or-treated with a lesbian flag sewn into my dress. Queerness isn't some distant hypothetical concept to me. It's right there. It always has been.

It's funny, because if you say the word *queer*, my mental image is Gretchen.

But I measure queerness against Edith. I've always measured it against Edith.

And Edith has always known she's queer. It's just never been a question. Even in preschool, Edith was into lesbians the way some kids were into unicorns.

If I were queer, wouldn't I at least sort of know?

It's my own brain. I have open access to it. No one's redacting parts of the story. *Especially* not something as fundamental as who I'm attracted to. And I know denial exists. But this *isn't* denial. Denial's a curtain with a clear truth behind it.

There's no curtain to pull back here. I'm staring straight at this question, shining every light on it, and still—

Scott, help, they're trying to make me sing!!!

I stare at my phone, at a total loss. Every possible response feels too flirtatious, too thirsty, too wistful. Too unbearably earnest.

And it *really* doesn't help that Tessa thinks I'm bi.

Because that's the thing about being straight. It's like having a built-in force field. It doesn't matter if you're laughing too loud or blinking a lot, or if that text was Too Much. When you're straight, cute girls literally don't have to worry about you catching weird, awkward feelings. Because you like boys, and she's not one, and that's the whole story.

I think I miss it.

Being straight.

I mean, I miss people thinking I'm straight. And by that, I mean I miss people *knowing* I'm straight.

Because I am. Straight.

One girl can't topple your entire sexuality, right?

DAY FIVE
TUESDAY
MARCH 22

Texts with Tessa

TM: Hello yes it's two in the morning

TM: And I'm writing to inquire about the 15 pounds of cat I ordered

TM: Upon careful consideration, I would like to request the front half please

TM: ie the soul, not the hole

TM: The tongue, not the dung

TM: The mouth, not the south

TM: ➡️🐈✔️

TM: 🐈⬅️🚫

TM: Okay I'm done I'm done I promise 😬

27

Unless it's not just one girl.

The thought lands in my brain with an echoing thud.

My eyes snap open, and I yawn my way into a sitting position, rubbing my eyes.

Unless—

I stare up at my poster wall until the images swim out of focus.

Unless it's not just one girl.

The words settle into my head, putting down roots.

Unless it's not just one—

But.

I don't get crushes on girls.

That's how I know Tessa is a fluke, not an actual crush. It's my brain trying to fit in with Lili's cool queer friends. Kind of like how Gretchen spent two weeks in Edinburgh last summer and came back with an accent and a whole new vocabulary.

If anything, it's some strange kind of role-play. Like method acting.

I mean, let's just call it what it is, right? I'm appropriating queer attraction. Like I did with Clea DuVall. And Nisha. And the le dollar bean girl. And all the others. *Not just one.*

But they weren't crushes. They *couldn't* have been crushes, because crushes aren't a thing you can hide from yourself.

Why am I even getting so stuck on this? I know what attraction feels like. I know what it feels like to want to kiss someone, and this isn't about kissing.

Though. It's not *not* about kissing.

But it's different, somehow, in a way I can't quite explain.

I guess you could call it a preoccupation. Or like a tiny pull I felt when I was near them. Not quite the same as a regular friendship.

Like taking the word *friendship* and underlining it.

Getting dressed feels like I'm sleepwalking. My weather app says it's chilly out. Sweater weather. As in, the actual weather outside. Not "Sweater Weather" the song, which TikTok says is yet another code for being bisexual. Kind of like lemon squares and cuffed jeans and not being able to sit in chairs normally.

I wish any of this made sense to me.

I settle in at my desk, pretzeling my legs in the chair. Which is how I always sit in chairs. I guess that's slightly weird?

How weirdly does a person have to sit to count as bisexual?

I keep turning the memories over in my head. The rustle of track pants against plastic chairs. The smell of butterscotch ice cream. The flat softness of felt rainbows. I remember all the details, but I can't quite conjure the feelings.

Maybe it would help if I was a little more methodical about it. I'm five months away from being in college, after all. Why not treat it like academic research? I could take one quick trip down the online rabbit hole, in the interest of triage.

Poke around for a second, rule it out, and be done with it.

Texts with Tessa

IS: Thank you so much for reaching out!

IS: The full contents of your shipment can be found in
        the attached inventory label

IS: For your reference, it states

IS: "The anus, not the brainus"

IS: We thank you for shopping with us

28

I can't believe how fast my heart's beating. I keep scanning the room, as if some stranger might pop out from under the bed to catch me in the act.

Of typing on my phone. That's the act.

This has to be a whole new level of unglued.

I open a private browser—which makes this feel like a bigger deal than it is.

It's not any kind of deal, really. Just three words and a question mark. No jumping to conclusions. I won't even jump to hypotheses—

My phone vibrates, and my heart leaps into my throat.

Text from Gretchen. **Heyyyy are you going to be home in like 2 hours??**

I catch my breath. **I think so, yeah**

Okay, noted! she writes, adding a winky emoji.

I feel so blurrily out of body. Like I'm my own reflection in water. I tap back into my browser, type three words, and press enter.

Pages and pages of results. Thousands of them. So many, it's hard to know where to start. I can't believe there are actually quizzes for this. It's like a television montage.

The definitive sexual orientation quiz

Are you bisexual or straight? Take this test!

Am I seriously doing this? Am I the biggest cliché on earth?

Though the fact that it's a cliché is wild to begin with, because you really shouldn't need a test to tell you your own sexuality. Maybe if you know you're queer and are just trying to home in on the exact label—I can see how that would be helpful. But the existence of queerness itself?

I pull back, staring at my posters for a minute before clicking the link. Don't want to seem too eager, I guess. True and utter clownery, given that I'm literally alone in a room. Also, why is my brain turning this into a capital-*E* Event? *Please rise for the momentous occasion of Imogen Scott confirming her hetero-sexuality via online quiz.*

I tap one of the links—an ad pops up for meeting singles in my area.

Then: a rainbow-flag stock photo that hasn't been formatted for mobile, followed by a paragraph of intro text. I keep scrolling until I reach the first question—though it's really more of a fill-in-the-blank statement.

I'm _____ *attracted to people of my own gender.*
only
sometimes
never

Only. Sometimes. Never. Only sometimes never.

I read it again.
I'm _____ *attracted to people of my own gender.*

It's a trick question, right? If I knew the answer to that, why would I be taking this test? I don't need the definition of bisexual. I want to know what it *feels* like. How do you know what counts as attraction?

Second question:
I have romantic daydreams about _____.
Only one gender (not my gender).
Only one gender (my gender).
Multiple genders.
No one.

Okay, got it, but . . . how literal am I supposed to be here? Do I round up to the choice that's most generally applicable? Or do I count every tiny little exception?

And what counts as an exception?

Also, how many exceptions until it's not really an exception?

202

I think about Clea DuVall and Kristen Stewart and Nisha and le dollar bean. And maybe the felt rainbow girl from Girl Scouts. And that girl Ilana, probably. And—

Tessa.

What if I'd stayed on campus. What if I'd gone to karaoke night.

What if we'd left early. Ended up in her room, with the door shut. What if we'd let the hallway chatter fade.

Maybe Tessa would have looked up at me with questioning eyes, smiling faintly.

Maybe I'd have smiled nervously back.

Tucked my hair behind my ears.

And maybe I'd have settled in softly beside her, my hands pressed flat on her gnome bedsheets. A millimeter from hers.

I can see it.

She'd draw a quick, shaky breath. "Hey."

"Hey," I'd say back. But—

My phone buzzes.

Texts with Tessa

TM: Oh you think you're so funny, don't you

TM: Psh I know your type

TM: Sitting right there with your giant kitty cat and your spoon applesauce and your little dimple

IS: What do you have against dimples???? 😭

TM: Oh I am emphatically pro-dimple, Scott

TM: I just think

TM: Certain people should be a little more mindful of how their dimples might affect the general public

TM: That's all 🫠

IS: I see

IS: Hmm

IS: 📎

TM: Okay that's just unfair

TM: 😭 😭 😭 😍

29

I stare at the photo on my screen, a little bit stunned by my own boldness.

I just sent that. To *Tessa*. And it's so—

Fully clothed. Nana-approved. Nothing but face and neck and shoulders. Let's be totally clear.

Just a random little selfie of me smiling. With my very visible dimple.

I feel fizzy with nerves. Or guilt. Both, really. I guess it feels like I'm trespassing. Like I've slipped backstage without a pass. I've crept out of bounds.

I mean, I can't even deny it at this point. I'm definitely flirting. With Tessa.

Tessa, who is definitely a girl.

I reread our last few texts, and my heart's not even a pinball machine. It's the entire arcade.

She's flirting back.

It's not a question. There just isn't any other way to read it.

Except—

It's Tessa. She does that.

Isn't that what Lili said? That Tessa's a flirty-pants who flirts with everyone?

So then, how do you tell in that case? How do you know if someone's flirting with you, or if they just have a flirty personality? And is it ever both?

How do you know—how do you *really* know if someone likes you?

Especially with girls. It gets so blurry sometimes. Two girls will hug each other right in front of you, and you'll have no idea if they're girlfriends or besties or what. Unless they're actively making out, you need floating heart emojis and a movie score to interpret it.

Is that where the queer aesthetic stuff comes in? Gretchen and her thumb rings? Edith's jean jacket?

But how could this be about *clothes*? Is the le dollar bean girl straight until she puts on the shirt? Is *every* straight girl just an out-of-uniform bisexual?

Maybe Tessa wasn't even flirting. She could have just been humoring me.

The mortification hits like lightning—a bright bolt of shame in my chest.

What if she's *not* flirting—but she thinks *I* am. Does she cringe every time she sees my name pop up in her texts? *Ohhhh, does this child have a crush on me? Yikes!*

It's the summer after fourth grade all over again. I remember how enthralled I was by Dad's new apprentice. Who, to be clear, was a literal grown man with facial hair. When he and Dad worked from home, I'd plant myself in the basement with a book or a cat, sneaking glances at his face when I thought he wasn't looking. We even had a real conversation once. He asked me if I wanted to be a contractor when I grew up. I said no. And then I walked around for the rest of the day with neon-red cheeks and a fluttering stomach. Me, a child, openly thirsting over a twenty-two-year-old man. In front of my dad. Undeniable clown behavior.

But this is at least a little different, right? For one thing, I'm eighteen, which makes me very decidedly not a child. In fact, it's the exact same age as Tessa. Unless my math is wrong, we're literally just four months apart.

Though I know it's not that simple.

She's in college. I'm in high school. It's a whole different universe, really. I'm pretty sure Tessa's not asking teachers for permission to pee these days. Nor is she holding the unlockable bathroom door shut with her foot while she does it. I'd even go so far as to guess that Tessa rarely has to pass through gauntlets of fifteen-year-olds dry-humping each other against banks of lockers every time she wants to grab a textbook.

And that's not even opening the whole living-with-your-parents can of worms. Imagine being used to the privacy of dorm rooms, only to be stuck frantically buttoning your shirt back up because your girlfriend's mom knocked on the door.

"Imogen?" My mom knocks on my door.

Honest to God, I practically jump out of my skin.

30

Mom cracks the door open, smiling. "You've got a visitor, sweetie."

I shove my phone away and spring out of my chair, stomach fizzing like a volcano.

There's no way. None. That's not how reality works. And it's definitely not—

"Helloooo!"

The door creaks open.

There's a tiny, sharp twist in my chest. "Hi! Oh my God, you're back! How'd you guys get here so fast?"

"By waking up way too fucking early." Gretchen sets a plastic bag down on top of my dresser and flops onto my bed. "Mama P was like, 'No, ma'am, I don't want to be anywhere *near* Manhattan at rush hour.'"

"Probably a good call." I scoot in beside her.

"Definitely. I'm just tired. Had a late night." She shoots me a sly, sidelong smile.

I raise my eyebrows. "Wait. Did you—"

"Mayyyy-be."

"With Brielle?" I shake my head. "You actually hooked up with your student host?"

Gretchen grabs one of my pillows and buries her face in it.

"That's, like, a God-tier college visit achievement."

"I knowwww." She lets out a muffled giggle.

"So . . . does this mean Sarah Lawrence is the one?"

Her eyes peep up from over the pillow's edge. "Well . . ."

I look at her. "Wait—did you hear back?"

"Um. So . . . I actually have some news." She dumps the pillow, slides off the bed, and swipes her plastic bag off the dresser. She hands it to me, eyes gleaming. "Open it!"

I reach inside, pulling out a fluffy pink teddy bear, the exact same shade as Gretchen's hair. He's wearing a red shirt that says simply: *Vassar.*

"So you'll have something to remember me by," she says.

My mouth falls open. "It's official? You're going to Vassar?"

"I'm going to Vassar!" Gretchen's eyes well up with tears— which makes me tear up, too.

I jump up to hug her. "Gretch! Oh my God!"

"I can't believe I got in!"

I bite back a smile, and she grins at me. "What?"

"Nothing!"

"Imogen Louise Scott. *What?*"

I laugh. "I just love your reaction. You're brilliant. You're the valedictorian. Teachers are obsessed with you, you crushed the SAT, you could probably publish your essay in the *New York Times* if you wanted—"

"Um, *what?*"

"Or at least the *Chronicle-Express!*" She rolls her eyes, but I keep talking. "I'm just saying, it's sweet! You don't even see how incredible you are."

"I just can't believe we're both in college." She exhales. "It's so *weird*. It doesn't feel like real life."

Turns out, Mama P's been in the kitchen this whole time—Mom appears to have talked her into some kind of weird floral tea. "Look at these college girls," she says, smiling in that same conspiratorial way that Gretchen sometimes does. It always makes me feel like I'm in on some unspoken joke.

"Congratulations, sweetie! Your mama just told me the big news." Mom squeezes Gretchen's shoulders. "You should be so proud. Are you excited?"

"Hasn't really sunk in yet." She laughs.

"Oh, well, that's because we haven't properly celebrated yet!" Mama P sets her mug down and stands. "I don't know about you all, but I think this calls for a Seneca Farms trip. Kelly, what do you think?"

Mom presses a palm to her forehead. "I wish I could! But we've got Curt coming to install the air-conditioning in the shed. And then I want to get the tape down so it's all prepped to paint tomorrow." She exhales. "Wow, this is turning out to be quite the production, huh?"

"Sure sounds like it! Kelly, why don't you take the morning off tomorrow? The girls can handle painting."

"Oh, that's too big of a job. I couldn't ask them to do that—"

"Nonsense. I'll send Gretchen over in the morning. Is eight o'clock too late?"

"Too *late*?" Gretchen blinks.

"Are you sure?" my mom asks.

"Our absolute pleasure." Mama P presses her palms together. "And we'll get out of your hair now, too. Is Edith around? Does she want ice cream?"

It's like shaking the cat treat container—Edith's in the doorway within moments, shoes tied and ready.

Texts with Tessa

TM: But it's not an actual farm?

IS: Haha no

IS: Totally not, it's just an ice cream shop

IS: But also fried chicken

IS: Though that's in kind of a separate building

IS: It's literally the best ice cream on the planet btw

TM: That's what Lili says!!!

TM: But idk man

TM: Can't forget the big gay ice cream shop!!

TM: Hmm maybe this calls for a taste test

IS: DO IT!!

IS: It's such a quick drive from Geneva!!

IS: Right in Penn Yan

TM: Just like 20-30 min, right?

TM: From Geneva to Pennsylvania Yan

TM: Omg shut up autocorrect

IS: Haha autocorrect is right though

IS: That's what it's short for!!

IS: Pennsylvania Yankee

TM: NO WAY

TM: Oh man, I dig it

TM: I mean, kind of a weird choice of name for a town in NY, not gonna lie

IS: Haha PY is weird choice central

IS: Has Lili told you about the griddle

IS: And the pancake

TM: Nooooo

TM: 👀

IS: Oh we're heading out!!!

IS: Hold that thought 🥞

31

It's too cold for ice cream under the pavilion, and there's a bit of a spring break crowd indoors. But we manage to snag the corner booth just as someone's leaving. "Gretch, slide in next to the girls for a second! I need a picture with those pretty cones." Mama P snaps a few horizontal pictures, popping them straight into her message app.

My phone buzzes a moment later with the notification. I have a whole text thread with Mama P, just for pictures. I bet there'd even be some from eighth grade if I scrolled back far enough.

Gretchen scoots back in next to her mom, tapping her screen. "Cute! I'm posting this."

I smile, watching her type one-handed, stopping every so often to lick away the drippy parts of her cone. "You know you don't actually have to post in real time, right?"

"Phone and cone, Immy," says Edith. "Do it for your fans."

"My fans. So, like . . . Mom?"

"Don't count her out! She's building her platform."

"Her profile picture is a bunny," I say. "From Google Images."

But of course I'm already tapping into Instagram, ice cream firmly in hand.

Gretchen's right—it really is a cute picture. With Edith in the middle, our side-by-side hair looks like Neopolitan ice cream. We're all smiling, cheek-to-cheek, behind double-scoop Oreo sugar cones that cover half of our faces. But you can still kind of see my dimple poking out if you look closely enough.

I wonder if Tessa will look closely enough.

By the time I press post, Edith's already halfway down to her cone. She swallows, licking her lips. "So, Vassar, huh?"

Gretchen smiles. "Are you guys surprised?"

"A little bit!"

Edith scoffs. "Come on. It's *Gretchen*—"

"Not surprised that you got in," I rush to add. "I just didn't know it was the frontrunner! I really thought you were suffering through it with that Live, Laugh, Love girl."

"I was playing it cool! Didn't want to jinx myself." Gretchen smiles. "Anyway, Piper's not the worst. We've been texting—"

"Wait—"

"Not like that!"

"Imogen, I want to hear about Blackwell! Your mama said that was your first real visit to campus, right? What an adventure!"

I shrug, feeling my cheeks go warm. "I mean . . . it's just Geneva."

"It's still exciting! Oh, you girls are just going to thrive in college. I'm telling you—Gretchen thinks I'm a broken record, but it's so true. These are such transformative years—"

"And you're going to learn *so much* about yourselves," Gretchen concludes, perfectly nailing her mom's intonation.

"Okay, smartass. You'll see." Mama P tugs Gretchen's ponytail, turning back to me. "Did you feel like you got a sense of what it's like there?"

"Oh!" Gretchen yelps. "Oh my God. Hot Tessa commented on my picture!"

I blink. "She—"

"Oh—wait. Ha. Okay, she commented on a picture I was tagged in. *Your* picture. But still! She said, and I quote, 'Is it gay, though?' With the little thinker emoji!" Gretchen laughs. "I want to reply! Is that weird?"

"Saying what?" Edith asks.

"Saying, 'Fuck yeah, it's gay!'" She turns to me. "Should I follow her? What do I do?"

My heart thuds so hard, I can practically hear it. "I—"

"Who is this, now?" asks Mama P.

"Lili's friend. And apparently Imogen's friend, too, even though she's *wasted* on you. Freaking heterosexuals." She shakes her head at me, smiling.

I swallow back a wave of annoyance.

216

And then I feel guilty for being annoyed in the first place. Gretchen can like Tessa. She can like whoever she wants.

I just wish she'd stop talking about Tessa like she's some kind of celebrity crush.

God, Lili would roll her eyes to the moon if she knew.

32

I used to think Lili was just being territorial. We both hung out with other people sometimes, of course, especially at school. But it was different with Gretchen. For one thing, she moved to our school in eighth grade—the year Lili started high school.

I remember the end of summer that year felt like counting down to my own execution. I had this recurring daydream where I was sitting alone at a lunch table, lit by a spotlight for some reason. Everyone in the cafeteria was staring at me, and all you could hear were amplified chewing sounds. I just couldn't get it out of my head.

And then this new girl showed up, with purple streaks in her hair and enamel pins all over her backpack. Gretchen wasn't even five feet tall back then, but her presence could fill entire rooms somehow. The last new kid I'd semi-befriended had moved here from New York City, and for the entire first month of our friendship, I legitimately thought that's where Gretchen was from, too. She just seemed to know so much about *everything*—gerrymandering, chaos theory, and what people meant when they used the eggplant emoji. And she especially loved to talk about things like compulsory heterosexuality and gender performance. She'd even post graphics sometimes to educate people online.

Of course, Edith followed her around like a little queer puppy. And my mom seemed charmed by her—adults always love Gretchen, because she isn't weird or shy around them. The only person she couldn't win over was Lili. There's just always been this undercurrent of tension between them.

I remember one particular Tuesday—May of last year, not long before Lili came out. Gretchen and I had stopped in for ice cream at Seneca Farms after our Pride meeting, and Lili had walked the four blocks from her house to meet us.

It's all right there in my brain, every detail. I'd grabbed a cup of ice cream for Lili and set it on the shadiest patch of table. But it was practically soup by the time Lili arrived, and I was already down to the last few bites of my cone. Gretchen's progress was slower—probably because she was doing most of the talking.

I guess you could call it debriefing. There'd been a new Pride member that day—a junior named Dallas who had declined to give labels or pronouns. Gretchen found the whole thing discomforting. "Like, I'm torn," she'd said. "Because on the one hand, no one should have to share that. But on the other hand, I felt a little unsafe, and I think that's worth acknowledging."

"Unsafe?" Lili had asked, sliding onto the bench beside me.

Gretchen nodded. "I feel like even having one cishet person there really changes the vibe. There's just this extra potential for judgment and scrutiny—not you, Immylou, you know that."

"But how do you know they're cishet?" asked Lili.

"Well, that's what's tricky about it! They could totally be closeted. Which is why I would never, like, kick anyone out or question their right to be there."

Lili's eyes narrowed. "But you . . . are questioning their right to be there."

"No . . . I'm literally discussing my lived experience as a queer person in a queer space."

Lili didn't respond, but the air felt so thick all of a sudden. I remember watching ice cream drip from Gretchen's cone onto the table—she seemed to have forgotten about it entirely.

Gretchen kept talking. "I guess I just find it kind of unfair that the onus is on queer people to come out and share our labels. Allocishet people don't have to because they're the default. So it just becomes this whole self-perpetuating dynamic that protects allocishets from having to declare their positionality—which makes queer people even more vulnerable."

"Right, but how do you know who's allocishet? You don't," Lili said, gripping the edge of the bench between us.

"I get that—"

"Okay, but do you? Because it sounds like you're talking about a specific person who showed up to a Pride meeting and—very pointedly—didn't label themselves? You're really reading that as allocishet?"

"I mean, Dallas clearly doesn't want to be called queer," Gretchen said.

"So don't call them queer! But don't act like they don't belong there."

"I didn't! I offered them doughnuts—Imogen, didn't I?"

I looked up with a start. "Um. You did. Yes—"

"Like, this is literally just me talking about my own safety in a *designated queer space*."

"But why would you assume bad faith?" Lili insisted. "Why would someone show up to a Pride meeting to be shitty to queer people?"

I remember how Gretchen's eyes flashed when Lili said that. I could practically hear the thud of my heart hitting the ground beneath me.

"You really think that doesn't happen?" Gretchen's voice cracked. "Lili, that's why the club at my middle school disbanded! Because every goddamn week, the same group of assholes from the basketball team would show up claiming a bunch of labels and pronouns they learned from some fucking cringe compilation. And they were blatantly doing it to mock us, but you couldn't say anything, because then you're invalidating them. Until eventually it was just too exhausting to deal with, and the group stopped meeting."

Lili exhaled then. "I mean, yeah, that's fucked up. I'm really sorry, Gretchen." Then she turned abruptly back to her cup of melted ice cream, fishing an Oreo out with her spoon. And she didn't say anything else about it all night.

But when she drove me to school the next morning, she ranted about Gretchen the whole way there. "I *hate* that she went through that. I hate it! But does she really think that's what's going on here? With this random unlabeled kid? Come on."

I hugged my backpack to my chest, flustered. "I mean, I don't think it's anything about that person in particular. It's more that the situation brings up trauma for her. It makes sense that she'd be a little hypervigilant."

"No, I get that." Lili was quiet for a moment. "But what's the solution? Not let anyone in the door until Gretchen decides they're queer enough?"

"No. I don't know." I turned to stare out the window. "I just feel like it's not really our place to decide one way or another, you know? Since Gretchen's queer . . ."

Lili didn't speak then, but her face in that moment is still pinned to the wall of my brain, like a photograph. Her lips, pressed so tightly together they were practically white; nostrils flared; dark eyes flashing. I didn't really know what to make of it. I never understood why Lili got so prickly about Gretchen's discourse.

Until she drove me back from Brianna Lewis's graduation party a month or so later. Then I got it.

Texts with Gretchen

GP: IMMY

GP: SHE FOLLOWED ME BACK

GP: AND LIKED MY COMMENT

GP: Okay okay it's ON

GP: And I never posted my thirst trap!!!!

IS: I thought that was for Brielle 🫠

GP: 2 birds, 1 stone lol

GP: Anyway thirst traps are for general audiences, remember 🫣

GP: How soon is too soon tho, hmm

GP: Also I need you to find out if she's single and what her type is and if she's open to long distance lol

GP: Signed, a uhaul bisexual

33

I feel like an overfilled balloon. The slightest touch, and I'll pop.

I set my phone down on my bed without responding.

I don't get where this is coming from—why Gretchen's suddenly so fixated on Tessa. They've never met, never talked, never even interacted online until now. The only thing Gretchen knows about her is that she's cute. Pretty. Beautiful.

Hot. Whatever that means.

She's never even heard Tessa's laugh.

I sink back onto my pillows, both hands pressed to my chest. It's still light out. Still at least an hour before dinner. It's just me staring at the blankness of my own bedroom ceiling.

I don't know how to shake this feeling loose.

I rub my eyes and sit up, reaching for my phone. But it isn't Gretchen I'm texting.

Okay I know this is probably super random, I write, but I was kind of thinking about stuff

Ellipses—Lili's already typing.

Stuff?

I don't know. I was talking to Gretchen at Seneca Farms today, and it reminded me of last year

With Dallas

Ah, that was a fun one, writes Lili.

I know. I stare down at my screen, eyes prickling. I was just thinking about what I said to you that day. Like how it wasn't our place to disagree with Gretchen's take, because she was actually queer.

I don't even remember you saying that, writes Lili.

I do. I pause. And I shouldn't have said it. I'm so sorry.

Immy, it's fine!! I wasn't even out yet. 😄

I start to reply—but suddenly, she's FaceTiming me. I tap accept, and she pops into frame with a smile that's halfway between baffled and amused. "So what's this about?"

"I don't know." I shake my head. "It was just weighing on me. Like, you were telling me something so important, and I wasn't even listening."

Lili opens her mouth and then shuts it. "Immy, no. You can't do that. You're really gonna beat yourself up for not magically knowing I was queer?"

"I guess." I swallow. "It's more the fact that I didn't even consider it. Like I just had Gretchen in one box and you in another. She was queer and you were straight."

"But that's how being in the closet works! I'm not saying it's fun, but . . ."

"Yeah." I scrunch my nose. "I'm just sorry I made it even harder."

"Okay, that's very sweet and totally unnecessary," she says, laughing. "Here, one sec, I'm taking you onto my bed." Lili's background jerks around for a second, while she crosses the room and resettles. "Okay! So, like—where did this come from?"

"The Seneca Farms stuff?"

"Yeah. Just looking for new stuff to feel guilty about, or what?"

"Nooooo—"

"So, yes. Immy, seriously. You're good. Can we just blame Gretchen? I love blaming Gretchen."

"I know." I smile a little. "She was being kind of weird today, I guess."

"Uh-oh. Was somebody discoursing again? Wait—let me guess." Lili pitches her voice higher. "Excuse me, I'm a real-life certified Actual Queer Person. Are you literally talking over me right now?"

"No!" A laugh tries to break through, but I choke it back. "She wasn't."

"Not this time."

"Okay, she's not *that* bad."

"Then why do you look so pissed off?" Lili asks.

"Me?"

"Mm-hmm." Lili peers into the screen, tapping her lip.

"Yes, I'd say you are . . . cloudy . . . with an eighty percent chance of precipitation."

"Is this a weather report for my face?"

"Ooh. Possible thunderstorms. Flooding, tornadoes. We suggest you take cover immediately."

I crack a smile. "I'm just being grumpy about stupid stuff."

"What kind of stupid stuff?"

"Just random stuff." I bite my lip. "Like—I don't know. She's buddying up to Tessa on Instagram. I don't know why I'm annoyed by that, but—"

"Tessa, like *our* Tessa?"

"I—yeah." I blush.

"Sorry, but—how do they even know each other?"

"They don't. Tessa just commented on one of my pictures, and then Gretchen followed her, and Tessa followed her back."

Lili's eyes narrow. "That's weird."

I shrug. "I think I'm overreacting, though. It's—"

"Hey, speaking of Tess." Lili sits up, her tone suddenly shifting. "I meant to check in earlier. Um."

I freeze. "About what?"

"I know you guys have been texting a lot."

"Is that—okay?"

"Oh, totally! Of course. I just . . ." She pauses, studying my face. "I didn't know if you wanted to, like, come clean about stuff. The backstory."

"Like—the ex-girlfriend stuff?"

Lili nods. "And the sexuality stuff. If you want! Up to you. Just wanted you to know I'd be fine with it. Either way."

"Oh. Okay." My heart flips. "I'm—"

"Or I could tell her," she adds. "I don't know. Just if you feel like—if it starts to seem relevant. You being straight."

I feel my cheeks go red-hot. "Like—I'm leading her on?"

"No! Oh—Immy, not like that. I don't know." She laughs nervously. "I'm reading way too much into this, huh? Okay, you know what? Pretend I didn't say anything."

"No, you're fine," I say slowly. "It's just—"

The sexuality stuff.

Speaking of Tess.

The words tiptoe to the edge of my tongue, then hastily retreat. Like a kid working up the nerve to dive off the high board.

It's not that I'm scared. Not exactly. It just feels so official to even broach the topic out loud. Especially when I can't quite decide if these feelings are real.

Because if I actually liked girls, wouldn't I be more like Edith? Or like Gretchen, who's basically an encyclopedia of bisexual memes. Or even Lili, who knew she was pan for years before coming out. *That's* what queerness looks like. Not me pulling muscles in my brain trying to figure out what even counts as attraction.

The whole thing just seems a little too convenient, you know? *Oh, Imogen? That girl who suddenly thinks she might be bi after spending a few days with the cool queer kids? Imogen, a known people pleaser? Couldn't be faking it!*

I just can't glue down the thought. The question sounds less real in my head every time I ask it.

Texts with Tessa

TM: FOUR!!!!

IS: Four? 👀

TM: Ahem
TM: Gory homebirth baby, lesbian elsa, cat
TM: Cheerleader!!!

IS: Ohhhh
IS: Gretchen posted her throwback, haha
IS: That was my eighteenth birthday 😊

TM: Pretty dang cute, Scotty
TM: I'd say it's your best since Lesbian Elsa

IS: It's actually a lesbian cheerleader!
IS: Like Natasha Lyonne in BIAC

TM: BIAC 🤔

IS: But I'm a Cheerleader!
IS: It's my favorite movie 🖤

TM: RIGHT! Duh
TM: Wow

TM: My lesbian credibility in tatters

IS: Nah
IS: Credibility fully intact

TM: Okay but what if I told you
TM: I've never seen it 😅😅😅

IS: Lol you're fine!!
IS: Neither has Gretchen
IS: Technically, they're not even BIAC costumes
IS: We're MUNA and Phoebe Bridgers from the Silk
        Chiffon music video!

TM: I LOVE THAT SONG
TM: Have never seen the video!!
TM: Is there a BIAC reference?

IS: Uh yes 😂
IS: Just a bit

TM: Okay, I'm finding it
TM: And I'm literally going to stream the movie tonight

IS: Omg, you don't have to!

TM: Imogen please, my reputation is on the line

IS: No seriously

IS: Idk, you may not even like it

IS: Gretchen has some kind of issue with it

IS: I think she thinks it's for straight people

TM: But I'm a Cheerleader?

TM: Doesn't Natasha Lyonne hook up with a girl?

IS: Yup Clea DuVall

IS: And yeah, Gretchen has a lot of opinions 👻

IS: I just mean don't feel pressured to watch it!

TM: But it's your favorite movie!!!

IS: Well what's your favorite movie? I'll watch that

TM: My favorite movie! Huh

TM: Hmm

TM: Can it be a tie?

IS: Totally

TM: Okay! Then I think . . . the princess bride and
        booksmart

TM: Oh! And mean girls

TM: And ET

TM: Back to the future

TM: WAIT ALSO

TM: DEBS!!!!!!

TM: And before sunrise/before sunset

TM: And inside out!!

TM: Joy is my girl 😊

TM: And Priscilla 👑🖼️

TM: Omg and Ferris Bueller!!

IS: Wow 😄

IS: You know what you're like?

TM: Uh oh 😄

IS: You know how sometimes you go to Wegmans for one thing

IS: Like a loaf of bread

IS: And you end up leaving with half the bakery section and a cart full of produce??

IS: You're that

IS: In human form

TM: Scott.

IS: 🤗

TM: Brutal

IS: I know

TM: Yet so accurate

TM: Wait

TM: Also Bend it like Beckham!!!

TM: That movie is SO GAY

TM: I mean it's not

TM: Like it actually hurts

TM: But I still love it

IS: Me too!! ⚽

IS: You have excellent taste btw

TM: 😊

DAY SIX
WEDNESDAY
MARCH 23

Texts with Tessa

IS: WOW okay 😂

IS: So you liked it, huh?

TM: Like

TM: I'm obsessed

TM: I need a rewatch ASAP!!

TM: You'll watch it with me, right?

TM: You don't have to wear your cheerleader costume

TM: You *can*

TM: But you don't have to

IS: Noted 😂

IS: Omg I'm so happy you liked it!!!

IS: My comfort film 🖤

IS: And Tessa, the princess bride 🏰

IS: Loved it

IS: How did I go so long without watching it??

TM: I need to rewatch that, too!!

TM: I haven't seen it in years, I feel like a fake fan

TM: Though to be fair I did frame a picture of princess
        buttercup for my bookshelf

TM: When I was like 10

TM: Nbd, just pretending she was my girlfriend

IS: Ohhh that's so cute 😆

TM: Definitely still on display in my room 😬
TM: I told my ex it was a picture of my cousin Annie from Westchester

IS: Ooh good call
IS: Wouldn't want her to think anything was going on between you and a fictional princess
IS: From a movie that came out in 1987

TM: Right!! Could have been catastrophic 🫨
TM: Though Jillian might actually have been pissed, who knows

IS: She was really weird about stuff, huh?

TM: Sometimes
TM: I mean we were really young too, so that was definitely part of it
TM: Dated sophomore year mostly and the beginning of junior
TM: Though we were friends first
TM: Like best friends
TM: For YEARS
TM: Kind of like you and Lili I guess?
TM: But waaaaay messier

IS: You mean the breakup?

TM: Honestly, all of it
TM: Like it was this really intense friendship
TM: But we were also kind of frenemies I guess??

IS: Omg, I can't imagine you having a frenemy!!

TM: Right?? I'm allergic to conflict
TM: I guess it was more like she was mad at me a lot and
        I didn't always know why
TM: I was just sad and confused mostly
TM: And then sometimes it was totally fine

IS: Oh, that must have been so hard

TM: Kind of? I don't know
TM: I think we were just so incompatible
TM: She's kind of serious about things
TM: Like she doesn't really joke around much
TM: Or maybe it's more that our senses of humor didn't
        really click

IS: Ahhh okay
IS: That's actually kind of a huge deal imo
IS: The humor thing

TM: Oh, 100%

TM: Honestly, that may be the most important thing

TM: For me, at least

IS: And you haven't really dated anyone since then, yeah?

TM: Nope 😅

IS: Can I ask why not?

IS: Seriously fine if you don't want to answer that btw

TM: I don't mind at all!

TM: Though I don't know if there's like a clear answer for that

TM: I think it's probably a combination of things

TM: Like I had a really stupid crush on a straight girl most of senior year

TM: Also I'm just a wimp about that stuff in general

TM: I don't know haha

TM: What about you?

IS: You mean with Lili?

TM: Yeah, or even just in general

IS: Haha well I'm definitely a wimp

IS: Idk, I haven't actually dated anyone

IS: Besides Lili

IS: Which barely even counts lol

TM: Wait, why wouldn't it count? 😂

IS: Oh I guess

IS: It was such a short period of time

IS: And the energy wasn't even really that romantic

TM: Huh

TM: Maybe that's why you guys were able to bounce
        back to being friends again so easily

IS: I guess so!

TM: Do you think it would get awkward though if one of
        you started dating someone

IS: Totally not

IS: I'd honestly just be happy for her

IS: Or vice versa

IS: I know that's probably weird!!

TM: Not at all!

TM: I think it's really cool

IS: Me too

TM: Hmm

IS: Oh my god
IS: Tessa it's almost 2:30

TM: Whoa!
TM: Look at us
TM: Hey maybe we're night owls AND early birds!!

IS: That sounds healthy

TM: 😛

IS: Seriously, don't you have class tomorrow????
IS: Today I mean
IS: Yikes

TM: Eh, not til 10
TM: I'll live
TM: I'll steal Kayla's Life Savers 😊

34

You'd think I'd be a total zombie this morning. Tessa and I didn't stop texting until almost three a.m., and even then, I was too amped to keep my eyes shut. It was probably close to four by the time I drifted off—but here I am, not even four hours later, in sweats and an old academic bowl T-shirt. Hair pulled back, heart still fluttering.

The doorbell rings right at eight, and I rush to answer it. "Wait." I pull open the door. "You're not Gretchen."

It's Otávio, looking only marginally awake in sweatpants and an already paint-spattered T-shirt. "I think your mom wanted the top half of the walls painted, too," he says, shrugging serenely.

"Rude." I grin, stepping back to let him inside. I kind of love that five-foot-nine Otávio is our token giant, but he definitely has some kind of point. Edith is five-five, I'm barely five-four, and Gretchen's *maybe* five-one. If you're being generous.

We step out the back door and straight back into the shed,

where Mom is crouched, stirring paint. There's blue tape along all the trim, and the entire floor is covered with a plastic drop cloth. It's so strange seeing the shed without its metal storage shelves or stacks of boxes. Between that and the white coat of primer, it actually looks weirdly spacious. A little smaller than Lili's dorm room, maybe, but not much. And I bet it's at least as big as Tessa's.

Mom coats one of the rollers in light mint green, running it along a plastic paint tray to squeeze off the excess. "Thank you so much again," she says, handing the roller to me. "You guys go ahead and get started. I'll send Gretchen back when she gets here. And then I think I'm going to just lock myself downstairs for a few hours and knock out my conference prep. Dad's home today, though. Is Edith still sleeping?"

"No idea."

"I'll investigate." Mom stands, pressing her palms to her thighs.

Otávio cues up some sort of instrumental guitar playlist on his phone—he can be very dreamy and timeless like that. He turns the volume up and sets it down on the drop cloth, as far from the rollers and buckets as possible. I used to help my parents with paint projects sometimes, and I forgot how much it calms my brain down. Even better is the fact that Otávio's sort of shy and quiet like I am, so we're perfectly happy working in silence. Slow and peaceful, like the first summer day on the lake.

Until Edith appears in the doorway, looking like her birthday came early. "Guess what guess what guess what!" She bounces into the shed, Gretchen trailing behind her. "Kara Clapstone came out!"

I laugh. "Gretchen, why are you wearing a trash bag?"

"It's a paint poncho!"

"Who's Kara Clapstone?" Otávio asks.

"An actress! She played the nerdy girl in *Shop Talk*, and she's about to be in that coven show. Here, you'll recognize her." Edith hands him her phone.

"Cool. So she's queer?"

"Yup—bisexual!" Edith grabs a roller, glancing back over her shoulder at Gretchen. "Still think *Shop Talk*'s for straight people?"

"Oh, one hundred percent," Gretchen says. "It's not about Kara. It's about the straight gaze."

"There are . . . straight gays?" Otávio looks bewildered.

Gretchen laughs, tapping just below her eyes. "Gaze like *gaze*. It's made for straight audiences."

"Right, of course," Edith says. "This movie about queer girls, written and directed by two queer women, starring a queer woman . . . is for straight audiences."

Gretchen smiles. "Don't get me wrong—I'm thrilled for Kara! And, like, it definitely helps."

"Helps what?"

"I don't know—the general optics, I guess? Obviously,

having a straight lead actress was kind of an iffy choice—"

"But she wasn't straight," Edith says.

"Sure, but she said she was. And sapphic representation is already so rare in Hollywood." Gretchen settles in cross-legged on the drop cloth. "So I can see why people would want those roles to go to actual queer people. It's about equity. And authenticity—"

"How is Kara not an actual queer person?" Edith's voice comes out sharp.

"She *is*! Of course she is. I'm just saying, I get where the Kara discourse is coming from."

I press my thumb to my lips. "There's Kara discourse?"

"I guess it's more like people rehashing some of the earlier discourse?" says Gretchen. "Like there were queer people who critiqued Kara's casting when they first announced it. Now everyone's turning on them and saying they pressured her out of the closet."

"I mean. They kind of did," Edith says.

"Well, I think they expressed valid frustration. It was a mainstream gay movie! Obviously, there's going to be backlash when people see *yet another* queer role go to a straight woman. What did she think would happen?" Gretchen tugs at the edge of her paint poncho. "It just sucks, because now people are using it as this gotcha moment. Like people should have some-how known not to criticize her work, because she'd eventually turn out to be bi?"

"But it's not about criticism of her work." Edith sets her roller on the paint tray. "They're mad that she said she was straight—"

"Right, because—"

"And now they're tripping over themselves to find reasons to still be pissed about it! We've already got Twitter randos questioning her motivations for coming out. 'Oh, she's just saying she's bi to get out of valid criticism!' 'Oh, she's doing it to get more press for the coven show!'"

Otávio wrinkles his nose. "That's kind of gross."

"Can we just be happy for her?" Edith shakes her head. "Plus, the shit she's getting from other actors. You know the girl who played the gay trombone player in that battle of the bands movie?"

"Jeanette Jaymes?"

"Yeah. So, like, five seconds after Kara's announcement goes live, Jeanette drops this shady Instagram post about how straight-passing bisexuals love to tweet about how queer they are from their boyfriends' beds." Edith scowls. "And then she dirty deleted, but seriously? Let the woman live!"

And just like that, I'm blinking back tears. Which is ridiculous. This is a ridiculous thing to cry about.

I mean, it's a ridiculous thing for *me* to cry about.

Because I'm not Kara Clapstone. I don't even know Kara Clapstone.

Gretchen exhales. "I mean . . . biphobes are gonna biphobe.

It sucks." She leans in to paint along the edge of the trim. "But at the same time, Kara's pretty straight-passing, so there's privilege there, right? She's not going to be harassed by bigots and homophobes. She's a wealthy white actress with a boyfriend! In LA!"

I pause. "Isn't she from rural Alabama, though?"

"She sure is." Edith does jazz hands. "And now she's got five thousand college sophomores explaining to her that if she's actually bi, she should have come out before the movie released. Because it would have meant so much to her fans."

Something twists in my chest.

I wonder if Kara Clapstone's town in Alabama is anything like Penn Yan. It's probably worse—at least Penn Yan gets to be in New York state. But we're not exactly Manhattan. I remember the summer Edith and I made a game out of counting all the aggressively right-wing T-shirt slogans at the Yates County Fair. We had to stop after an hour because it was too depressing. *Don't tread on me. God, guns, and glory. I oil my gun with liberal tears.* And at school, you basically can't even pee without having to read whatever fresh slur just popped up on the walls. Otávio and I started bringing Sharpies into the bathroom to black them out, but it's like Whac-A-Mole.

I think people forget how different things can be in different places.

"It's clown behavior," says Edith. "I'm sorry, no. Kara Clapstone doesn't need to set her coming-out timeline according to your weird parasocial entitlement."

"Totally agree! I'm glad she waited until she was ready!" Gretchen says.

"So stop discoursing," Edith snaps, "and leave her alone!"

Then she storms out of the shed, letting the door clang shut behind her.

Texts with Tessa

IS: Hello I just painted a shed

IS: And there was discourse

IS: And now I need a shower

IS: 😭 😭 😭

TM: Okay wow I have questions

TM: What was the shed discourse???

TM: And can it be fixed by a shower? 🤔

IS: Haha I wish it was shed discourse

IS: I love shed discourse

IS: This was

IS: I don't even know where to begin

IS: 😵

IS: OKAY NEW TOPIC

IS: How was your morning

IS: Did you make it through stats

TM: Hahahahaha oh man

TM: Soooo

TM: Want to see what falling asleep while taking notes looks like?

TM: 📎

TM: womp womp womp ▓

IS: Omg are those your notes??

IS: AHHH I'm so sorry

IS: Can you get a copy of someone else's?

IS: I feel so bad

TM: Scott, omg no!!! Don't feel bad

TM: It's fine! I can get the TA's notes

TM: It's legit one of my accommodations, I just always
        forget it's an option 😄

TM: Please don't feel bad!!!!

TM: Honestly stats is basically math, I promise I don't get
        it any better when I'm awake 🫠

IS: I don't get tit either

IS: *IT

TM: OH 👀

IS: Oh my god

TM: I mean, you definitely could 😈

TM: Lots of tit

TM: All the tit

IS: TESSA NO 😆

IS: NO MORE TIT DISCOURSE

TM: *titcourse

TM: 😏

35

Otávio's on the track team, but I've never seen him move like he does when we finish the shed. He's probably halfway home before Gretchen and I have a chance to wash the paint off our hands.

Dad's in the kitchen, assembling a makeshift lunch buffet—bread, jelly, SunButter, fruit, and tortilla chips. "How's the shed looking?"

"Amazing," says Gretchen, smiling so brightly it makes my head spin. If it weren't for the angry nineties music blasting from Edith's room at top volume, I'd almost think the tension in the shed never happened. It's like when you're reading a book and you accidentally skip a whole page. That same little tug of, *wait, what?*

Did I just misread the entire mood of that interaction?

I mean, Otávio looked like he wanted to jump out the window, and Edith was practically boiling over. But here's Gretchen, casually pulling the crusts off her sandwich and chatting with my dad about where she thinks the futon should go.

What did she think would happen?

I always feel so out of my league when it comes to queer discourse. It's like I'm surrounded by people doing synchronized dances on tightropes, and I'm just trying to keep my feet planted.

Like the whole gay-media-for-straight-people meme. The straight gaze. Or when the topic of queerbaiting comes up sometimes in Pride Alliance. Not just about scripted TV shows and movies—I guess queerbaiting happens with certain celebrities, too. Like when allocishet influencers hint at being queer, just for clout. Or when they make money from media with overtly queer themes. Sometimes cis straight musicians will even make their lyrics ambiguously queer on purpose.

I'm always a little unnerved when the subject of queerbaiting comes up, though. Maybe because I'm not good at spotting it in the wild. The problem is, I can't always tell if someone's allocishet in the first place.

I guess it goes back to what Gretchen always says, about how queer people are hardwired to recognize each other. That would explain why no one else in the group seems to have trouble seeing it.

Though.

Sometimes they almost seem to see it *too* well.

That's the thing that keeps throwing me. Obviously, it's not my place to speak over queer people on this. But I can't shake the thought.

It isn't only Kara Clapstone. Just a few weeks ago, a Broadway actor got dragged for taking a role that should have gone to a queer guy.

Turns out, he was one. He ended up coming out on Instagram, just so people would stop hassling him about it. I remember reading his caption over and over, feeling sick to my stomach. I'd never even heard this actor's name until that day, but I was on the verge of tears for a week. Something about that discourse sliced straight through me.

Something about this discourse does too.

"So I joined the admitted students Discord server," Gretchen says, dumping her crusts into the compost. "But it's not super active yet. The Reddit admissions megathread is popping off, though. People have been sharing their stats—like scores and grades and stuff. I'm kind of intimidated!"

"Sounds really intense," I say vaguely.

"*So* intense! You haven't joined the Blackwell Discord, right? Do they have a Discord? I don't know how it works. Does someone in the incoming class have to make one?"

"I don't know." I yawn, tucking my ankles around the legs of the barstool. Now Gretchen's talking about some kind of summer orientation meetup, but my mind's still swirling with questions about Kara Clapstone.

Like whether she just came out to her family, too.

Maybe they already knew. Or maybe they'd wondered. Or not.

The first time she said it out loud, was she scared?

Was she sure it was real?

"You should see if Blackwell has one," says Gretchen.

I nod fuzzily, watching my dad put all the lunch stuff away. Lids on jars, loaves sealed off. "Okay."

"I'll poke around Reddit and see what comes up," Gretchen says. "Also, I kind of feel like watching a movie. Is that weird? Why do I feel like that's such a nighttime activity?"

Dad looks up at me. "Peanut, where's Edith?"

"Oh. Um. Probably in her room?"

"Talking to Zora." Gretchen shakes her head affectionately. "Wait, you know what we should watch? What was the documentary Nicole was talking about last week?"

I stare at her, more than a little bit gobsmacked. Does she really think Edith's just chilling in her room right now, Face-Timing her girlfriend? She has to know Edith's pissed at her, right?

"The one about that wellness influencer cult guy. Here, I'll look it up—"

"Oh, you know what?" Dad's eyes meet mine, for just a moment. "Immy, I actually need you to go through the boxes today. Your sister, too."

"Oh!" I open my mouth and then close it. The relief I feel is so unexpected, I'm practically speechless. "Okay. Um. Gretch, maybe tomorrow?"

256

"No. Ugh. We're going to the outlet mall. She shakes her head, looking glum. "Friday?"

I give her a thumbs-up. "That works."

The moment the door shuts behind her, it's like my brain comes off mute. I'm wide awake for the first time all day.

Texts with Tessa

TM: Feeling any better?

TM: Did you get to shower off all that discourse?

IS: Haha yes!

IS: Shower actually did help I think

IS: I was in such a bizarro mood, I don't even know

TM: What was the discourse??

TM: Only if you want to talk about it of course

TM: I don't want to rehash stuff!!!

IS: Oh no, it's fine! You're not rehashing

IS: Idk if you've seen that Kara Clapstone came out

IS: From shop talk

TM: I saw!!!!

TM: Ohhhh man, was there discourse?

IS: I guess? I haven't really gone down the rabbit hole yet, but Edith and Gretchen were arguing about it

IS: Long story

IS: Anyway, better now!! All showered with an elderly kitty in my lap

TM: Is it Quincy??????

IS: Of course

IS: He's the only one who gets to stay in my room

IS: Bc he's the only one who can be trusted not to eat his little hamster sister

TM: We love an uneaten hamster!!!

TM: Wait hold on one sec

IS: Okay!

TM: I'm back!! Sorry

TM: The himbos are being insufferable

TM: I swear to god it's like having ten older brothers who adore you

TM: But give you shit literally all the time

TM: Thus I am now in the hallway outside Dan's suite

IS: Omg, go hang out with your ten brothers! Sorry!!

TM: No thank you 😌

IS: No for real, I'll let you go!

IS: I should go anyway

IS: Edith and I are supposed to go through some boxes from the shed apparently?

IS: Like old storage stuff, should be interesting

IS: Definite potential for embarrassing Lili content

TM: Oh well in that case 😄
TM: Counting on you to send me everything

IS: I will!

TM: I know 😏

Texts with Gretchen

GP: On Privacy, Privilege, and Positionality: Is Kara Clapstone's Announcement Too Little, Too Late? 🔗

GP: Okay I actually really like this take

GP: Kind of unpacks some of the issues I had with how everything's being framed

GP: Curious to know what you think!!

36

I don't click Gretchen's link. Even the headline puts a pit in my stomach.

I never know how to navigate this stuff. Of course I want to listen to queer perspectives. But what do you do when there's no consensus? How do I know which queer perspective to defer to?

Either way, I'm just a straight girl talking over queer people. Unless I'm not.

Okay, but what are the odds of that? Occam's razor says the simplest explanation is probably true. So what's actually more likely? That I magically turned queer over the course of a weekend?

Or that I'm doing what I do in every situation—trying to be exactly what everyone wants me to be.

Something thuds near the bottom of my bedroom door— Edith, knocking with her feet. "Hey, help me with these," she says, peeking out over a pair of stacked cardboard boxes. But when I make a grab for the top one, she clarifies, "No, I mean, there are like six more in the basement. Dad actually does want us to go through them, apparently?"

I laugh. "Yeah, why else would he have asked us to?"

"To rescue you from Gretchen. You know that was the whole point, right?" Edith sets the boxes down on my bed, herding me out the door for another load.

"You don't think you might be projecting?" I side-eye her as we step into the hall. "Just a little?"

"I mean, that's what he literally told me."

"Wait, really?"

"He said, and I quote, 'I think your sister needed a little bit of a Gretchen detox today.'"

"Dad said *detox*?"

"He's a king! What can I say?" She taps a short stack of boxes with her toe. "Here, these three are ours, plus the two big plastic ones by the couch."

It takes us three more trips downstairs to get them all, plus a quick stop in the kitchen to fuel up on Mom's fancy Lindt chocolate.

"Okay, what does he want us to do with this stuff?" I ask, settling onto the rug with one of the big plastic tubs. "Just, like . . . go through it?"

"And consolidate it. We're supposed to decide what to keep, donate, throw away . . . I don't really remember what's in them, though."

I nudge the lid off the first tub. "Looks like clothes." I pull out a tiny white hoodie covered in hand-painted black spots, with a pair of black socks sewn on as ears. "This is from *101 Dalmatians*, right?"

"My theatrical debut!" Edith tugs it out of my hands, hugging it close. "Okay, I'm starting a pile. Definitely keeping the sentimental stuff."

Of course, the entire tub turns out to be sentimental stuff—tie-dyed camp T-shirts and costumes and my favorite cat-patterned dress from preschool. I stop short at the sight of Edith's perfectly preserved Lesbian Elsa dress, stomach twisting with guilt. There's no soft way to spin it. I'm literally holding a lie in my hands.

By the time we reach the bottom of the tub, every single piece is in the keep pile. "Marie Kondo is shaking and crying right now," says Edith.

Luckily, the next few boxes are a little easier to trim down. Old school assignments go straight to the recycling bin—other than the obvious gems, like first-grade Edith's drawing of "The Horniest Unicorn." Then there's a full box of plastic figurines and favor-bag prizes for the donate pile, and a few tattered squishies for the trash. Edith casually sets aside a small collection of stray Barbie limbs for unspecified purposes. "This is fun. It's like going through a tiny serial killer's trash." She pulls out a small plastic treasure chest. "Hello, are you full of baby teeth?"

"Why are we saving this?" I hold up a hardened blob of

air-dry clay covered in sequins.

"Because it's a beautiful, timeless work of art?"

I stick it in the trash pile, alongside a collection of pipe cleaner bracelets and dried-up slime. I legitimately think I could scrawl a smiley face on an orange peel, and my parents would save it for decades. There's an entire box of original Imogen and Edith drawings, too, plus a few of Lili's old horse pictures. We used to hide out in the barn with our sketch pads, tucked up next to the hay bales for hours. Lili knew how to add dimension and shading, and she could blur her pencil lines with two fingertips. Sometimes she'd let me color them in, too, because I was good at keeping things inside the lines.

It's strange, seeing all these relics lined up like that, side by side. Santa letters and movie tickets and the dress I wore to freshman year's homecoming dance. All strung together like beads on a necklace.

I break into a box of old photos, while Edith settles in with her own fifth-grade diary.

"Listen to this masterpiece. 'Hi, Diary. Here are all the reasons today was bad. Number one, Mr. Dye is a buttwhole'—" She looks up. "With a *w*. Butt. Whole."

"I mean, it kind of works."

"'Number two, we had kickball in PE but Patrick bunted and that is cheating but he didn't get in trouble. In conclusion, number three is there were no middle seats left on the bus, only the back which is bullies and the front which is buttkissers and now I always have to sit alone because Imogen doesn't go to my school because she is in sixth grade. Love, Edith. P.S. What starts with F and ends in u-c-k? A firetruck! LOL. Otávio heard it from Lili!'"

"Oh." I look at her. "Edie."

"Right? Fuck Patrick!"

I press my cheek. "I made you ride alone with the butt-kissers."

"No way. I picked the bullies." She pokes me with a Barbie leg. "Please tell me you're not blaming yourself for graduating elementary school."

"I'm not. I'm blaming that buttwhole Mr. Dye."

"Why did I talk so much about butts and men?" Edith makes a face, flipping to the next entry.

I turn back to the photo box, lifting out a short stack of prints. Me, perched on Dad's shoulders, hands pressed flat on his head. Baby Edith staring into a mirror. The two of us dangling our feet off the dock at Nana's house. Me at the library, proudly holding up my plate of award-winning Rice Krispies Treats. Edith in her heart-shaped glasses. There are so many with Lili and Otávio, too—lined up beside hay bales or sprawled on the couch. Lili and me manning a table stacked high with boxes of Girl Scout Cookies.

I look up at Edith. "You know, I felt the same way you did in fifth grade—when Lili moved up to middle school. Eighth grade, too."

266

"And now," Edith adds.

I pause. "College is different, though. You kind of expect that to change things."

Edith looks at me. "Do you think it has?"

"What do you mean?"

"Changed things." She sets her journal on the rug, stretching. "What about this weekend? Did it feel different with Lili?"

"No! I mean, not really? Not in a bad way." My heart twists. "I don't know. It's probably easier, because Geneva is so nearby."

"Yeah, but nearby isn't here," Edith says.

"Yeah."

For a moment, neither of us speaks. But then—

"I'm kind of dreading it," says Edith.

"Dreading college?"

"Dreading you leaving for college!"

"Wait." I stare at her. "Really?"

"I mean, I'm taking your room," she says quickly, "so that's good. It's gonna be my greenhouse. I think I'm going to try being a plant mom."

I nod slowly. "Huh."

"All I'm saying is it's going to be a little weird when you're gone." She shrugs. "And I'll probably miss you."

I press a fist to my mouth. "Edie—"

"Like a little bit! Enough to passive-aggressively remark upon it in my diary sometimes. That's all." She shakes her head, laughing. "Stop looking at me like that!"

It's just funny, I guess. We've always been so attached at the hip, but I've never really thought of it as Edith needing me. Or missing me.

I would have sworn it was the other way around.

Texts with Tessa

IS: Oh hello 🐐

IS: 📎

TM: Omg IS THAT DAISY?!????

TM: The most beautiful goat!!!

TM: Oh my heart

IS: She was the best 🐼

TM: So that's clearly you on the left

TM: Edith on the right

TM: You guys look so much alike, it's wild

IS: I know 😄

IS: Her hair is blonder

IS: And she's like an inch taller than me now

IS: But otherwise 👻

TM: I love it

TM: We're like that too!! Let me find a pic

TM: 📎

IS: TRIPLETS!!! Wow, even Dan

IS: Is this from your bat mitzvah?

IS: Wait no

IS: Must be Rachael's bat mitzvah, right??

TM: Actually I think it's my cousin Walter's bar mitzvah?
TM: That's Annie aka Buttercup's little bro haha
TM: But he's Rachael's age, so same era!!
TM: Don't worry, I would never spring a pic of 12 year old me without warning
TM: Your body isn't prepared for that level of titcourse
TM: Or lack thereof 😬

IS: 😆
IS: I think I can handle it
IS: I mean 📎

TM: Oh
TM: WHAT
TM: Is that 12 year old Imogen 😱

IS: Eleven 🥺
IS: First day of sixth grade

TM: Scott
TM: Your shirt
TM: Cattitude 💀

IS: As you can see
IS: I was very cool in middle school

TM: You were 😄

TM: Okay hold on, let me find my bat mitzvah pics

TM: Just know

TM: You won't be able to unsee this

IS: I'm ready 💪

TM: Ok wait

TM: I'm going to show you two

TM: A case study

TM: All right, the backstory is that my parents made me wear a dress to the ceremony, but I got to pick my own clothes for the party

TM: So here's me being awkward as fuck outside the temple 📎

TM: And then

TM: Taken literally the same day . . .

TM: A twelve year old tomboy icon 🕶️ 📎

IS: OMG

IS: These are both incredible!!!

IS: Aww were you really tiny or was that just a big Torah 😄

TM: Both 😄

TM: Idk, I think they're all kind of big

IS: Also, you are legitimately so cool???

IS: Your little pinstriped pants and suspenders 🎩

IS: And all the socks!!!!

IS: You look so happy

TM: Those were our favors!!

TM: The bottoms say "shut up and dance at Tessa's bat mitzvah"

TM: I was OBSESSED with that song

TM: Actually they say "Shut ⬆️ and dance" because my mom thought it would be more polite? Idk

TM: and they have like those traction dots on bottom so you can wear them on the dance floor

TM: I still wear the extras sometimes ☺️

IS: I would literally only wear those socks if I had them

IS: I'd do laundry every day

TM: I'll get some for you!!!

TM: Next time I'm home!

IS: Omg I promise I wasn't hinting!!

TM: No I know!! Haha

IS: I seriously can't get over these pictures

IS: The contrast 😂

IS: You're like that lesbian tiktok trend

TM: Wait what 👀

IS: Where they're like 'oh, you're into masc girls? no
         problem!'
IS: And they whoosh their hand in front of their face
         and BOOM 😌

TM: I literally have no idea what you're talking about 😂
         😂 😂

IS: Really???
IS: That was like my entire FYP for two weeks!!!

TM: Ma'am, that is between you and your algorithm 🙊

IS: 🙊
IS: Wait hold on, Edith just busted in
IS: Oh I think we're gonna watch Shop Talk 🖤

TM: Okay, but no discourse allowed 🖤

DAY SEVEN
THURSDAY
MARCH 24

37

Edith spends the night in my bed, which is how I know she's still upset about Gretchen.

It's what we've both done since we were tiny, anytime we feel sad or stressed or adrift. Like the time we couldn't find Adrian for two entire days, or the night before Edith got her tonsils out. Even really trivial stuff, like when Edith's kindergarten teacher said she couldn't wear her Jason mask in the Halloween parade. There's just something about the rhythm of her breathing that reels me back to shore. I think it must be the same for Edith, too.

We watched all of *Shop Talk*, even the bonus footage. But we don't even mention Kara's announcement. Or Gretchen. Or the discourse.

And I don't click Gretchen's link.

I haven't texted her back since she sent it. I know that's pretty spineless of me.

It's just—when I pick up my phone, all I want to do is talk to Tessa. I may be getting slightly addicted.

I'm trying not to overthink it.

Tessa FaceTimes me just before ten in the morning, and I can barely catch my breath in time to press accept.

"Hi!" Her face pops into frame—wide brown eyes, pink cheeks, hair tucked behind her ears, the dull green of campus behind her. The image is just a little too blurry to make out her freckles, but my brain fills them in. "I was just—" She stops short, breaking into a smile. "Okay, wow, it's you! It's your face!"

It's my face. I touch my cheek as if to confirm it.

I think my heart's trying to kick down my rib cage. "That's kind of FaceTime's whole thing."

I settle in cross-legged on my bed.

"I *know*. But I've gotten so used to texting you now! It's like—wait, sorry, is this okay? FaceTiming?"

I laugh, slightly breathless. "Of course."

"Okay! Sorry. Yeah—I was trying to text and walk, but it was taking too long, and then I almost tripped off the curb. So I was like, 'Okay, you know what, Scott, I'm just gonna'—anyway, hi! This is my walk to class."

"Ooh, what class? Stats again?"

"No, thank God. Social psych today. Stats is tomorrow. Hey." She looks suddenly flustered. "So. Speaking of tomorrow—I've got an idea."

I scoot back toward the headboard. "An idea?"

"Mm-hmm." Tessa grins, and I grin back, and I can't quite pinpoint why this moment feels so surreal. "So, I think—"

Someone screams, just out of frame, and Tessa's eyes dart sideways.

"Oy. Okay. Frat bro swiped some girl's hat, and now they're both laughing. All good. Anyway! I think you should come tomorrow."

"Oh!" My heartbeat quickens. "You mean—"

"To the party. Just think about it, okay? Rumor has it you already have an outfit."

"That's true."

"And I checked with Quincy. He said he's totally chill holding down the fort."

"Well, in that case . . ."

"Wait, is that a yes?" Her tentative smile makes my heart catch.

I smile back. "It's yes-adjacent." I pause. "Let me talk to Lili."

Texts with Lili

IS: Okay, question for you

IS: If I wanted to attend a certain party tomorrow night

IS: On a certain college campus

IS: Would that still be an option, maybe? 😆

LC: Wait, seriously??

IS: Only if it wouldn't be any trouble!!!

IS: I know this is so last minute

IS: Totally totally understand if it's a bad time

LC: No, it's good!

LC: I'm just surprised 😄

LC: You seemed totally not into it on Monday

IS: No no I promise I was into it 🫣

IS: I'm sorry

IS: I was just overthinking some stuff

IS: And then Tessa mentioned it again today

IS: Idk, I figured it was worth checking?

LC: Ohhhhhh so you just needed the invitation to come from Tessa

LC: I see how it is 😄

IS: What? No!!!

IS: I didn't mean it like that!!

IS: I'm sorry 🫠 🫠 🫠

LC: Immy omg I'm kidding

LC: I'm so glad you're coming!!!

LC: Like I'm fucking hyped

LC: Actually, why don't I come down and pick you up tomorrow

IS: No!! I think I can get the car

LC: Seriously, I need to grab some costume stuff at home anyway

LC: It's perfect

LC: And I'll just drive you home in the morning, or whenever you want

IS: You sure? 🫣

LC: Look he's already waiting for you 📎

IS: Aww, hi Puppy

IS: See you soon 🐴

Texts with Gretchen

IS: Hey! Okay so

IS: I think I'm actually going back to Blackwell tomorrow night

IS: For the dark academia party

IS: I'm so sorry, G!! I know we were talking about hanging out then

IS: Maybe Saturday??

IS: Anyway, sorry, go have fun at the outlet mall!!!

IS: Get those deals 💪

Texts with Tessa

IS: So

IS: Looks like I'll see you tomorrow 😊

38

I press send.

And then I spend a full minute of my life staring at my phone screen, before remembering Tessa's in class.

Class. Not avoiding me. Not scrambling for a way to explain she was actually kidding about the party. Literally no reason to think that. Because she's in class. Which I know for a fact, since I walked her there.

Therefore, I'm chill now.

Until a text comes through, and I grab my phone so forcefully, the entire charger unplugs and comes with it.

It's just Mom. **Sweetie, are you busy? Building a bookcase for the shed, could use a hand!**

I plug the charger back in, feeling almost light-headed. It's unsettling, if you think about it—the way your whole mood can be hijacked by nothing but words on a screen. Tiny black lines on a glass rectangle.

When did everything but Tessa start feeling like background noise? At what point, exactly, did my brain decide we were doing this?

Doesn't even feel like I'm in the driver's seat at this point.

I leave my phone plugged in on my nightstand. I don't want to be weird in front of Mom.

I find her on the floor of the shed, surrounded by wooden planks and little plastic bags of bolts and screws. "Oh, hey." She looks up from some kind of instructional diagram. "Does this make any sense to you? I can't figure out how it's supposed to line up. It's the one with the three holes, but I think they're on the wrong side."

She hands me the sheet, and I stare at it for a moment. "Are you sure you're not holding the board upside down?"

"But shouldn't the white part be faceup?" Her brow furrows.

"Eventually, but I think the whole thing's upside down when you're building it. You just flip it over at the end. Here, I just need the little wrench thingy."

Mom hands it to me. "Huh."

And for a minute, my brain seems to settle. I'm just tightening screws and lining up corners, while Rufus Wainwright's voice ripples through Mom's phone speakers.

But then—

"So tell me about this costume party," she says, tucking

her elbow over her head for a stretch.

"Oh! Um. It's not really a costume party? Just kind of a theme party, I think . . ."

My mind veers off course without warning.

Tomorrow. The party. *Tessa.*

If her class started at ten, it's probably over around eleven, right?

Though maybe that's just Monday-Wednesday-Friday classes. Maybe Tuesday-Thursday classes have to run longer to make up for that missing third day. Ninety minutes, maybe? Eleven thirty?

Also, what time is it right now? I don't wear a watch. Normally, I just check on my phone, but I left it upstairs so I wouldn't be weird and obsessed. Clearly, that's going great.

"I think that's as tight as they go, right?"

I look down to find I've locked my screw in so tightly, it's almost level with the wood.

"Oop," I say, blushing.

The problem is, the more I worry about weirdness, the weirder I get. And the harder I try not to act like I have a crush, the more it's starting to feel like one.

By the time we screw the last shelf in, I've turned into a line of ellipses. Nothing but stuttering anticipation. I should be in my room by now. My phone's gravitational pull should have reeled me in straightaway.

But I linger in the shed for some reason, long after my mom heads in for lunch. Even though there's nothing out here yet but an empty bookcase.

Nothing but space.

It feels bigger than my bedroom somehow, even though it's not.

There's just something appealingly half-baked about it. Unfinished, in progress, suspended in time. I try to imagine its final form, but every time I picture it, it's different.

"Immy?" The shed door creaks open, revealing Gretchen. "Your mom said you were out here. You okay?"

"Oh—yeah! Hi! I thought you were shopping today."

"I was." She laughs. "I texted when we left, but then I just figured I'd drop my mom off and swing by. Had to make sure I saw you before you headed back to Blackwell."

I flush. "I'm so sorry about tomorrow."

"What? Immybean, no—you're good! God, I mean. At least one of us should get to experience a college party this week. Here, wait, let's head back in." She reaches both hands out, and I let her tug me up.

"You're not pissed that I ditched you?" I dust off my jeans, following her back out of the shed and in through the kitchen. Of course, Adrian and Binx are immediately on the scene, double-teaming us with a whole repertoire of meowing and ankle weaving.

"Do I look pissed?" Gretchen bends down, petting them both. "Aww, hi, kitties. Anyway, I bought you something today!

Just wanted to drop it off."

"What? No, you already—"

"Had to. It was screaming your name." She swipes a tiny brown shopping bag off the counter and hugs it to her chest. "Don't worry, it's small. Super cheap. Here, let's go to your room."

"Cheap?" I fall into step beside her, peering at the bag. "Does that say J.Crew?"

"J.Crew Factory! Plus, it was on sale."

When we reach my door, Gretchen opens it without the slightest hesitation. She's forever at home, wherever she goes. I've always been a little in awe of that. She pulls out my desk chair and turns it toward me. "You sit here."

I laugh. "What is this?"

"You'll see! Close your eyes," she commands. A moment later, there's a soft tug on my ponytail. "Wait, where's your little circle mirror?"

"Dresser, maybe? Or the bookcase?"

"Yes! Aww—Vassar Bear looks so cute with your books! Got to take a picture of that for the 'gram."

There's a pause, a quick patter of footsteps, and then—

"Okay! Open your eyes, but you're going to need both mirrors, so . . ."

She grips my shoulders, nudging me toward the full-length mirror on the back of my door. "You ready?"

She hands me the smaller mirror, and I line up my reflections so I can see the back of my head. "Oh!" I say.

"How cute is that?"

It's my regular ponytail, but now there's a perfect black bow tied around it.

"You don't actually have to tie it," Gretchen says, like she's reading my mind. "It's like a little rubber band. You just slip the bow on top, and the ribbons kind of hang down the sides. And it's velvet!"

I reach back to touch it—it's soft and stiff all at once. "Oh, I love it."

"It's for the party! Isn't it so dark academia?"

"Ohhhh." I nod. "Definitely. Wow. It's perfect."

"Couldn't resist." Gretchen leans her head in closer, smiling into the mirror like we're posing for a picture.

Texts with Tessa

TM: OH MY GOD

TM: Are you for real?????????????

TM: Scott!!!!!!!!!

TM: I'M SEEING YOU TOMORROW

TM: I mean

TM: Obviously I'm really chill about this 🙈 🙈 🙈

IS: Me too, yup, totally nonchalant 🙉

TM: 🙀 🙀 🙀

TM: Also btw I'm obsessed with this 📎

IS: Haha I didn't even know she posted that

TM: Scott, how are your bookshelves so gay????

TM: They make mine look like a church library

TM: And I'm not even Christian!!

IS: 😅

TM: Can you explain to me

TM: Why you have three identical copies of One Last
       Stop 🫠

IS: Oh I mean

IS: One's signed, one's my reading copy, and one's for emergencies

TM: Emergencies 💀

39

Gretchen perches on the end of my bed, eyeing me curiously. "Who are you talking to?"

"Oh! Um, Tessa. Lili's friend."

"I know who Um Tessa is." She waggles her eyebrows. "Do you always smile like that when cute girls text you?"

I look back at her, speechless.

"Oh my God, your face right now." Gretchen nudges her foot against mine. "Come on! You can admit Tessa's hot, right? Please tell me you see it. I don't care if you're the straightest girl on earth."

"No, she is. Yeah. She's—cute." I press a hand to my cheek. "I don't know if I'm the straightest girl on earth, though."

I stop short, feeling like my heart's trying to break free from my chest.

"Oh?" Gretchen tilts her head toward me, eyes gleaming.

"I don't know," I say again, quickly. "Maybe. I'm just sort of thinking about it. Am I really . . . fully straight? You know?"

"Oh, sweetie! Did Tessa turn you gay?"

"I—"

"Kidding! I'm kidding. Oh, you're so cute. Okay, don't panic. You're not gay."

"Right—I know. It's just, like. Crush feelings, I guess?"

She laughs. "About Tessa?"

I shrug, hugging my knees to my chest.

"Ah yes. Okay, so Tessa's got what I like to call the Ruby Rose effect, right? Like, the specific vibes are different from Ruby, of course, and I think Ruby's genderfluid. But it's still that straight-girl-magnetism thing."

"Oh, no. Tessa's not straight—"

"I knowwww. I mean she *attracts* straight girls. Like you."

I pause. "Oh."

"I'm just saying, it's normal! Seriously—Tessa's super cute."

"No, I know." I tuck my chin between my knees, a lump starting to catch in my throat. "Yeah. I just feel . . . like it's different. Maybe? I don't know. It might just be in my head. Nothing's, like, happened," I add quickly. "And she's not—interested. I think. It's just a crush. Maybe."

Gretchen smiles a little. "Okay. So. You don't think she's into you. And you . . . don't know if you're into her?"

"I know it's weird."

"Have you tried passing yourself a note? 'Do we like her? Check yes or no!'" She giggles. "You could try reading your own diary."

"This is so embarrassing—"

"Oh, honey! No, no, no—sorry!" She scoots closer, her arm encircling my shoulders. "I don't mean to embarrass you! I'm just not sure what you mean."

"What I mean?"

"When you say you're not sure if it's a crush. What would keep you from knowing that?" She pokes my cheek. "Like, how do you know when you have a crush on a guy?"

"I mean. I just know? But this is different." I shake my head. "I don't know how to explain it."

"Well," Gretchen says slowly. "If you had a crush on her, it would feel like a crush."

"I think it does, though? Just a different kind of crush."

Gretchen draws back, eyeing me appraisingly. "Okay, how about this?" she says finally. "Do you want to fuck her? No? Then you're safe."

I open my mouth and then shut it, head spinning in a million directions at once. *Safe?* Like being queer is some kind of dreaded outcome?

And is "wanting to fuck" the only indicator of attraction? That can't be true, right?

I try to imagine what sex with Tessa would feel like, but my brain won't even go there. Kissing? Yeah, maybe. But *sex?*

There's no way she'd want that. And even if she did, I'm pretty sure I'd be awful at it.

"I don't know," I say finally, voice barely louder than a whisper. "I haven't really thought about it."

Gretchen smiles, squeezing my shoulder. "Then I think you

have your answer."

Suddenly, I'm blinking back tears.

"Oh, sweetie!" Gretchen's expression softens. "Aww. Hey. You know it's okay to be straight, right?"

I swallow thickly. "I know—"

"You're already enough, Immy. Okay? Don't forget that."

"Thanks." I scoot forward, feet on the ground. "Um. I should probably—"

"Wait—oh, I didn't mean to upset you! Are you mad?"

"No! Yeah, no, I'm fine." I stand, turning to shoot her a quick, forced smile. "Just realized I was supposed to help Edith with, um—"

"Immy."

"I'm fine!"

Texts with Gretchen

GP: Hope you're not upset!

GP: I just think it's important to understand the nuance here, yk?

IS: I'm not upset

GP: Ok good lol

GP: Oh!! Can you let Edie know there's a little surprise waiting for her on your porch

GP: It's a 🌱

GP: Apparently she's planning to become a plant mom?? 👻

DAY EIGHT
FRIDAY
MARCH 25

Texts with Tessa

TM: OMG SO

TM: I just talked to Declan

TM: Not only did he find 🥒

TM: He found it on Tuesday!!!! And didn't tell us 🗄

TM: Wait til you hear what he's planning

TM: It's diabolical 🙊

TM: ANYWAY, MORE IMPORTANTLY, HI

TM: I'M SEEING YOU TODAY 🫧

40

"Whoa." Edith appears in my doorway. "Hi. What are you doing?"

I tuck another sweater into my suitcase. "Packing?"

"That giant-ass suitcase? For one night?" She shuts the door, strides across the room. "Why are you bringing fifty cardigans?"

"You mean four?"

"It's one night!" Edith swipes my argyle green sweater out of my hands, peering into my suitcase. "All right, intervention time. What do you actually need? Pajamas, toiletries, clothes for tomorrow morning, party clothes. That's it! You're done!"

"No, I'm not. My pinafore still has a hole in the butt." I exhale, pressing my hands to my cheeks.

"Okay? That's literally gonna take five minutes. When's Lili coming?"

"Around eleven?"

"Immy, that's in two hours. You're fine. Ooh, I like this."

She holds up the black velvet bow. "Very on-theme."

"It's from Gretchen. Oh, I'm supposed to tell you she got you a plant? In the kitchen, on the windowsill."

"Of course she did." Edith shakes her head, smiling wryly.

I tilt my head. "Is this a thing? Gretchen buying you plants?"

"No . . ." Edith pauses, removing another cardigan from my suitcase. "But Gretchen stirring shit up with people and then making up for it with gifts is a thing."

I look at her. "I—didn't know you guys had ever really argued. Until the Kara Clapstone thing, I mean."

"We haven't. I'm talking about you."

I freeze. "What do you mean?"

"Come on. It's *Gretchen*. She lives for drama. Remember when Otávio gave money to the Salvation Army guy?"

"I mean, I wouldn't call that drama. She was just trying to explain the issues with that organization."

"I know. And I'm not saying she's wrong. She's just a little intense about it sometimes."

"I think she's just challenging us to be better allies."

I mean, I *like* that Gretchen's good about checking me on stuff. Sometimes I really need it. Like when I used to think bisexual meant someone could only like two genders. Or when Quinn Santiago asked for ideas about where to buy a binder in person, and I—with mortifying sincerity—suggested Staples or OfficeMax.

Do you want to fuck her? No? Then you're safe.

I keep thinking about the way Gretchen's eyes glinted when

she asked it. She didn't even pause to let me answer.

Not that I have an answer.

Should I have an answer?

Edith's still looking at me. "Look, I love that girl to pieces. You know that. I'm just saying, it's not always so black and white."

"I know, I know."

"Good." She flips my suitcase closed. "Okay, you go sew up your pinafore's butthole—"

"Butt-*whole*. With a *w*."

She splays her hand over my face. "Goodbye. And don't even think of sneaking any cardigans back in."

The second I slide into the passenger seat, Lili turns to me, beaming. "Big news!"

"Ooh—what?"

"Declan found the sausage!" she says, and I open my mouth to reply. But then her expression shifts. "Wow. I got scooped by Tessa, huh?"

"Er." I blush. "Yeah."

We buckle up, and Lili turns the car on.

"You guys have gotten pretty close this week, huh?"

"Me and Tessa?" My voice jumps. "Did she say that?"

"I mean, she hasn't put her phone down in days." Lili glances at me. "You trading me in for a new bestie?"

"Lili, no—oh my God—"

"I'm kidding!" Her smile flickers. "Look, as long as you

don't replace me with Gretchen, we're good."

I try to laugh, but it comes out like a sigh. "Yeah . . ."

"Wait." Lili stops at a red light, twisting to look me straight on. "What did she do?"

"Gretchen?"

"Mm-hmm. Definitely getting Gretchen-was-discoursing-again vibes."

"No!" I laugh. "I mean, yeah, but that's not . . ."

I trail off, suddenly not sure where my brain's even heading.

The thing is, Gretchen's not even doing anything wrong. It's just this dynamic that's always kind of been there with us. Basically, there's a version of me who lives in Gretchen's head, and as long as I stay within a certain radius of that, we're fine. But when I veer too far off course—I start to feel kind of hazy sometimes.

Maybe I'm more liquid than most people are. I always seem to take the shape of my container.

Usually, it's a sort of relief, letting Gretchen remold me.

41

Everything at Blackwell is just how I left it: the same white paths and stone arches and vine-covered fairy-tale buildings. The weather's cooled down again—jackets and scarves are out in full force, even this close to noon. But the courtyard's still bustling with laughter and footsteps and faint strains of music. You can almost taste that it's Friday.

My stomach hasn't stopped fluttering since we got here.

I hoist my suitcase up the front stairs, loving that I know which dorm is Rosewood. I call the elevator while Lili signs me back in at the front desk, and once we're in it, I know exactly which button to press. It's as automatic as home.

Third floor. Same cinder-block walls, same posters, same paper mural of quotes. I don't even think anyone's wiped a single doodle from their white board.

My eyes go straight to Tessa's closed door.

"She's in class," Lili says flatly, unlocking her door. "Don't worry—she'll be back for the party."

My cheeks go warm. "Oh—"

"Guess you'll have to hang out with me in the meantime!" Lili steps inside, leaving the door open for me—but she doesn't glance back. She just crosses to her desk chair and opens her laptop, like she's settling in to write a thesis.

I pause in the entryway, watching her.

"Are you coming in?"

"Yeah. No, definitely." I nod quickly, dragging my suitcase and pulling the door shut behind me. "Hey—um. Are you—"

"Not mad at you." She exhales.

I press my lips together. "It kind of seems like you are, though?"

"Okay, well, I'm not."

I sink onto the edge of Lili's spare bed, scooping Puppy into my lap. We're both quiet, but the air itself feels taut and charged. Telephone-wire silence, my dad calls it.

But then Lili tucks her legs up into her chair, circling her arms around them. "Ugh. I'm sorry."

"For—what?"

"For being a grumpy little bitch?"

I laugh. "You are *not*—"

"It's just." She stares at the floor for a second. "I don't know. I feel like I'm missing something? You've been avoiding me for months—"

"Avoiding—"

"Immy, you *have* been. How many times have I invited

304

you here? A dozen? I didn't know if you were mad at me, or if I'd hurt you somehow without realizing it. I couldn't believe it when you told me you applied here. I couldn't even talk you into visiting for a weekend."

I stare at her, almost speechless. "I—I promise it wasn't like that. At *all*. I'm so sorry. You didn't do anything wrong. Oh my God." I blink back tears. "Lili, I'm sorry."

"I don't need an apology! I just—I don't get it, you know? You refuse to come visit for literal months, but now you're back a week later? Because *Tessa* invited you?" Her voice catches. "And I'm glad you get along with my friends! Seriously. I'm just, like—what's the deal? What am I not understanding?"

"You're not—" I cover my face with both hands. "I'm sorry. I wasn't—I didn't mean for it to seem like I was avoiding you."

"Okay?" A tear breaks through, but she wipes it roughly away. "So—"

"Lili, I was so—" I try to push down the lump in my throat, but it's hopeless. "Intimidated," I say.

"By my friends?"

"By them. Or, like—the idea of them. And by how happy they made you." I sniff. "I didn't know if they'd like me—"

"Okay, well, they're obsessed with you, so."

"I don't know." I exhale shakily. "You're so happy here—and God, Lili, I love that. I love that you get to just live, and be queer, and you've got this whole little family of queer people. It's amazing."

305

She wipes her eyes without speaking.

"I just wasn't sure how I fit into the picture, you know?" I shake my head. "It felt like you'd found this really sacred space, and I didn't want to invade it."

Lili looks at me incredulously. "Immy, I *cried* when you told me you were coming here. I was so fucking thrilled. You're my best friend."

"You're mine, too!" I say, eyes watering all over again.

"Ha! Suck it, Gretchen." She wipes another tear with the heel of her hand, smiling triumphantly.

I laugh, but it comes out flat.

Lili raises her eyebrows. "You're still not going to tell me what Gretchen did to you?"

I pause. "I mean, I'll tell you if you want. It's just not much of a story, I guess? Basically . . . we were talking about crushes, and she was kind of weird about it. That's it."

"Weird like—making fun of you? Making fun of the guy?"

"No, no. Not like that. Not . . ." I trail off, rubbing my still-damp cheek. "It was subtle. Kind of hard to explain. Like, she wasn't being mean? She just wasn't, like, taking it seriously."

"Okay." Lili rolls her chair closer. "So you have a serious crush."

"No! I don't know. I don't even know if it *is* a crush." Lili stares me down until the tops of my cheeks go warm. "I guess that's what I was trying to . . . decide. But it kind of felt like Gretchen decided for me."

306

Lili taps her lower lip with her thumb—neither of us speak for a moment.

"Okay, so." She pauses, shooting me a look I can't quite decipher. "You were like, 'Hey, I think I have a crush on this person,' and Gretchen's like, 'Ha ha, no you don't'—is that kind of what happened?"

I open my mouth and then shut it.

On this person. That's—

Neutral.

Person. *Person.* Not guy.

I tuck my chin into Puppy's rainbow mane, making his horn flop sideways. "Yup. Basically."

We're quiet again.

Until Lili suddenly leans forward. "Remember Brianna Lewis's graduation party?"

"The party or the car ride?"

"What do you think?" She laughs a little. "You know I was scared shitless, right? You were the first person I came out to."

"Other than your family."

"Nope," she says. "You."

I look up at her, finally. "I thought you said—"

"I know. I was just—I don't know—trying to take the pressure off, because I knew you'd feel this huge responsibility to make it into some big perfect moment."

My hand goes still on the edge of the bed. "I had no idea."

"I know."

"I'm so sorry. God. I should have—"

"Made it into some big perfect moment?"

"I mean . . ."

Lili meets my gaze. "But you did! You made space. You took it seriously. You know there's not a script for this, right?"

I nod.

She pauses. "You know. If you ever had something you wanted to tell me, I could make space for that, too."

42

Something you wanted to tell me.

It's not like the code's hard to crack here. Lili clearly knows something's up, and she's just waiting for me to say it. She's practically holding up cue cards.

I'm sort of dying to know what kind of vibe she picked up.

Right now, she's staring into the mirror with laser focus, a bobby pin clenched between her teeth. "See, this is why I never wear my hair up."

"You sound like an amateur ventriloquist," I say.

She slides the last bobby pin into place. "Not sure being a ventriloquy expert is the flex you think it is."

I laugh, hugging Puppy to my chest. As if that's going to tamp down my drumrolling heartbeat.

It's impossible to explain what I'm feeling. Joy plus wistfulness plus early spring sunset. Faint laughter from the courtyard seeps through Lili's open window, intermingling with the "getting ready" playlist streaming from her phone.

It occurs to me that we've never done this, in all the years we've known each other. I don't think we've been to a party that was worth changing shirts for.

I sing along under my breath to the music, smiling at Lili.

She shakes her head, smiling back. "I can't get over you knowing every word of every gay song ever."

"I'm the one who introduced you to 'Silk Chiffon'!"

The first time I saw the music video, I seriously thought I was dreaming. My favorite movie, in song form. One verse in, and I'd already texted it to half a dozen people.

"You know that's why Gretchen dyed her hair pink, right?" I add. "Phoebe Bridgers in that music video is, like, her entire aesthetic."

"I hate agreeing with Gretchen." Lili plops down beside me on the bed. "Man, your *face* right now. You look like someone offered you a million kittens."

My cheeks go warm. "I'm just happy to be here."

"Okay, Pollyanna Banana. Let's fix your cute bow."

I gather my hair back and release it, shifting sideways so she can adjust the bow around my half ponytail. You could say I'm slightly obsessed with how my dark academia outfit came together. It's pretty simple—gray plaid pinafore from the thrift store, buttwhole-free at last. I'm borrowing Lili's black button-up boots, but everything else is just stuff from home—my white Peter Pan–collar shirt, black tights, black cardigan.

When Lili's done with the bow, she tugs some of my hair

forward, arranging it over my shoulders. "Love it. You look like a Samantha doll."

I laugh. "You look like someone who writes letters with a quill and uses sealing wax."

"Mission accomplished." She taps open the selfie camera on her phone, scooting in beside me, and I'm pretty sure this is the most I've ever liked my own face. My cheeks are flushed, my hair's the right amount of wavy, and the light from Lili's window makes my eyes look navy blue. Lili holds her arm out and smiles, and the scent of her hair makes me think of Goldfish crackers and YouTube and Snoopy sheets and the time she got stuck in the baby swing at my house and my dad had to chainsaw her out of it.

The quintessential Lili smells. She really is my whole childhood.

"O . . . kay. Posting now, tagging you. Caption is"—she stands and paces while typing—"'Dark academia party aesthetic on point.'"

Gretchen texts me a screenshot literally five seconds later. *INCREDIBLE, LIFE AFFIRMING, 12/10!!!*

I set my phone down on the bed without responding.

"Uh-oh. That's not a million-kitten face." Lili shuts one eye. "Who are we ghosting?"

I shake my head. "No one. I mean—Gretchen. But I'll write back later. I'm just not in a Gretchen mood right now."

"Not being in a Gretchen mood is a mood," Lili confirms.

Texts with Gretchen

GP: STILL NOT OVER THAT PIC!!! 🔥

GP: Okay fine fine don't text me

GP: SIGH

GP: No jk you're living your college life and I love that for you

GP: You look gorgeous Immybean, go have FUN

43

"The troops are assembling in Kayla's room," Lili says, shutting her window and sneaking one last glance in the mirror. By the time we step out into the hallway, my heart's firmly lodged in my throat.

Tessa's door is closed. And Lili doesn't even knock when we pass it. Which is—

Fine.

I mean, I'm sure she's coming. She's the one who talked *me* into coming.

But as far as I know, she hasn't been back to her room all afternoon.

I spend the whole walk to Kayla's trying to figure out how to casually ask Lili about it, but every version of the question feels about as subtle as screaming into a microphone. Not that I've been particularly subtle up until now, I guess.

If you ever had something you wanted to tell me.

Normally, we'd need a keycard to get into Kayla's dorm, or

we'd have to call her to come down and open the door. But a guy Lili knows from orientation group lets us slip through the entrance behind him. Already, there's this palpable buzz in the air. The entire first floor feels like a block party—people drifting from room to room in one messy jumble of laughter and music, liquor, and weed.

Kayla's in a double room on the third floor—apparently her stoner roommate is out of town all weekend. There's no question that the side plastered with anime art prints is Kayla's. Above her desk, there's a little gallery of family photos, arranged around a framed vinyl collector's version of Janelle Monáe's *Dirty Computer* album. Whereas Audra's decor pretty much boils down to one giant cloth tapestry and a bunch of string lights. But somehow a few flickering candles pull the whole thing together, softening the chaos to something cozy and intentional. Kayla, Declan, and Mika are piled onto Kayla's bed, drinking out of teacups, while music streams from someone's phone.

Not a Tessa in sight.

"The triumphant return of Imogen!" Kayla half sings. "You two both look amazing." But my chest feels so hollow and sharp, I can barely muster a proper response. Ten minutes ago, I was so in love with this outfit. Now I just feel vaguely overdressed.

"Those are some classy cups," says Lili, sinking into Kayla's giant beanbag chair. She scoots to make room, and I plop down beside her.

"Beverages, ladies?" asks Declan. He stretches his legs out, hooks his feet around the base of Kayla's desk chair, and slowly reels it back toward the bed. There's a dining hall tray perched on top of the seat, holding two large bottles and a few empty teacups. "Rolling bar," he says, winking.

"He's wearing his actual prep school uniform blazer right now," Kayla says, sipping her drink. "Just putting that out there in case you thought this boy was even a little bit dope."

"Babe, it's fine. No one cares that you weren't cool in high school." Declan grins back at her. "Speaking of corrupting the youth! Imogen, what can I get you?"

"Um. What are the options?"

"Literally only raspberry vodka and orange juice."

"And water." Mika holds up their cup. "Goes down better with Zoloft."

"Exactly. Water if you're on anxiety meds," says Declan, "and vodka if you *should be* on anxiety meds."

"Raspberry sounds good! Thanks," I say, which makes Lili full-on gape at me. But I'm not in the mood for a big Baby's First Drink announcement, so I just pretend I'm absorbed in Declan's bartending skills. And I guess Lili gets the message, because she doesn't say a word about it, even when I almost choke on the first sip because it tastes like a Starburst soaked in rubbing alcohol. She just watches me warily until I shoot her a forced grimace-smile.

The second sip's a little better, though.

By the fifth, I'm hardly shuddering at all.

Then, before I know it, I'm past the halfway point of my

teacup, and there's this happy fuzzy feeling curling around the edges of my brain. Because tonight's going to be top tier, Tessa or no Tessa. How could it not be? It's my first college party, I'm dressed like an old-timey schoolgirl, and I don't know who made this playlist, but it's A+, the most perfect vibes—Hayley Kiyoko, Lil Nas X, King Princess. It's actively hard to keep from singing along.

"You good?" Lili murmurs.

"Magnifique, Monsieur LePoisson," I say. The song switches to Clairo's "Sofia," and I gasp, which makes Lili laugh. I could go on for hours about how Clairo is an actual genius. But I feel a little boxed into my own head right now. Almost like bunny mode. The words are *there*, but they keep dying on my tongue.

I really thought alcohol was supposed to make the talking part easier. So far, it's just making my brain louder.

I try to focus on the song, because I don't want to miss the line about Clairo loving Sofia with her hair down. It makes my throat catch every time—there's just something so earnest about it. Imagine being loved with your hair down. Loved without an agenda, without an audience. Never having to earn and re-earn it. Love without modulation.

The door creaks open.

And Tessa walks through it. Wearing a brown tweed suit. With a vest.

She fingers the collar of her shirt, flushed and breathless. "Sorry! Laundry catastrophe. Some dude took my clothes out of the dryer—*dumped* my clothing on the floor, soaking wet, and put his gross boxers in there. Like, BRO, I PAID FOR THAT CYCLE. And there were no other free dryers, so now I've got clothes hanging all over my room. And *then* I had to borrow a shirt from my brother. But! I'm here!"

I don't know how to stop staring. Tessa in an old-fashioned suit, hair already starting to break out of her ponytail. Her frantic energy, her sweet flash of a smile. She looks like a hot young professor on the first day of class.

Our eyes meet, and in my brain, it's like daybreak.

44

Tessa asks if anyone wants a refill, and she's looking right at me, so I hand her my teacup. Then she settles in on the floor, half-turned toward Lili and me, one leg bent at the knee in a triangle. Like a menswear catalog.

I'm feeling warm and kind of spinny, and second drinks really do go down easier than first drinks. And the talking part's easier too. Normally there's a whole security system in my brain, checking and rechecking every single thought before it's allowed to leave my mouth. But now the guard's gone off duty.

"Wait." I set my cup down. "Is *this* the party?"

Kayla laughs. "Imogen, no! We're just trying not to show up too early."

"Right. Totally. Definitely." I nod. "It's totally early. It's only . . . nine."

If Gretchen were here, she'd be calling me a sweet baby nerd. An innocent bean. I don't mind it for the most part. But I guess I'm kind of glad to be out of her orbit for a second. It makes tonight feel a little more mine.

Tessa nudges my foot with her shoe and shoots me an early-bird-solidarity yawn. The song switches to Conan Gray's "Heather," and the opening chords make me feel so wistful, I almost can't catch my breath for a second. But Tessa's still smiling at me, so I smile back, except now I'm blushing, and I'm pretty sure the eye contact should have ended by now. Only I can't look away, because Tessa's so cute, and her smile is like sunshine on water.

I think I've slipped inside a daydream. Something about the flickering candles and the music and the pinballing conversation. Kayla starts talking about Sailor Moon, and somehow it turns into a whole confessional story hour about our first crushes. Our first *queer* crushes.

Am I still problematic if I say Clea DuVall?

I mean, I can't say Tessa. You can't just *say* that.

"Robin Wright in *The Princess Bride*," Tessa says, shooting me a split-second glance.

"Truly the Starbucks of white-girl lesbian awakenings," Declan says, and Tessa does that low Tessa giggle. Which is pretty much a declaration of war against my heart.

"Mine was Jade," Mika says. "I just didn't know that it was a queer crush until later."

"Excuse me—you and Jade? That's not a crush. That's *love*." Kayla presses her hand to her heart. Mika just bites back a smile.

Then Lili starts talking about this regional Girl Scout

convention we went to when she was in fifth grade—I was in fourth. "We had to make these little pin crafts to trade with troops from other counties, like as an icebreaker—Immy, do you remember this?"

"SWAPs? Of course I remember."

"Yes! SWAPs. So the idea is that you end up with a whole collection of different ones. They were pretty cute. I think ours were pompom horses?"

"No, *yours* were pompom horses, because you're a horse girl," I say. "Mine were bunnies."

"So what happened?" asks Mika.

Lili clasps her hands. "So there's this one girl from, you know, some other town in central New York. Curly hair, and she was wearing overalls. And her pins were—"

"Felt rainbows," I say.

Lili blinks, shooting me a surprised half smile. "How do you remember that?"

"Um." My cheeks go warm.

"Hold up," Kayla says. "You're telling me this girl literally shows up at Girl Scouts to turn girls gay?"

I sip from my teacup and shrug.

Kayla shakes her head. "Goddess behavior."

"Patron saint of queer awakenings," adds Mika.

"Well, it wasn't my awakening." I pause. "I mean, it wasn't my *first* awakening."

"Ooh, spill it, babe," says Declan.

I can practically hear Lili's jaw slamming to the ground, but

I keep my eyes fixed straight ahead. "So. Um. This new girl had just moved here—not *here*. I mean home. Penn Yan. Anyway, she moved from New York City, and she had double-pierced ears, so third-grade me was like, holy crap, I have to be friends with her. Also, I was pretty sure we were *meant* to be friends, because she was Ilana with an I, and I'm Imogen with an I, and we hung out on the playground the whole first week. And I had this daydream where me, her, and Lili were a group of three best friends. It was so vivid. Like, to the point where I used to get stressed out about hypothetical future friend rivalries."

Lili looks both stunned and amused. "How did I not know about this?"

"Because she got absorbed into this group of popular girls who used to coordinate their outfit colors, and she never talked to me again."

"*Mean Girls* is real." Kayla nods gravely, and I laugh.

"I mean, she wasn't Regina George or anything. She was just in that group. And she moved back to the city a few years later anyway."

When I look up, everyone's still watching me expectantly, like they're waiting for some kind of punchy reveal.

"Oh! That's it," I say, flustered. "Sorry. That was—wow, I just told you guys a really pointless story."

"Not pointless," Lili says faintly.

Here's what I don't say: I looked Ilana up on Instagram last year. Out of nowhere—she just popped into my head for some reason. It was strange—she looked completely different than

I remembered. Less makeup than she used to wear in middle school, for sure. And her nose was pierced. But I think it was mostly the way she was smiling in every photo. A lot of her pictures were with this one particular girl, though I never figured out if she was Ilana's girlfriend. I don't even know if Ilana's queer. But I spent hours investigating the issue. And in retrospect, maybe that means something.

All these moments, scattered and separate. All these disconnected dots.

45

It's close to ten by the time we set off for Rainbow Manor, and the air's so cold it makes my cheeks prickle. Lili waits until the others are a few feet ahead before linking her elbow through mine. She looks at me hesitantly. "So, Ilana and the overalls girl. That's not fake backstory."

I shake my head, heart tugging sharply.

"We don't have to talk about it," she says. "Unless you want to. Immy. God. We don't have to go to this party."

I laugh. "But I want to go to the party. That's literally why I'm here!"

"Okay, but—" She stops short, and I realize Tessa's circled back to meet us.

Lili releases my elbow, side-hugs me, and jogs to catch up with the others. "Scotty Scott," Tessa says, falling into step beside me. "I liked your queer-awakening stories."

Which gives me this quick spike of panic. It suddenly occurs to me just how far I've strayed from my stolen Lesbian

Elsa narrative. Though Tessa's smile is so wide and sincere, I'm pretty sure she doesn't think anything's off.

"I like yours too, but"—I lean closer—"do they know she's your cousin?"

"Okay, you know what? That's enough of your cattitude." She tilts her head, smiling.

"Keep it moving, slowpokes!" Declan hollers, gloved hands cupped to his mouth. "Less flirting, more walk—"

Kayla slaps a hand over his mouth, herding him forward. "Carry on," she calls out over her shoulder. "Take your time. All is well."

"*He's* a slowpoke," Tessa mutters, but my brain's still stuck on the part where we're *flirting*. Is this flirting? Just . . . this? Joking and talking?

Do I want it to be flirting? Because I'm—

My foot slips off the curb, just enough to make me lose my balance—but Tessa hooks her arm around my waist to catch me. "Whoops!"

I turn toward her, burying my face in the wool of her blazer. "Did you steal this jacket from an old-timey professor, or what?"

"Yes, actually! From my dad."

"You're the real deal, Minsky," I say, and her last name feels thrillingly strange on my tongue.

Tessa looks down and then back up at me, her smile almost shy.

Okay, I'm pretty sure this is flirting.

"You guys ready?" Lili asks, stopping in the middle of the sidewalk. The house looks bigger, somehow, than it was last weekend, with even more Pride flags on display. The walkway's lined with tiny LED tea lights, and muffled music seeps through the walls.

Stepping closer, I see there's a sign on the door.

Welcome to Rainbow Manor: If you're out, come on in!

46

The entryway funnels us straight into Rainbow Manor's living room. It's crowded—not as bad as a movie frat party, but denser than any house party I've been to. The furniture's been pushed to the perimeter to make space for a makeshift dance floor, girl in red streaming from a speaker on one of the side tables. The decor's pretty simple, but some of the details are cool—fake candles, beige globes, stacks of books, dark velvet cushions. Overall, kind of a moody vintage library vibe.

Either Mika, Declan, and Kayla have already moved to another room, or they've been absorbed into the throng of people on the dance floor. "Here, link up," Lili says, grabbing my hand. So I grab Tessa's, and we move through the crowd like a chain.

"Lili!" calls out a brunette in a suit and a newsboy cap. They hug Lili, wave to Tessa, and smile at me. "Hi! Vitoria. They/she," they say, glancing over their shoulder. "Sorry, I've lost Nora *and* Alix."

"Nora's right behind you." Lili laughs, pointing to a pony-tailed blond girl with a bunch of piercings. She's wearing a turtleneck sweater and trousers, and I catch a flash of a woven striped bracelet when she waves—black, white, gray, and purple. Lili leans closer to me. "Okay, Vitoria's from Brooklyn, and they're a classics major, and, um, I don't know Nora's major, but I'm pretty sure—you're from the South, right?"

"Yup! Georgia." Nora nods.

"Right! So—okay, you know Tessa. And this is Imogen—she'll be a freshman here next year."

"Very cool! Are you visiting from Philly?" Nora asks.

"Oh, no, just Penn Yan. It's like thirty minutes away."

"She's my BFF from home," Lili adds.

I release Tessa's hand, cheeks burning.

"Go dance! We have to find Alix," Vitoria says as the song switches to Lorde.

We end up on the edge of the dance floor, where people are dancing in clusters or grinding or making out. I don't know if I'm dreaming or if my mind's just gone blank. It's beyond bunny mode. This is just . . . a totally different league from trivia or the tunnels, or even drinking in Kayla's room.

Lili spots Mika on the dance floor and waves. Then she turns back to Tessa and me. "You don't see Kayla or Declan, do you?"

Tessa shakes her head. "If they're making out—"

"I will ascend," Lili says. Then she pauses. "Oop—okay, no, Dec's dancing with some guy."

Mika's already a little flushed and sweaty by the time they reach us. "Hi!"

Lili tugs one of Mika's suspenders back onto their shoulder, raising her eyebrows. "You look like you've been having fun."

Mika laughs. "I'm dancing—come on!"

There's nothing delineating the dance floor from the rest of the space, but it feels like stepping onto the moon. Even dancing as an awkward quartet is the coolest moment of my life, by a mile. Except then the song switches to Doja Cat, and people rush to the dance floor, filling every pocket of space. Now I'm pressed so close to Tessa, I can feel the quiet curve of her breasts.

She meets my eyes, and her face is bewilderingly close. I've never been this aware of my body before. Every inch I move feels like a decision.

Suddenly Lili's hand is on my upper arm, but I can't quite hear what she's saying.

"What?" I lean closer.

"Bathroom! Come on." She grabs my hand—and the next thing I know, she's leading me past the kitchen and down a short hallway. But the bathroom's occupied, so we just lean against the wall, side by side.

"I don't actually have to pee," Lili says, and then she stops short. "Okay, now I do, but more importantly." She stares me down, and I guess she's still a little drunk, because she pokes me in the forehead. "You."

"Me?"

"So like." She pauses. "I don't know how to ask this. I don't know. I just—"

The bathroom door swings open, and someone in a full-on raven costume lurches toward us, wings raised. "NEVER-MORE."

We stand in stunned silence for a second.

Then Lili yanks me into the bathroom, shuts the door, and locks it. "Okay, you stay there," she says, stepping back into this sort of toilet nook, separated by a sliding partition door. "Immy, you're gonna hear me pee!"

"I've literally wet your bed."

"Ha ha, true." She starts peeing. "Okay, listen, I'm not trying to do the overbearing big sister thing, but I just want to make sure you're good. Like. You're happy?"

Staring at myself in the mirror is a little like watching myself in a movie. I'm so flushed, but in a good way. Almost like I'm glowing.

I wonder what Tessa thinks when she sees me.

"You okay?"

"Oh! Yeah, of course!"

"Immy." The peeing sound stops. A moment later, Lili flushes the toilet and slides the partition back open, studying me in the mirror while she washes her hands. "You're not—you know you don't have to prove anything to anyone, right?"

My cheeks flood with heat. "I know."

"Okay." She pauses. "'Cause you know—like, you *know* I'm in favor. As long as it's for you. Not, you know, 'the backstory.'"

She does air quotes, still studying me intently in the mirror. "It's real, right?"

I nod quickly, throat feeling thick all of a sudden.

"Oh no. No no no. No crying." Lili shoves me softly. "Immy."

I laugh, a little breathlessly.

She hugs me, quickly and tightly. "Okay! You gonna pee or what?"

On the toilet, I cover my face with both hands. I—

I think I just came out?

Sort of? Or did the coming out part happen back in Kayla's room, when I talked about Ilana and the SWAP girl?

Or maybe none of it counted, because I didn't say the words.

Bi. Bisexual. *Lili, I'm bi.*

It feels bigger than I want it to be. Do I really have to announce this? Can't I just feel something and live inside it while it's happening and not analyze it to death?

47

By the time we're back, Mika and Tessa have retreated to the edge of the dance floor again, joined by Declan, who's apparently ditched the random guy. I don't think they see us yet, though. Tessa's nodding along to something Mika's saying, laughing a little, and I'm just so fascinated by every detail of her. The way her sleeves are a little too long. Her fidgetiness—the way she's always bouncing on her feet, pushing her bangs out of her eyes. The way her smile never needs a warm-up. Then she catches me staring, and her whole face lights up. My heart jumps into my throat.

We make our way toward them. Declan's clearly drunker than he was when we got here. He grabs both of our hands, tugging us closer. "Where's Kayla? She's not answering her texts!"

Lili shrugs. "Maybe she's hooking uppppp."

"That's what I said!" says Mika. Declan glowers at both of them.

Tessa steps closer. "Hey, you're back."

"Back," I say faintly. I'm so nervous, I'm practically shaking. I think talking about this with Lili might have made it real. The song slows down, but my heartbeat doesn't.

Tessa bites her lip. "Want to dance?"

"Dance, like . . . dance?" I nod. "Okay, yeah."

She puts her hands on my waist, and I lean in closer, letting my fingertips graze the ends of her ponytail, the wings of hair at the nape of her neck. My heart's beating so hard, it feels like my ribs might crack open. I've slow danced before—at homecoming, junior prom, even the eighth-grade dance.

But this already feels different. Not because Tessa's a girl. The difference is quieter, tucked away in my chest. It's a shift from a spiraling *I hope I'm doing this right* to the ache of *I hope.*

Tessa's eyes catch mine, and her lips tug up at the corners, just barely. And the noise in my brain falls away.

All the times I said I'm straight. All the times everyone's said I'm straight.

There it was, underlined and written in bold. How could I miss it?

Like finding Waldo and realizing he was never really hiding.

48

By now, the music's louder, the dance floor's fuller, and the air smells like candles and sweat. People keep stripping off layers, flinging them on the couches and chairs that line the room's perimeter, and there's a pair of broody-looking schoolgirls making out right in front of me. But I feel a little removed from it all. Lili and I are leaning against a stretch of wall near the entryway, basically taking turns yawning.

"Where are they?" Lili groans. "I'm starving."

She's been trying to round everyone up for at least twenty minutes, but Kayla and Declan have disappeared again, and Mika's gone off to find them. Plus, Tessa's been in the bathroom line for approximately a century, and I'm not trying to be dramatic about this, but it feels like someone turned off the sun.

My gaze drifts back to the schoolgirls. I've never been more painfully aware of the fact that I've never kissed a girl before. Or anyone, of any gender. It's funny how I lived without kissing for eighteen years, and now I think I might die if it doesn't happen tonight.

But how on earth do I get there? How does anyone get there? Kissing isn't something you can be measured and gradual about. Once you start doing the tilty-head thing, I mean—your cards are pretty much on the table, right?

Maybe the schoolgirls will make it easier to broach the topic. *Looks fun—should we try it?*

I can't picture those words coming out of my mouth. I'd need a million more raspberry vodkas and a lobotomy and at least two hours to practice my lines in front of a mirror. But Tessa's already crossing the dance floor, so I guess the lobotomy's off the table. I don't even have time to catch my breath.

She's taken her ponytail out. And what am I even supposed to say about that? What is there to say that Clairo hasn't already said?

She reaches us just in time to hear Lili let out an emphatic "Holy *shit*."

"You okay?" Tessa asks. Then she scoots in beside me and smiles. "Hi."

Lili's staring at a photo on her phone. "Mika took this." She shoves the screen in front of us. "Am I losing my mind, or . . ."

I study the photo—it's clearly taken outside, on what looks like a deck. Other than a few blurry light spots—Christmas lights, maybe—the image is dark and grainy. But there's just enough contrast to make out two figures leaning against a railing in the background of the picture, and it's really unmistakable.

On the left, Declan's bright blond hair. Right beside him, Kayla's Sisterlocks and choirgirl posture.

Tessa frowns. "I don't get it."

"That's Kayla and Dec," Lili says, tapping the screen.

"I know, but—"

"The hands," I say.

"Thank you!" Lili pinches and zooms until the screen basically looks like a blurry screenshot from an ultrasound, but still.

Those are clearly hands. And they're clearly twined together.

"Oh shit," Tessa says.

Lili exhales. "I KNOW."

"Are they . . . secretly together?" I ask.

"I don't know!" Lili looks at Tessa.

"I mean—like, it would be one thing if they were making out, right? Like, okay, whatever, it happens. But hand-holding?" Tessa leans closer and gasps. "Is Kayla wearing the sausage gloves?"

I stare at the screen, mostly so I won't stare at Tessa.

Is kissing really that small of a deal to her?

Another text from Mika pops up. **So I'm just gonna back away slowly 🙈 meet you out front?**

49

The air hits like a slap the second we step through the door.

"Scott, you're shivering." Tessa starts to shrug off her blazer. "Here—"

"No, I'm fine! I promise."

Mika rushes toward us, bouncing on their feet. "Wow, this weather. Let's move."

"How are Kayla and Dec sitting out there in this?" Lili asks, falling into step beside Mika.

Tessa hangs back, next to me. "I know you think you're Elsa," she says, and I let out a shivery laugh. "Come *on*. It's a cool jacket. At least do it for the outfit."

"I don't want to ruin *your* outfit. And it's really more my face and hands anyway. I need gloves and one of those robber masks."

"Hmm." Tessa turns to face me, grabbing both my hands, and my stomach does a quick-drop roller coaster swoop. I can't take my eyes off her face—the curve of her freckled cheeks, her short hair falling loosely into place around her ears. She presses my hands together in prayer position and cups her own hands around them, rubbing them a little on the sides with her thumbs.

Lili glances back, shooting me a questioning eyebrow raise over her shoulder.

I flash a quick smile, and she and Mika keep moving.

"How's that? Warmer?" asks Tessa.

My chest flutters. "Yeah."

"Good. Let me get the palms."

I try to twist my hands around, back-to-back, and the awkwardness makes Tessa giggle. "No, no. Here. This one"—she takes my right hand, crosses it over my chest, and tucks it into my armpit—"goes here, and *this* one . . ." She presses my left hand between both of hers, and suddenly we're standing so close, the tips of our shoes are touching.

Then she switches my hands out to warm the right one. "There," she says, finally.

I drop my hand but don't step back. I may or may not still be breathing.

She's just the tiniest bit taller than me—two inches, maybe. If I stood on my tiptoes—

"Is that what Kayla and Declan were doing back there?" I blurt. "Warming each other's hands?"

Tessa laughs. "Yup. And now they're probably warming each other's lips."

I swear to God, I'm like a pointillist painting of myself. I'm just colors and dots.

"Okay, but it's *whatever*, right? It happens?"

"What?" She studies me, grinning.

"You said that!"

Her quick, shaky laugh makes me melt. "But I don't actually think that. Kissing's not *whatever*."

"I've never done it."

"Never done what?"

"Kissed anyone."

Tessa's eyes flare wide. "You and Lili never—"

"Oh, yeah. Obviously. I meant other than Lili." Fuck. Fuck. "Lili and I kissed . . . so much. We were always kissing. Wow, I'm talking a lot about kissing, aren't I?" I laugh sharply. "Sorry—I'm not, like, obsessively thinking about kissing."

"Me neither. Totally not."

Suddenly, I'm on the tips of my toes, kissing her lips so quickly, it barely feels real.

She stares back at me, wide-eyed. But if she's surprised, I'm downright dumbfounded. I just—

Kissed Tessa. I *kissed* her.

I mean, it's not that I haven't pictured the kissing. But I've always imagined it as a thing that happens to me. Something I get swept up in. In my mind, I'm *never* the one who initiates it.

I can't be. Because that would mean this is something I'm certain about.

Tessa lets out a soft breath. "I'm—"

"Immy?"

Lili's voice.

Tessa and I spring apart, even though I know Lili's too far up the path to see us—not that she'd be weird about it either way. But the whole thing's inherently weird, given that I have no idea how Tessa feels about what just happened.

Or how badly I want it to happen again.

By the time Lili reaches us, she's breathless. "Sorry! I was gonna let you catch up, but, uh. Gretchen's here? And my brother, and your sister—"

"Wait—what?"

"Yeah . . . they're outside my dorm. I mean, they're inside now—I let them in. But I didn't want you to be surprised—"

"But." I shake my head slowly. "It's almost midnight."

"I know. I know. Are you—I don't know if you want to, like, talk to them, or . . ."

My heart feels like it's bouncing off the walls of my chest.

I can't—

I mean, I barely feel up to the task of existing as Gretchen's cishet best friend. Or Edith's straight big sister. And I'm *definitely* not up to being straight in front of the girl I just kissed.

Lili pats my arm. "Hey. I've got your back."

"You okay?" Tessa asks softly.

I'm pretty sure my lungs have shut down.

DAY NINE
SATURDAY
MARCH 26

50

Gretchen, Otávio, and Edith have taken over a cluster of chairs in the lobby, overnight bags piled at their feet. I breathe in, trying to steady myself. I feel completely unstrung.

"Surprise!" Gretchen's the first to jump up and greet me with a hug. "Couldn't miss the chance to see Dark Academia Imogen in person."

I barely register any of it. So many questions are jostling for space in my brain, I don't even know where to start. Did Gretchen plan this? *When* did Gretchen plan this? Also, how did they find Lili's dorm, and does Gretchen need a visitor parking permit, and are they staying overnight, and where are they sleeping, and, most importantly, what on earth is happening? Why—literally *why*—are they here?

"What's up," Otávio says, fist-bumping Tessa.

Right. Otávio would know the dorm. One mystery down.

Tessa turns to smile at my sister. "Hi! You're definitely Edith."

"I definitely am!"

"Oh man, even the dimple." Tessa looks from Edith to me.

"Tessa, right?" Edith says. There's this tiny lilt in her voice that makes me wonder what Gretchen's told her.

"So you guys just . . . decided to come up here?" asks Tessa.

"Oh, we were in the neighborhood." Gretchen says, with this little hand wave she does when she's trying to show off her thumb ring. She turns to Tessa. "It is . . . very cool to meet you in real life."

Tessa looks slightly bewildered. "You too."

"You've been taking good care of my bestie, right? You haven't been throwing her into any parties with no training wheels?" Gretchen hooks an arm around my shoulder.

"Everything's—great," I croak.

"Good." Gretchen squeezes my shoulder, reclaims her hand, and turns right back to Tessa. "Okay, wow—your suit is perfect, by the way."

I need a pause button. I need to sort through my thoughts, but everything's moving so fast. The party feels like it happened a century ago. And that lightning-fast kiss feels like it never happened at all.

I always forget that Gretchen has game in ways I can barely imagine.

It probably helps that she's actually queer. Like, I'm pretty sure she wouldn't have thrown down one chaste kiss and called it a night. How do I even compete with someone like Gretchen? And why would I? How could I stake any sort of claim here when I'm not even sure I'm really bi?

That word again. How could two letters wreak so much emotional havoc? *Bi.*

Why do I feel like I'm stealing?

"Okay," Lili says. "So, I'm gonna take these guys upstairs to drop their stuff off, and then we'll all head out to the diner. I can fill them in on . . . everything we've been up to this week."

I shoot her a quick, grateful smile—even though I'm not sure how she's planning to spin things. I guess she'll make sure everyone's on the same page about the backstory, for one thing.

Maybe she's just trying to buy me time for a talk with Tessa.

The talk, I mean. Because at this point, it's inevitable. I've been careening straight toward it since the moment I kissed her.

I wait until they're in the elevator before turning to face her. But the words get stuck in my throat.

How am I supposed to talk about this here, with drunk strangers stumbling in and out of the front door every second? How do I lay out the full messy truth under the fluorescent lights of Lili's dorm lobby?

Deep breath. "Can we go outside?"

"Only if you take the jacket," Tessa says with a flash of a smile.

"Fiiiiiiine."

She helps me into it, giving the collar a quick tug, and then we step back out to the courtyard. It's not particularly private out here, given the big lobby windows. So.

No kissing, I guess.

344

Not that Tessa's going to want to kiss me again once she finds out I'm straight. Or that I *was* straight? But was I?

How does this work? Am I stepping into a room or turning on a light?

I aim for a smile, but it doesn't quite stick. "I have to tell you something," I say in a rush.

The ground feels like it's tilting beneath me. The thought of dropping this bomb here and now makes me dizzy. But I kind of have to come clean, right? There are too many ways this could fall apart. This can't be a thing Tessa hears from anyone but me.

I shut my eyes for a moment. "You know the whole thing about Lili and me? How we used to date? That's . . . not quite true."

Tessa's eyes widen. "Oh—"

But then the door to the lobby swings open. "We're back!" Edith says.

Gretchen looks me up and down. "Cute blazer," she says slowly.

Her voice is as sharp as the edge of a knife.

51

It's sheer panic all the way to the diner. I feel like I'm on an airplane—strapped in tight with no legroom, tens of thousands of feet above my own life.

Gretchen sidles up to Tessa, who keeps glancing back at me with an expression I can't quite decipher. Tessa, who probably feels completely betrayed. Or at the very least, I'm sure she thinks I'm a total liar. That's basically where we left off, right? I lied my face off about dating Lili, and now she knows. Really, the only question is whether she's pieced together yet that I'm straight.

Was straight? Thought I was straight?

The diner's surprisingly crowded for one in the morning. All college kids, of course—flushed and tipsy, sharing plates of cheese sticks and French fries. "They do soft pretzels on weekends," Lili says, scanning the space for an empty table. She points to a booth near the back. "Okay, tight squeeze, but I think that's the best we're gonna do."

Now I'm picturing myself pressed up close beside Tessa, not a single molecule of air between us. I'd blow my own cover to bits before we even put in a drink order. I mean, Otávio could probably be talked into thinking I was just playing a part for the sake of the backstory—and God only knows what Gretchen's thinking right now.

But Edith? She'd know.

Of course, the problem solves itself when Gretchen scoots into the booth right behind Tessa. Which means the only seat left is on the other side of Gretchen.

It's the one spot where I can't see Tessa's face. Which is—

Probably for the best. Looking at Tessa is almost as dangerous as touching her. At least I won't accidentally stare my way out of the closet.

But the funny thing is, the more I think about coming out, the more I kind of want to do it. I want to hear what the words sound like out loud, in my voice.

But not here. Not right now.

If I do it here, I'll have to come out in two directions at once. There's just no way to spin it without admitting to Tessa that I wasn't out to begin with. That I thought I was straight.

Even though I'm not. And I wasn't.

I don't *think* I was.

But then again, do I *really* know that? Does anyone really, truly, one hundred percent know? Like, there has to be a chance

I talked myself into this, right?

This is what internalized biphobia sounds like. I know that. I know.

And I swear it's not something I'd ever think about bi people in general. It's just—me.

I've always had such a pliable center. I *like* being who people expect me to be. It's not that I'm trying to change who I am. I just want who I am to make sense. In every context. Without any uncertainty or contradiction. Which means pinning down who I'm supposed to be in any given situation and adjusting my feelings accordingly.

Here's a fun riddle: a people pleaser walks into a diner with five other people, and every single one of them wants her to be someone different.

Is that what's happening? People saw me as queer for a week, and it stuck?

A waitress stops by for our order—soft pretzels, pancakes, and coffee. Every core food group represented. Then Lili dives in with a full slate of meandering party anecdotes, clearly an attempt to steer the conversation toward neutral ground. But I only really start to relax when Otávio admits he's never heard of dark academia—which basically guarantees a good thirty minutes of collaborative explanation, complete with YouTube clips and probably a detailed analysis of my vision board.

Maybe we can stretch that until the part where we pay and leave. If I can just get through this meal, I'll find a way to pull Tessa aside on the walk home. I'll tell her everything.

And then I'll come out to everyone else. Separately. In orderly succession.

But then our food arrives, and Gretchen turns to Tessa in the pause that follows. "So, you're a lesbian, right?"

"Yup! Or gay. Or queer. Whichever."

"Cool. Okay, question." Gretchen grips the edge of the table. "Would you ever date a bi girl?"

I stare at my plate. The outline of my pretzel starts to blur.

"Uh. Yeah. Of course," Tessa says, sounding puzzled.

I can hear the smile in Gretchen's voice. "Really? Isn't that kind of unusual? I think it's amazing, don't get me wrong."

"I . . . don't know what you mean."

It's the softest I've heard Tessa speak, the whole time I've been here.

I really wish I could see her face.

"No, for real," Gretchen says. "It's a thing. I mean, I honestly get the hesitation. You get a lot of straight girls pretending to be bi, which makes a lot of lesbians think we're *all* faking it."

Edith shakes her head. "Gretchen, what are you talking about?"

"I mean, I definitely don't think that," says Tessa.

"Okay, but let's say you like a girl, and then it turns out that she's faking it. What would you do?"

Tessa laughs uncomfortably. "I *really* don't think that's a thing."

"You'd be surprised," Gretchen says, so cheerfully, she's practically singing.

349

Lili's fork lands on the table with a clang. "Well, that's biphobic as fuck."

"Uh, I'm literally bi," Gretchen says. "And I'm sorry, but this actually affects me? Straight girls who do this are why everyone thinks bi girls are undateable."

"I don't think bi girls are undateable," Otávio chimes in.

"I don't either!" Tessa says.

Lili slams her hands down. "Great! New topic."

"I don't think we're done with this one," says Gretchen.

Edith is looking straight at me, brow furrowed and tense. Lili, on the other hand, looks like she wants to commit murder.

Otávio appears to be enjoying his pancake.

Gretchen shrugs. "I'm just saying—"

"Okay, you want to talk about it?" I cut her off, anger coursing through me so suddenly, it feels like it could split me in two. "Fine. Lili and I aren't exes. I lied."

"No." Lili shakes her head. "Nope. *I* lied. Months ago. And then I roped you into it! This is so completely not your fault—"

"Yeah, but I still went along with it!"

"So you guys . . . are still together?" Tessa asks.

"What? Oh, no," I say quickly. "We never dated."

"Fuck." Lili covers her face. "Okay—"

"I've never dated a girl," I add. "Or a boy. Or anyone. And I wasn't Lesbian Elsa. I was Straight Anna."

Lili cuts in. "Okay, here's how it went. I was an insecure little fuckhead who made up a whole backstory that Imogen didn't even know about until this week. And the only reason she went along with it is because she's the best friend on earth."

"Oh." Tessa's voice is barely audible. "So you're—you're straight?"

"A hetero queen," declares Gretchen.

I turn to her, dumbfounded.

"This isn't Imogen's fault," Lili says, looking distressed. She turns to Tessa. "You can't be mad at her."

"I'm not mad."

"I'm not straight," I say, eyes prickling with tears. "Gretchen, I told you that."

"Did you? Because what it sounds like is a pick-me straight girl appropriating queerness because she thinks it will make everyone happy."

Lili shakes her head, looking like she's about to explode. But before she can even open her mouth, Edith swoops in. "Uh, why the fuck do you think you get any say in Imogen's identity?"

"Because it's my label!" Gretchen says, eyes pooling with tears. She wipes them angrily away with her palm. "And it's not some fun fucking afterthought. This—being queer, being *bi*—I don't get to turn it off when I'm not in the mood. You know when people started clocking me as queer? Elementary school. Ever been called a slur in front of your mom at Walmart, Imogen? Have you ever been told, 'Oh yeah, my dad's not really comfortable with you spending the night'? I used to get off the bus crying my eyes out because some sixth grader kept saying I was going to hell. And then, when I finally, finally have *one* safe

351

place, the fucking basketball team burns it to the ground." She lets out an angry, choked laugh. "How about the girl from the movie theater with her fucking skirt up her ass. 'I'm not interested. I date boys.' Uh, cool story. You're not even cute. And I'm exhausted. It's exhausting. And now you—do you even like girls, Imogen? Like, are you actually attracted to girls?"

I try to speak, or even breathe, but it feels like my throat's caving in. I just—

Don't know what to think. Maybe she's right. It's not real. I don't want to kiss Tessa. Not that it would matter if I did. There's no way in a million years she'd want to kiss me at this point.

I can't stop blinking. "I'm gonna go."

It came from my mouth, but it doesn't sound like my voice. It doesn't even feel like I'm speaking.

"Alone? Immy, it's one in the morning—"

"I can walk you back," says Otávio.

"I'll wait outside. Just let me—" I jump out of the booth, feeling like the whole world's watching me stumble. Tables and tables of blurry faces. I push through the door, barely even noticing the cold anymore. There's a shadowy spot a few feet from the door, where I can settle in beneath an overhang. It's not private. I guess nothing ever is.

I cover my face with both hands.

A bell chimes faintly a moment later, and the door to the diner swings open. "Imogen?"

My sister.

"Hey." She scoots in beside me. "Guess who's getting a brand-new, freshly ripped, Lili-shaped asshole right now."

I let out a tearful laugh. "Oh, I bet."

"God. Immy. I'm so happy for you." She hugs me. "So you're—I'm guessing you're not gay. Are you bi?"

"I think so?" My heart skips a beat. "I'm not faking."

"Okay, first of all, fuck Gretchen—"

"She's right, though! It makes no sense." I shake my head. "Like it just suddenly pops up? That's not normal. You've always known you were queer. Lili's known for years—"

"Doesn't matter! Immy, you can't let her get into your head about this. Everything she said, all of that"—Edith gestures vaguely at the diner—"that's Gretchen's baggage. It has nothing to do with you, okay? She's being awful, and she knows it!"

I smile a little. "I don't think—"

"Look, on some level, she knows it. She has to. She's just—you know, she's scrambling right now. You sort of flipped her world upside down with this one. You being queer means she's been wrong this whole time. Which is why she's telling herself you're faking, or you don't *deserve* to be queer, or whatever the fuck she's implying. Because otherwise, she has to sit with the fact that she just treated a fellow queer person like absolute shit."

For a moment, we're both silent. I swallow back a lump in my throat. "But what if I'm the one who's wrong?" I say, finally.

"About who you like?"

I press my cheeks. "How do I know it's not a fluke? What if I only ever fall for one girl?"

353

"Then you're bi." She pats my arm.

"What if I'm talking myself into it?"

"Not a thing—"

"Okay, but what if the girl I like is kind of—I don't know—boyish?"

"Is she a boy?" Edith asks.

"No."

"Sounds pretty bi." I laugh, wiping my eyes, and Edith hugs me again. "She likes you, too. You know that, right?"

"She—"

"Come on. You're not subtle—"

"I'm not?"

"Immy, you're literally wearing her jacket. And let me tell you, she's not even *trying* to hide it. I was sitting right across from her. That girl is—" She stops short, glancing through the window behind me. "Uh, coming out here." Edith kisses my cheek. "I love you. I'll see you back at the dorm. Or not! Live your life."

52

Tessa steps out of the diner, and I forget how to breathe.

This girl, in her vest with no blazer, cheeks flushed from the cold. She looks around, smiling a little when she spots me leaning against the brick facade. "Hi. So. Um. The others are going to hang for a minute, but"—she swallows—"maybe you and I could walk back?"

As soon as she says it, I know. Category five *letting you down gently* vibes. My first big bisexual heartbreak, coming in strong on day one.

No way out but through, though, so I nod quickly. And then I pretty much keep my eyes glued to the sidewalk.

She hesitates. "So that was—"

"A shitshow. I'm so sorry."

"No! You didn't do anything wrong!"

"I mean, I lied to you about Lili," I say, as we veer down the side street, toward campus. "And about being bi."

"But you are bi."

I shoot her a faltering smile. "Okay, but I'd get it if you were skeptical."

"What?"

"Under the circumstances."

"No. God. Imogen." She stops, turning to face me. "I'm not skeptical. I would never be."

I finally look up at her.

And instantly burst into tears.

"Oh! Oh no. Scott—Scotty. Hey." She hugs me, and I bury my face in the spot where her chest meets her shoulder. "Don't listen to the pink-haired girl, okay?"

I laugh tearfully. "I'm getting your vest wet. And I stole your blazer."

"I love it on you," says Tessa.

The air rushes out of my lungs.

She studies my face, wide-eyed, and it's like the entire universe shifts. She touches her fingertips to mine for a moment.

Then she takes my whole hand in hers. "This okay?" she asks softly.

"Yeah." I nod, wiping away a tear with my other hand. I smile back at her. "Sorry."

"Hey. Are you—God, you just *came out*. Oh man. That's really big. And at the diner!"

"I know!"

"Did you ever think you'd come out at a diner called Diner?"

I laugh. "I didn't think I'd come out. I didn't think I was

queer. Which—God, it's so obvious, too. How did I miss it?"

"Too busy looking for Waldo?"

I face-palm. "Not me spending my whole life bragging about how observant I am."

"Comphet's a bitch." Tessa squeezes my hand. "And it probably didn't help to have Little Miss One True Queer Gretchen screaming in your face all the time about how straight you are."

I laugh, but it comes out half as a sigh. "I promise she's not usually that aggressively wrong."

"You mean the girl who just informed me I don't date bi girls?" Tessa stops walking, turning to face me again. "Because I'm pretty sure all I've been able to think about this entire night is dating a bi girl. And kissing a bi girl. And—"

I kiss her. And this time, there's no hesitation, no second-guessing, not a single beat of *Wait did that just happen, did I just do that, and why and how and what does it mean?*

None of that. Just a full-force, hands-in-hair, forget-where-I-am, holy-shit kind of kiss. She cups my cheeks in her hands and our foreheads bump together, which makes both of us giggle for a second.

But then she presses even closer somehow, moving her mouth against mine, and it cracks my heart wide-open.

"Sorry. Uh. Excuse me," someone mutters, stepping around us on the path.

Tessa draws back a bit, flustered but smiling. "Okay, new plan. Do you want to go back to—"

"No. Nope. Absolutely not," I say—but the look on her face

stops me short. "Wait, you mean go back to the diner, right?"

"Oh my God, Scott." She leans in to kiss me again. "I meant my room."

"Ohhhhhhh. Yeah. Yes." I laugh.

Somehow our hands find each other's, fingers fitting together like notes in a song.

53

The five-minute trip back to the dorms is somehow the slowest walk of my life.

"Minsky!" a guy calls out as soon as we enter the courtyard. "Tess!"

"We didn't hear it. Keep walking," she mutters.

Waiting for the elevator is agony.

But when it arrives empty, Tessa smashes the button for the third floor, and then we kiss the whole way up. Kiss in the hallway. She's got one hand in my hair as she fumbles with her carabiner in the other, and then we kiss again as soon as the door shuts. Aching and frantic, like a movie. Every surface of the room is draped in the laundry she set out to air-dry. We kick our shoes off. I drop the blazer.

"So you've never kissed a girl," Tessa says, smiling and breathless.

"No, I have."

"Wait—"

"Tonight," I say. "Right after we left the party. Really cute freckle-faced girl from Philly." I touch her cheek.

Tessa touches my mouth. "How are you real?"

The way she's looking at me gives me this liquid-gold feeling. I sink back until I'm sitting on the edge of her bed, pulling her down with me. She tucks a lock of hair behind my ear and kisses me again, until I can barely sit upright. She kisses my forehead, my cheeks, the crook of my neck, and I don't know if I'm falling or blooming. The way our ankles overlap. The ache below my navel. I kiss her again, and my mind's as quiet as snowfall.

A week ago, Tessa was just a face in Lili's college pictures. A week ago, I'd never been kissed. A week ago, I thought I was straight.

It's like learning to read—the way the letters and phonemes click into place. That sudden burst of meaning.

I smile up at her. "I always thought I'd have my first kiss in front of the pancake griddle."

"Okay, what is this mysterious pancake griddle?"

"The world's biggest pancake griddle! It's in Penn Yan."

"And people just, like, kiss in front of it?"

"No, they made a pancake on it! 1987. The world's biggest pancake ever—well, at the time. My parents actually got to eat part of it."

She sits up suddenly. "You're descended from pancake royalty?"

"I mean, yeah," I say, "but deep down, I'm just a normal

girl. You don't have to treat me differently in pancake situations."

"Pancake situations," agrees Tessa. "Breakfast, for example."

"Exactly."

"Okay, so"—she flops back down, rolling onto her side—"*do* they let people make out on the griddle?"

"In front of the griddle! It's mounted to the outside of a building. So . . . I mean, as long as the clothes stay on, I guess so?"

She taps her finger to my lip. "Interesting."

I pause. "Speaking of whether or not clothes stay on—"

"Also interesting," she says, eyes going wide.

"I don't mean—" I blush. "I'm not saying, like—get *naked*—"

"You sure?"

"Oh—"

"I'm joking!" she says. "Sorry. I mean—I'm not joking. I want to—like, I definitely want to, but not until you want to. Or *unless* you want to. You know what I mean. Now I'm shutting up."

I giggle. "I know."

She studies my face like she's memorizing a poem. "Hey, let me know if *any* of this is too fast. I know it's been, like, an emotional night. And your sister's here—"

"Let's not talk about my sister."

"Oh man. I was always so scared I'd randomly butt-dial

Dan or Rachael or, like, my parents in the middle of hooking up."

"Oooh. Don't do that."

"I won't." She reaches back and pulls her phone out of her pocket. "See? No butt-dials."

"Love that for us!"

She taps my nose. "Wait."

I smile up at her, taking in the soft lines of her profile while she opens her music app. Her eyes crinkle at the corners—I know she knows I'm watching.

"Okay!" She stretches over me, setting her phone on the nightstand. The audio's a little quiet—just a regular phone speaker—but even the first few instrumental notes make my heart flip. I trace her freckles with my fingertip from one cheek to the other and sing the first word along with David Byrne.

Home.

"It's my—"

"Favorite." I kiss her. "I know."

"You're my favorite," she says, and I laugh. Then I sit up just enough to peel my tights off. And my cardigan. "Not trying to get overheated," I explain.

"Oh, yeah. Good point. Very dangerous." Tessa pauses—then taps her belt buckle. "Should I, um—"

"Yes. I mean. Belt. Pants. Whatever. If you want—"

"Okay. Yeah." She nods quickly, and I could swear it's my heart that's unzipping.

I shut my eyes for a moment, letting the music fill every crack in my surface.

This must

be the place.

My phone buzzes under my thigh, almost startling me off the bed. Turns out, I've missed a whole stack of texts from Lili.

Okay Gretchen went home

Followed by a GIF of Harry Styles waving goodbye and blowing a kiss, and then:

The kiddos are still here tho

They're gonna crash tonight in my room

Which means we're a little short on beds in here, you should probably find alternate lodgings for the night 😌

And then a frantic addendum:

OKAY BUT JUST TO CLARIFY you are welcome to come back to my room anytime, we're in here, we love you, door's open!!!!!

"Are they like, 'where are you'?" asks Tessa.

I set my phone next to hers on her nightstand, turning to face her. "No, they're—"

My words melt away when I see her. Tessa in an undershirt, white with short sleeves, the straps of her sports bra faintly visible underneath.

Nothing on bottom but boy shorts.

My heart's spinning cartwheels. I don't think I realized

until this moment just how much clothing she usually wears. Hoodies and jeans and shorts. Even her dark academia clothes had extra layers. I guess she was *technically* naked under a bathrobe when we met, but if I think about that too long, my heart might combust. She's so pretty, it's actually kind of unbearable. Boyish and girlish, all at once. She's a little huskier than I realized. Narrower than I am, but with an unexpected softness.

What would it feel like to touch her bare skin with mine?

I fidget with the hem of my skirt, unsure if I should take off my pinafore, too. I wonder what she thinks I look like underneath. If she's thought about it at all. To be honest, it's weird that *I'm* thinking about it. I don't typically get too wrapped up in body stuff. I'm kind of in that in-between space where I'm bigger than most actresses but small enough that people aren't shitty to me, and it just hasn't really been an issue for the most part.

But maybe that's because no one's actually *seen* my body before. I don't even really wear bathing suits, other than summer trips to Nana's house on Cayuga Lake. And this is very much not Nana's house on Cayuga Lake.

The song restarts itself. *Home.*

I imagine Tessa unzipping my pinafore, unbuttoning the shirt underneath it. Maybe she'll think my stomach's too soft. Maybe she'll find the twin scars on my back where a doctor scooped off two birthmarks. Or she'll feel the little connect-the-dot zits running along my spine. Or she'll—

"Hey." She reaches up with both hands, tugging me down beside her. When she leans onto her side, our faces aren't even an inch apart. Her hand falls to my waist. "I can't tell if you're thinking or panicking or—"

"Both. But in a good way?"

"Oh, right, the *good* kind of panic." She cups my cheek with her hand. "Let's not rush this, okay? It's so new. You should take the time to figure out what you want."

"I want this, though."

"Yeah, me too! But—"

"And I promise this isn't just, you know. Me figuring stuff out. Or experimenting—"

"Oh! No—Imogen. I know you're not. I just mean, like—I don't want you to think you have to be some cool, sophisticated queer seductress girl, you know? You don't have to try stuff because you think that's what I want."

I sit up. "You don't think I'm a cool, sophisticated queer seductress girl?"

"Totally not." She sits up beside me.

I scoff, tugging her backward onto the pillows, tangling our bare legs together. She touches my lips with hers, just for a second, and I smile back up at her.

She lets out a quick, breathless laugh. "Oh my God, this is—you know that part of *The Lion King* where they're having sex in the forest—"

"People had sex in *The Lion King*?"

"No, lions had sex in *The Lion King*—"

"*What?* Sorry—when?"

"'Can You Feel the Love Tonight'! Imogen, they were rolling around the whole jungle—"

"I thought . . . I thought they were just, like—being in love?"

"Yeah, but then Nala gives him that look—remember? Like. *Heyyyyyy.*" Tessa leans in and kisses me. "And that's us! We're lions having sex! Except we're *not* having sex, because we're not gonna rush!"

"To be clear, we're also not lions," I say, shooting her a smile that turns into a yawn halfway through. "Sorry—"

"No—geez—what time is it?"

I crane my neck toward the pair of phones on Tessa's nightstand. "Almost three in the morning. Yikes—sorry! I can give you your bed back—"

"I don't want my bed back. Sleep here."

I look up at her. "Really?"

"Imogen." She rolls back down beside me, scoops my hair back, and kisses me. "Do you need me to spell it out? I've been"—she kisses me—"losing my goddamn mind"—she kisses me again—"ever since that dog wandered over, and you just—boom"—another kiss—"dropped down and hugged her. The look on your face. And then you're like, 'My goat was named Daisy.'"

"She was!"

"I know!" Tessa laughs, tucking a lock of hair behind my ear.

Then she buries her face in the crook of my neck, and every breath she breathes feels like a love letter.

54

My eyes don't want to stay closed. It's been like this for at least an hour—me, staring dazedly into the dark, memorizing every inch of Tessa's blank white ceiling.

My head's a shaken snow globe, glitter suspended in liquid. When I touch my lips, they feel tender. I don't know how to make any of this feel real.

I kissed a girl.

She kissed me back.

And now I'm in her room, in her bed, close enough to feel her chest rise and fall as she breathes. I don't know how people do this. How do you turn your brain off after kissing? How do you stop cataloging every point of contact between your over-lapping bare legs?

Also, how do you unremember the fact that you didn't wash your face before bed? Not to mention brushing or floss-ing, which is why your breath now tastes like the apocalypse, and also your bladder keeps chiming in to say, *What's up, hey,*

Imogen, hey, about that alcohol last night, about those liquids—

I just have this feeling that getting out of bed will break the whole spell. What if Tessa wakes up regretting everything? What if she sits up in bed, hugging the edge of her blanket in horrified silence? *I was in my underwear,* she'll realize, *and Imogen didn't even try to breach the waistband.*

Does she even like girls?

Does she want to fuck me, or not?

Except—no. Nope. Tessa wouldn't think that. This is my warped little bunny brain freaking out for no reason. Last night was perfect. I mean, other than the part where Gretchen called me a pick-me straight girl. But the rest of it was dreamy perfection wrapped in starlight, and now I'm lying here with bee-stung lips and a hundred new doors unlocked in my brain. Miles of uncharted territory.

Here I was, so sure I'd mapped out every inch of myself.

How do you get your own sexuality wrong? How is that even possible?

I feel on the verge of tears all of a sudden. But I can't tell if it's exhaustion or panic or just the fact that every part of this is light-years away from my normal.

And there's Tessa, sound asleep on her side, hand curved sweetly around the edge of the pillow. A stripe of dark hair falls over her cheek, tickling the corner of her mouth.

I want to tuck it behind her ear and kiss her. I want to click my heels and teleport home.

Close my brain for renovations. Imogen Scott, currently

under construction.

If I could call a time-out. Just for a second.

I slide out of Tessa's bed as carefully as possible, scanning the room for Lili's boots from last night. But since they've apparently vanished, I grab a pair of Tessa's flip-flops instead, strangely thrilled to find they fit me perfectly. Queer girl Cinderella.

The hallway's totally empty. Good. No one here to witness me wandering out of Tessa's room like I'm coming out of sex hibernation.

Which I'm *not*. Because we didn't. Have sex, that is.

The bathroom's lit only by a night-light, but by the time I'm done peeing, I can make the cubbies out well enough that I'm eighty percent sure it's Lili's toothpaste I'm borrowing. I attempt to finger-brush, studying my face in the mirror.

I look like the end of an action movie—flushed cheeks and dark circles, hair haphazard. Stripped totally raw.

55

"But what if Gretchen's right?" I blurt.

"Uhhhh." Edith stares at me, blue eyes glassy with sleep. "Have you . . . been here this whole time?"

"I mean, think about it! If I was wrong about it before, how do I know I've gotten it right this time? Like, how am I supposed to trust myself? And now I've dragged Tessa into it, and—"

"You didn't"—Edith yawns—"drag Tessa into anything. What time is it?"

"Nine seventeen."

Edith pulls herself up, gaze flicking from Lili's empty bed to Otávio's nest of blankets on the floor. "Where'd they go?"

"Bathroom, I think? I don't know."

She nods slowly.

"Do you think I was using her?"

"Lili?"

"Tessa!"

Edith blinks. "For what?"

"For attention? Or to make people like me, or to seem more interesting—"

"Oh, are we just listing out biphobic stereotypes?"

"What if I *am* the biphobic stereotype?" I cover my face.

Edith lets out a startled laugh. "This is wild. I don't think I've ever seen you just, like, completely lose your shit like this."

"No, I always lose my shit like this. Just not out loud."

She looks at me. "So this is what your brain sounds like?"

"I mean. Pretty much?"

"Huh. All the time, or just after sex?"

"You think I had *sex*—"

"You had SEX?" I look up to find Lili wide-eyed in her bathrobe, Otávio a half step behind her. I didn't even hear the door open.

"Noooooo!" I cover my face with both hands. "I didn't have sex! We just—you know."

"What did I miss?" asks Otávio.

Lili pats his shoulder, turning back to me. "I didn't even hear you come in last night."

"Yeah, no—it was late."

"And now she's freaking the fuck out," Edith chimes in.

Lili pauses—but then she stabs her finger in my general direction. "Oh, hell no. I know what this is."

"Er . . . what?"

"This is that thing where you're like, 'Oh no! I'm freaking out! She totes doesn't like me!' and she's in there like, 'Oh man

372

oh man—"

I laugh. "She does say *oh man*."

"Yeah, but this is like a sad *oh man*. Like, 'Ohhhhhh maaaaaan, that girl is SO not into me.'"

"Right!" Edith punches my arm. "And meanwhile, we're all like, 'YOU ABSOLUTE DUMBASSES, OPEN YOUR GOD-DAMN EYES—,'"

"THANK YOU!" Lili clasps her hands. "But nooooo. Rather than talk it out like normal people, you're gonna avoid each other and then—I don't know—maybe throw in a grand gesture later, but that's not going to happen until you're both *completely* miserable, and for what? WHY?"

I open my mouth and then shut it. "So . . . you think I should go talk to her?"

"Immy, I mean this in the nicest way possible, but I will physically drag you next door to make this happen," says Lili. "There will be rugburn. On your ass, probably."

Edith grins down at her phone.

"Um. Okay." I slide off the bed, and it's like I've lost the reins of my own body for a second.

I put Tessa's flip-flops back on. Cross the room. Pass Lili's desk.

But I stop short before opening the door. "Wait!" I whirl around. "What's the etiquette, though? Do I knock?" I pause. "Okay, yeah, I should knock. Obviously. Sorry. Never mind."

I take a deep breath and step into the hall.

* * *

373

Thirty seconds later, I'm back in Lili's room. "She's not there," I say.

"Uh, what?"

"I mean, I knocked, but . . ."

"Nope. Absolutely the fuck not." Lili hooks an arm around my shoulders, marching me back to Tessa's door. "Tess?"

She knocks. Then knocks again.

No answer.

Lili pulls her phone out of her back pocket, opens her texts, and starts typing. Her phone vibrates in her hand a moment later, and she makes a noise that's half exhale, half scoff.

"What—what happened?"

"Nothing. She's in her brother's room." Lili presses a hand to her forehead.

"Oh! When did she—"

"I don't know. I assume sometime after you left and dove into bed with your sister. The two of you. I swear to God. Same exact kind of weird." She taps her screen again, biting her lip. "Okay, you know what? I'm gonna get some laundry to do at home when I drop you guys off. And while it's running, maybe you fill in some of the gaps for me here? Like . . . she knew you were leaving this morning, right?"

I nod, a lump rising in my throat. "Yeah."

"Okay." Lili's brow furrows. "Hmm."

"I mean . . . she disappeared right when she knew I'd be leaving. Seems pretty straightforward, I guess."

"You think she's avoiding you?"

I shrug.

"But . . . you haven't texted her."

"No." I shake my head. "Yeah, I don't know. I don't want to pressure her or make it a big deal—"

"Yeah, but." Lili pauses. "I mean, you sort of left in the middle of the night, yeah? Which is fine! But, you know. You might want to text her so she doesn't think you ghosted?"

"Oh." I nod slowly. "You think I should—"

"If you want! Sorry—I'm—yeah. I'm not trying to give you unsolicited advice—"

"No, you're fine! I'm just—I don't want her to think I was ghosting. I wasn't!" My brain feels a little swirly. "Not on purpose. I should text her, huh?"

Lili tips her palms up. "I mean—I think so."

"Okay. Yeah. I'll just, um." I look down at my phone and back up at Lili. "What should I say?"

"That's all you, Immylou. You've got this." She pokes the tip of my nose. "Okay! Grabbing my laundry!"

She disappears into her room, but I'm still frozen in place. Alone in a dormitory hallway, staring at Tessa's shut door.

56

I keep sneaking glances over my shoulder, little quick scans of the courtyard. When we step off the curb into the parking lot, I legitimately almost trip over my suitcase.

"Hey." Lili slows her pace to wait up. "Everything's going to be fine. This isn't, like, your last chance to talk to her. We're talking about a thirty-minute drive. Not even that."

"I know—"

"Seriously, drive back up next weekend. Drive up tomorrow if you want!"

"Yeah." I nod. "Maybe."

Lili grabs my suitcase, rolling it around to her trunk, and I take one more glance back. Just in case of—I don't even know what.

Something.

But there's nothing. Only murky gray skies and Edith and Otávio trailing behind us like sleepy ducklings.

I take my phone out again, staring down at my text chain

with Tessa until it's just a blur of blue and gray bubbles. The problem is, no combination of words seems right. Or even in the vicinity of right. I keep deleting every message I start.

Just wanted to say how much I loved last night—
How much I liked last night—
Just wanted to say last night was really fun—
Hi, we made out last night and then I disappeared and then you disappeared and now I'm going home, and I know you don't want to be official girlfriends or anything, obviously, lol, but I just want you to know I really liked it—more than liked it. Unless you disagree, in which case I liked it just enough that you should feel good about your kissing abilities, but not enough that you should feel ANY pressure, okay?? And maybe you can respond with an emoji or something? Just to give me a clue where you stand??

I think about how the delete button looks like a house knocked on its side.

I tap it and watch the words unravel backward, letter by letter.

Edith dives into Lili's passenger seat before I even think to call shotgun, and her first order of business is hooking her phone up to Lili's Bluetooth. For a minute, everything's silent, apart from the low hum of the engine.

Until the soft instrumental notes start to rise like a church hymn.

"Oh? Oh? What's that?" Edith twists around the passenger

seat, holding her fist up like a microphone. "Could it be the iconic 1987 hit song 'Faith' by the late and great George Michael?"

Otávio rubs his temples. "Oh boy."

Edith ignores him. "Presenting . . . live in concert for the first time since Christmas break . . . the Scodoso siblings!" She revs up her air guitar.

Lili laughs. "Fuck yes. After this, 'Dancing Queen,' okay?"

"Nope," Otávio says. "No ABBA before noon."

"The way you say that like you're not the lead singer on 'Waterloo.'"

"Immy!" Edith cuts in. "Pay attention! Your part's coming—"

"Maaaaaay-be," I chime in, right on cue.

Lili shoots me a grin in the rearview mirror. "Still got it."

I don't miss a single lyric. It always amazes me how music can do that—the way it puts down roots in your brain. Close your eyes, and you're time-traveling. I could be eight years old, singing into Lili's unplugged karaoke microphone for an audience of stuffed bears. *Downright majestic*, Tessa had called it.

With my eyes shut, it's almost too easy to slot her into the picture, too—smiling and sleepy, squished into the back seat between Otávio and me. Eyes rimmed with dark circles, hair winging out in a thousand directions. Honestly, this girl could revolutionize the whole aesthetic of sleep deprivation.

I really, really need to text her.

"So what's the plan for telling your parents?" Lili asks. *"Are you gonna tell them?"*

I look up with a start. "About Tessa?"

She laughs. "About you!"

"I can help you write your coming-out speech!" chimes Edith.

For a moment, it doesn't quite compute—the idea that coming out exists outside the context of Tessa.

The fact that me being queer is just—mine.

"I don't want to do a speech—"

"Yeah, no, totally. Speeches are overrated. Ooh, you know what you should do?" By now, Edith's fully twisted in her seat, eyes gleaming. "Invite Tessa over, but sneak her out into the shed. And then I'll be like, 'Hey, Mom and Dad, can you guys drop this totally irrelevant item off in the shed for me?' And we'll time it so they show up and find you guys just making out—"

"That's—"

"And they'll be like, 'Edie, stop making out with girls in the shed,' but then you'll turn around and say, 'Guess what, bitches—it's IMOGEN.'"

I stare at her. "Wow."

"Okay, first of all," says Lili, "Imogen's never said the word *bitch* in her life. Second of all, what's the point of having a shed if you're not going to use it to make out with girls?"

"How often *do* you make out with girls in the shed?" Otávio asks.

"Never. My girlfriend lives five hours away. We've literally never met in person. Guys, this is all hypothetical. Just trying to inject a little creativity here."

"Oh. Yeah, no, I'm okay," I say, nodding politely. "I think

I'll just do it the regular basic-bitch way."

Lili's jaw drops. "I stand corrected!"

I shoot her a smile, before turning to peer out the window. The sky looks even more foreboding than it did when we left. It's definitely about to start pouring. Any minute now.

We're almost home at this point—though it looks like Lili's taking the long way to my house, right through the middle of downtown Penn Yan. Maybe she misses it.

I try to imagine myself a year from now, turning at all the same stoplights. Driving through the town I've always lived in, down streets I know so well, they're practically a part of me—Clinton Street, past Hamilton, and a left on Main. Coming back home. I know moving thirty minutes up the road to Geneva isn't some big, earth-shattering transition, but it's still going to be different, right? I don't think I've ever left Penn Yan for longer than a week or two.

I catalog the stores as we pass them. Long's Cards and Books, where Edith and Gretchen sometimes rearrange the YA section so all the queer books face out on the shelves. And the candy emporium, where Otávio once cried for ten minutes after trying a chocolate bar with pop rocks. There are a couple of artisan shops, where you can buy hand-painted wineglasses or cutting boards engraved with the outlines of all the Finger Lakes. And the Pinwheel Market. Milly's Pantry.

"Tessa would like Main Street," I say.

In the rearview mirror, I catch Edith and Lili exchanging quick glances.

"She would!"

"Want me to go get her?" asks Lili. "I'll do it. I will turn this motherfucking car around so fast, so help me, God—"

"Wait! Pull over!" I lean forward, far enough to see out Otávio's window.

Edith twists around, raising her eyebrows. "At the griddle?"

My cheeks flood with heat.

"I want to post a picture," I say.

Texts with Gretchen

GP: Wait are you home??

GP: Can I come over

GP: Please

GP: I want to talk about what happened

GP: You were hurt and I feel bad

57

"Yeah, that's not an apology." Lili hands my phone back, rolling her eyes.

It's just us now—other than Mel, who's snuggled between us, sleeping. We've already dropped Edith off at our house, and Otávio's inside. Even Lili's parents are MIA. So now we're just hanging out on Lili's metal patio glider while her laundry runs, waiting for the rain to start. Lili's always loved that moody, thick air that comes just before the sky breaks.

"So is Gretchen, like, tracking your location or something?" she asks, yawning.

I laugh. "I mean . . . it could be the iconic, highly visible Penn Yan landmark I posted."

With a kiss emoji for the caption.

Tessa hasn't liked the post, though.

"Still a shitty apology." She scowls. "She really sat there and typed, 'You were hurt.'"

"I know, I know."

"Can't you just see her waving a bloody knife around? 'Oh, you were stabbed? I feel bad!'" She scrunches her nose. "Are you gonna talk to her?"

"I mean . . . probably not today."

"I vote never," says Lili—but then she shakes her head. "Sorry, I'm trying to be less of a piece of shit about this."

"Lili, you're not—"

"I'm just, like, *incandescently* angry. This is primal rage. *Reptilian* rage."

"At Gretchen?"

"Yeah, at Gretchen! And, you know what, I knew she was going to pull something like this. I fucking knew it. She can't handle anyone sticking one goddamn toe outside of whatever little box she's shoved you into."

I ruffle Mel's fur, tilting my head toward the trees. "So you kind of . . . knew?" I ask, after a moment.

"About Gretchen being a nightmare? Or about you being bi?"

I smile faintly. "About me."

"I mean—before this week? Not particularly." She tilts her head. "I guess I always saw it as a possibility? Like, you wouldn't be the first *very* committed ally to . . . level it up a little."

I let out a sheepish laugh. "Yeah . . ."

"You know, you and Tess were off-the-charts funny this week."

I look up at her. "Really? Was it totally obvious?"

"Totally. Well, at least on Tessa's end." Lili pauses to tuck her legs up. "It was very cute. Tessa, on, like, Tuesday, developed

384

this sudden sociological interest in the ethics of dating your friends' exes. Totally hypothetical, of course. Just taking a casual poll, you know—seeing where I stood on the issue in general. I'm sitting there, like, oh, honey, you are *not* as subtle as you think you are."

I giggle. "What did you say?"

Lili leans her chin on Mel's head. "I mean—I said I didn't have an issue with it, because I obviously don't, but—Immy, that was a tough one! Because at that point, I assumed it was one-sided. You know, like, I didn't think you were gonna be interested in dating a girl. And since I'm the one who planted the seed in the first place by telling everyone you were bi—I just didn't want to put either of you in a weird spot."

"Oh. Right—"

"So then I tried to put out feelers with you, but of course you gave me absolutely nothing. Nada."

"I'm sorry." I press a hand to my cheek, grinning.

"Oh my God, please don't be. That's literally not—yeah, no. I'm the dumbass who lied in the first place—" Mel lifts her head with a start, and Lili lowers her voice. "Desculpa, anjinha—you're okay. Back to bed."

"Hi, cutie." I stroke her head.

"But then I started getting the feeling it *might* not be one-sided? Like when you suddenly wanted to come back for the party—I was like, *huh*. And then yesterday, when you were telling me how Gretchen was such a dick about your crush."

I nod slowly.

"Right, so. By the end of that conversation, I was like—I don't know—maybe sixty percent sure the crush was Tessa? Sixty-five percent? Just a hunch. It was the way you were talking about it . . . the fact that Gretchen didn't believe you. Which, by the way, is *profoundly* fucked up."

"Yeah, definitely." I pause. "Though it wasn't so much that she didn't believe me about Tessa. She basically just said Tessa's some kind of magic lesbian who attracts straight girls."

"Wow. Yeah. That's not a thing." Lili lets out a short laugh. "I mean—okay, fine, if you're out there crushing on girls and you want to call yourself straight, you do you. But Gretchen Patterson of Penn Yan, New York, is not the final fucking word on other people's queerness."

I laugh, a little sadly. "I know."

Lili's quiet for a moment. "It's like the Kara Clapstone thing. People saying she should have come out sooner because it would have meant so much to her fans or whatever. Even Gretchen talking about that unlabeled kid in Pride Alliance. I'm like—how did we get here? When did we decide this stuff needed our input?"

"But I get where she's coming from." I bite my lip. "You want to know your safe space is actually safe."

"Safe for who?" Lili counters.

"Yeah. That's—hard. It's complicated."

"Right." Lili pauses. "You know, I feel guilty sometimes for not coming out in high school."

"Guilty?"

"I don't know. I was talking to Mika last week about the DMs they get from baby queer kids. Trans kids. Some of them are like twelve years old. Mika's account means so much to them. And it's literally just the fact that Mika's this cool Japanese American nonbinary college kid out there existing and thriving and making art. Because some of them don't know *any* openly trans people in real life." Lili shrugs. "Maybe I could have been that for some little Brazilian pansexual kid in Penn Yan."

"Are there other Brazilians in Penn Yan?"

She laughs, scratching Mel's head. "Totally not. But you know what I mean."

"Well, yeah, but"—I glance at her—"isn't that just like what people were saying to Kara? That she should have come out sooner for her fans? But she didn't owe that to anyone. And neither do you."

"I know, I know."

"Also, you're my Mika. You know that, right?"

She snorts. "I am not."

"Lili, the whole backstory thing? That was actually really helpful."

"You mean when I lied to all my friends and made you go along with it?" She eyes me skeptically.

"It did! I think it helped just having people take it as a fact. Like. I'm Imogen, I'm bi." My breath seems to catch for a second. "I was so entrenched in thinking of myself as the token straight, world's best ally. You know? Like, that was my autofill. And the idea that I might not actually be straight seemed . . . a little too convenient, I guess? Or unrealistic. You can just picture someone rolling their eyes about it, right? Like it's some kind of peer pressure thing. All my friends are queer—"

"Maybe because you're drawn to fellow queer people?"

"I guess." I scrunch my nose. "Why do I feel like I'm just making all of this up?"

"Probably because of toxic-ass Gretchen. Or the five million other Gretchens out there on the internet. Some queer people just really seem to love shitting on other queer people. Every day, someone's out there weighing in about whether bi and pan girls even count as queer to begin with. Or we're only queer under certain circumstances. They'll say it with their whole chest. Absolutely zero awareness that their very specific queer experience isn't one hundred percent universal. And it's almost always this very white, very Western framework—completely rooted in colonization. No acknowledgment of regional differences, generational differences—just the same people relitigating the same semantic fuckery. But it still gets in your head! I feel like half of us are just drowning in imposter syndrome all the time. More than half, probably. I know I've been there."

I look at her. "Really?"

"Why do you think I made up the whole thing about us dating?"

"Yeah, but that was pretty much right after you came out. You seem so confident now."

"Sometimes I am," she says, "and then ten minutes later, I'm convinced I'm somehow faking it in my own head."

"That's how I feel!" Suddenly my eyes brim with tears.

"It's the worst. And it's such bullshit." She shakes her head. "And like, there's this whole other part of it where I'm pretty sure I'm panromantic asexual, actually. Or demisexual. I don't even know. And I haven't dated anyone. Which isn't *because* I'm asexual." She shrugs. "Sometimes I feel like, oh my God, why am I giving this so much mental energy? I'm literally home watching Netflix. Like. Who the fuck even cares? But I care! It matters."

"Of course it matters. It's a whole big piece of who you are."

Lili's phone alarm rings. "Oop—laundry's done! Hold that thought."

She scoops up Mel and stands.

"Hey," I say, peering up at her. "I love you."

She makes a face.

"I do!"

"I knowwww. And now I have to say it back, or else I'm an asshole." She rolls her eyes, smiling faintly. "You earnest little bisexual. I love you, too."

Texts with Gretchen

GP: Hey, I'm sorry

GP: Just wanted to say that

GP: I'll stop now, you don't have to reply

GP: But I'm sorry

58

Gretchen's texts pop up all at once just as Lili starts the car. "Tell me that's not who I think it is," says Lili, turning in her seat to back out of the driveway.

"Okay, but to her credit, she said sorry this time. Twice!"

"Baby learned a new word?"

I smile wryly. "I guess so."

I set my phone in Lili's cupholder, and neither of us speaks the whole way down Lili's street. But at the first red light, she shoots me a glance. "I keep thinking about everything Gretchen said at the diner. All the bullying—the basketball team. The guy at Walmart."

"She's had a pretty rough time." I nod.

"Yeah, she has." Lili pauses. "And obviously, it hasn't been like that for me. I know I'm not signaling queerness when I walk down the street. I'm not trying to hide it. I just—I just wear what I like. So am I less oppressed than Gretchen? I don't know! No one's called me the d-slur. But am I gonna tell the truth, the whole truth, and nothing but the truth to my Catholic grandmother in São Paulo? Uh. Maybe one day? Like, you know what I mean, right? I'm pretty sure Gretchen's not navigating that. So which one of us is more queer?"

"Well." I pause. "I'd have to see the two of you trying to sit in chairs."

"Yeah, what even is that? I'm *great* at sitting in chairs."

I look pointedly at her left leg, currently propped in an awkward triangle on the driver's seat.

"Shut up." She bites back a smile.

"But you're right," I say. "It's like there's this idea that you have to earn your label through suffering. And then you have to prove it with who you date, how you dress, how other people perceive you."

Lili nods. "Yup. Or else you don't count. Fuck that shit, though. We don't have to prove anything to anyone."

"Fuck that shit," I say.

Lili lets out a startled laugh. "Okay, new plan. Reply to Gretchen now. Like, right now. When you're in this exact mood."

I turn to the window, smiling. It's finally started drizzling, but there's no way this is all the rain we're getting. Lili bypasses Main Street—Route 14 is always faster. "Maybe you should hang at my house until it passes?"

"The rain, or my reptilian rage toward Gretchen?"

"Both?" I laugh and reach for my phone, sneaking another quick peek at the likes on my griddle post.

None from Tessa.

Which makes it all feel like a dream. The whole week, even. The tunnels and Declan's closet and texting until three in the morning. Coming out at a diner called Diner. Kissing a girl on the way back to her dorm. Now that I'm home, it feels almost preposterous.

I touch my lips again. Top and bottom.

"Edie grabbed your suitcase, right?" She glances back at the trunk. "Okay! I should probably try to beat this rain, huh?"

"Lili, I don't know—"

"If it gets bad, I'll swing back home." She leans over to hug me. "Hey, let me know when she comments, okay?"

"If," I say, and Lili makes the weirdest face ever. Like a smile trying to sew itself shut.

Texts with Gretchen

GP: IMMYYYYYYYY

GP: Can you just let me know you're seeing these??

IS: Hey, I'm here

GP: YES!!!! HI!!

GP: Okay, hi! Don't be mad

IS: . . .

GP: . . .

GP: ?

GP: What do the ellipses mean

IS: I mean

IS: I guess I'm just wondering what that was about

IS: At the diner

GP: Um, jealousy?

IS: Of me and Tessa?

GP: Kind of

GP: Idk, more like the idea of Tessa

GP: Or I guess

394

GP: The idea that you could bumble along as straight
and then fall into a relationship with a girl because
why not

IS: Okay first of all, closeted and straight aren't
interchangeable
IS: You get that, right?

GP: Yeah but
GP: Idk Imogen
GP: Can you really call it closeted? You literally thought
you were straight

IS: Then call it questioning

GP: But you weren't!
GP: I'm sorry, but were you really actively interrogating
your straightness
GP: Sorry, it's just like
GP: Labels have meanings, you know? It's how we're
able to talk about shared experiences
GP: That's like the whole foundation of the queer
community
GP: I know you probably think I'm trying to nitpick here,
but I'm not
GP: Just trying to understand I guess
GP: Obviously I'm happy for you

GP: And Tessa

GP: You know that, right?

GP: Anyway, hope you guys are having fun ♥

GP: You should take her to the candy emporium next!

59

I sink onto my bed, trying to scoop Quincy into my lap. But he shoots me a withering look, standing and stretching in defiant silence.

I puff my cheeks out and sigh, leaning all the way back on my pillows. It barely even looks like daytime in here—not a single wink of sunlight spilling through the gaps in the blinds. And of course I didn't bother flipping on the light switch.

Bumble along as straight.

Could you really call it closeted?

Maybe I just need to explain it more clearly. I could walk Gretchen all the way back to the beginning. To the girl with felt rainbows, to Ilana, to the le dollar bean girl. That tiny pull—so easy to miss in the moment, so painfully obvious in retrospect. I could take her through my entire unabridged history of attraction.

I could show her the quizzes in my private browser history. Shut her down, point by point.

I could ask her why she gets to decide what counts as questioning. And who counts as queer. And when she talks about the queer community, who does she mean? Who gets let in? Who gets shoved out? And what do you do with the fact that no two people seem to do queerness in quite the same way?

Maybe shared experiences shouldn't be the foundation at all.

Maybe it should be a promise to hold space for variation.

I could ask her why I wasn't allowed to have the crush I absolutely, one hundred percent had on Clea DuVall.

I could ask.

But then I might have to ask myself some things too.

Like why I thought I needed her permission in the first place.

Or why I tied myself in knots wondering whether I was allowed to love my favorite movie. Especially when the real question was tucked behind it all along.

Why? Why do I love it?

Why am I completely enthralled by this movie about a girl who doesn't know she's queer?

Who thinks she can't be queer, because she's a cheerleader.

Because she doesn't look queer. Or seem queer.

I tap out of my messages and into my camera, flipping to selfie mode. But I don't take a picture. I just stare at my face.

Sleepy blue eyes, ponytail coming undone. I smile at myself, and my dimple breaks through.

Hi, Imogen, I think.

I stand and cross the room to my bookcase. To my absurdly gay bookcase. Past my absurdly gay poster wall. My childhood bedroom, screaming at the top of its lungs this whole time.

There are still a few storage boxes stacked near my wall.

I pluck the pink teddy bear from my bookshelf, drop him into a box, and press the lid down. And then—

I freeze.

You should take her to the candy emporium next!

My heart flips upside down.

Tessa's not—

I pull my phone from its charger, checking my post again.

Nothing. No Tessa. But then.

I pull up her pictures.

Suddenly, the clouds rip wide-open.

60

I don't bother with socks. No boots. No raincoat. I don't care.

I leap for the door, while Quincy stares at me, gobsmacked.

But just as my hand hits the knob, it bursts open. "Immy!" Edith holds her phone up, bouncing on her heels. "Look—"

"I know. I'm—I need the car. Where's Mom?"

"No way. She's not going to want you going out in this. Here." She thrusts the car keys into my hand. "I'll deal with them."

"Um. Okay." I inhale. "Don't tell them—"

"Imogen. I would literally never."

"I know, I know. I'm just—I'm definitely going to. Tonight. Maybe. But—"

She hugs me. "Go!"

The windshield's getting pummeled—my wipers can barely keep up. But I take the roads at a turtle's pace. Thank God I'm not going far.

Main Street's a ghost town in the rain. Empty intersections at every light. But I see it as soon as I pass Cam's Pizzeria. The rain blurs out the words painted on its flat metal surface, but I know them by heart. *Birkett Mills. The Annual Buckwheat Harvest Festival. Penn Yan, New York. This is the original griddle used to make the . . . WORLD RECORD PANCAKE. September 27, 1987, 28' 1".*

There's a Subaru Outback parked in front. I pull my twin Outback beside it, opening the door the second the car stops. Then, squinting through the rain, I see Tessa break away from the narrow overhang by the mill's entrance. Soaked within seconds. Then again, so am I.

I swipe a lock of hair out of my eyes, but it clings slickly to my cheeks. Totally pointless. I can't stop smiling. I reach for her hand. "Hop in!"

"No way." She tugs me closer, laughing. "We're already wet! You hop out."

So I do. Slam the door shut. I run straight into her arms. "You're here!"

She lets out a breathless laugh. "I saw your picture! I should have just texted, but—" Her eyes meet mine. And my heart does a whole ballerina leap in my chest. "Oh man. I don't know. It wouldn't have been dramatic enough. Anyway, I suck."

"Wait—what?"

"I should have texted you first thing in the morning. I shouldn't have made you put out a bat signal." She bites her lip. "I shouldn't have left."

401

"But I left first! I'm the one who should have texted you! You must have thought I was ghosting—"

"No. No way. I just—thought you might have had second thoughts, and I didn't want to make it weird for you. At least that's what I told myself." She wipes her cheek, uselessly. "Really, I was just scared."

"Of me?"

"I really like you." She blurts. "And this doesn't usually happen. Not, like, this much, and this fast, and—this is *so* not fair to you. You've barely even had a chance to work it all out in your head. I know last night was a lot. Like, it was so much, and I completely understand being freaked out. I think I overstepped—"

"You didn't! You didn't overstep. I'm not freaked out. I shouldn't have made you feel like I was."

"No! No, it's just—Scott, I'm kind of the veteran here, you know? Like I know how huge this is. It's kind of seismic, right? And I think I should have let you settle into it more. Or checked in more about how you felt."

How I felt.

Dizzy, off-balance, unsteady. Like my bones were too big for my body. Like I couldn't zip myself closed. Like I'd colored outside my own outline, stepped out of frame, made myself three-dimensional.

"I couldn't sleep," I say softly. My lips are so close to her ear, I don't know whose raindrops are whose. "I was so aware of you."

Tessa nods.

"I've never existed in the same space as someone like that. It's so different from what I expected. Kissing's so different from the inside. And I don't think I really thought about what happens after—"

"Like—"

"Not sex," I say quickly. "I mean, not just sex. It's the whole afterward part. Like brushing your teeth, washing your face. Looking in the mirror. That stuff. And everything's the same, but you're different. Like you've unlocked this whole new part of yourself, and now you're moving things around to make room for it. Recalibrating." I bury my face in the soaked shoulder of her hoodie for a moment. "Does that make sense?"

"Yup. Yeah." She draws in a breath.

"And I just kept thinking—*Am I doing this right? Do I kiss like a straight girl?* I thought I *was* a straight girl until this week—"

"You don't kiss like a straight girl. Also, that's not a thing. But even if it was a thing—listen, I believe I speak for every person you've ever kissed, and you. Do not. Kiss like a straight girl. Case closed."

I laugh. "Okay."

Tessa leans closer, just barely.

She's looking at me like I'm something to pin a wish on. A shooting star, a line of birthday candles, 11:11.

I almost lose my breath for a second. I can read every freckle on her nose. "Hi."

She pushes a wet strand of hair aside to kiss my forehead. And then she kisses my lips.

So I cup my hands around her face and kiss her back. In the middle of the day. In the middle of Penn Yan's beautifully deserted rain-battered Main Street.

Tessa's so close, but I press in closer, and she lets out the softest-edged sigh. Her hands trail the hem of my waterlogged shirt, and I swear it feels like taking off sunglasses. Clarity and brightness.

I want to laugh until I sob. I want to memorize this feeling—every shade, every shadow, from every angle. I slide my fingertips along her cheekbones, catching raindrops.

The way she's watching me makes me feel boundless. Doors flung open, no fences. Earnestness, all the way down.

I still can't believe this moment is real, that I get to live inside it. Everything's clammy and cold, and we're both completely soaked through. But it's worth it.

Obviously.

I feel like sunlight through lace.

61

But kissing in dry cars is nice, too. Tessa digs two towels out of the back seat, both covered in Labrador hair from some himbo-related dog-park adventure. They barely dry us off, and they make us both smell like wet dog. It's so gross. I'm so happy.

"Perfect," Tessa says, kissing the crown of my head.

It's the kind of kiss that screams *girlfriend*. I think? As opposed to friend-of-a-friend you made out with a few times?

I twist in my seat to face her. Suddenly the word's in the center of my brain, lit in neon.

Girlfriend.

I don't know what's more surreal—the thought of having a girlfriend or being one.

But how do you broach the question? *Do* you even broach the question? Am I a clingy high school girl just for thinking it? A naive baby queer who imprints on every cute tomboy who glances in her direction?

Then again, she's *here*. In my town.

That has to mean something. Right?

Tessa takes my hand over the gearstick, threading our fingers together. "What do you think, Scott—should I just set up a tent by the mill for five months?"

"I mean, I do have a house." The tips of my cheeks go warm. "It's just that my house comes with parents."

My voice sounds like a baby cartoon mouse. Perfect.

She taps the heel of her hand to my nose like she's honking it. "Look, I'm happy to hang with parents. Parents love me. Well, not the homophobic ones, probably, but in general? I'm a parental love machine." She stops short, pointing at me. "Not, like, in an I-want-to-hook-up-with-your-parents way, though. God. Yeah, no. First of all, you know I'm not into dads."

I blink. "Hey, I'm kind of obsessed with your brain."

"Oh, you know. Just a little move I have called ADHD. Chick magnet. Works like a charm."

I grin. "Really?"

"Absolutely not. I mean. Yes ADHD. No magnetism."

"None? You sure?" I scoot closer, leaning over the gearstick to kiss her.

She grins and exhales. "Okay."

"I don't want you to go."

"Me either." She presses her forehead against mine. "Though . . . we should probably think the parent stuff through."

"I mean, I know they'll be cool about it. They didn't bat an eye with Edith."

"I know, but it's still a pretty big moment, right? Coming out to your parents." Her eyes go soft. "I don't know. I just want you to be able to be in control of this one. You didn't get that last time."

"Yeah." My heart flips.

I think about Gretchen asking Tessa if she'd ever date a bi girl. Her voice was so casual, almost cheerful, but I could sense the storm brewing just beneath its surface. It's that shift in pressure you feel before the thunder's even audible.

But I actually think the worst part came before that.

When I stumbled over myself, trying to explain how I felt about Tessa.

The way Gretchen treated the whole conversation like a movie she'd seen before. She was so amused by it all. So certain my feelings weren't real. She didn't leave even an inch of space to entertain the idea they could be.

"You know it's okay to be straight, right?" she'd said.

Gretchen was the first person I came out to.

Gretchen will *always* be the first person I came out to.

Maybe one day we'll talk about it. Maybe I'll find the words, and she'll find a way to hear them. Then we'll cry and hug and years will pass, and we'll move past it. It'll be just a little bump in our backstory.

Or maybe for us, it ends here.

Maybe Gretchen's my backstory.

Group Chat with Kayla and Tessa

KR: omg the wurst thing happened, and your expertise is needed

KR: and I do mean wurst 😌

KR: y'all around?

Kayla changed the subject to sausage party 🌭

IS: Noooo 🏠 back home

IS: Like Penn Yan home

TM: I am also currently in Penn Yan 😳

TM: Heading out in a few min though, what's up

KR: imogen!! ngl, I legitimately forgot you don't already go here

KR: come back sooooon

IS: I will 🖤

IS: So what's the wurst news??

KR: ah yes

KR: a tale of treachery

KR: starring everyone's favorite token white boy

KR: so dec ends up in my room last night

KR: to be clear, this was after the party

KR: and he did not stop at home first

KR: straight back to my room

KR: anyway, i wake up, reach for my phone, and guess what's on my nightstand

IS: 🌭 😵 ??

KR: yeppp. so, like

KR: kind of shady

KR: keeping in mind that the circumstances of him being in my room were not sausage related

TM: OR WERE THEY wink wink 😉

KR: cool, thanks for including the wink emoji, that really clarified what you meant by wink wink

TM: No prob

KR: anyway, i go to brush my teeth, open my toothbrush holder

KR: guess what's jammed in there

KR: ANOTHER FUCKING SAUSAGE

KR: so i go back to my room and

KR: sausages EVERYWHERE. all the same goddamn brand

KR: did he buy them in bulk????

KR: and i cannot emphasize enough that this
        motherfucker came straight over after the party
KR: like either this man had 15 sausages on his person
        all night or he stashed them earlier while we were
        pregaming
KR: clearly premeditated!! AND HOW DID HE KNOW
        HE'D BE COMING BACK HERE

IS: 15 sausages?? 😱

KR: MAYBE MORE!! I DON'T KNOW! I KEEP FINDING
        THEM
KR: guys we gotta go BIG
KR: i want a long con

TM: YES, draw it out
TM: One a day

KR: right, that was my initial thought
KR: but then i realized i'm the one who'd have to sneak
        around in there 15 times

IS: Could you mail them?

KR: 🤔
KR: tell me more

IS: Like, sending them anonymously

IS: In envelopes

IS: One by one

IS: I guess that would be kind of expensive though

IS: Maybe illegal

TM: Hahahahahahaha

TM: Imagine being the FBI dude assigned to this case

KR: okay, so we've got some possible felony charges in the mix

KR: and yet

KR: possibly worth it 😈

TM: I mean if you're not willing to risk an FBI investigation, is it even really revenge??

TM: At some point, the sausage casing's gotta come off

TM: Okay not literally, though!!!!!! 😨

TM: Please continue practicing safe sausaging

IS: Okay wait

IS: What if you didn't go big

IS: What if you went . . . small 😊

KR: 👀

IS: I just wonder

IS: How long it would take him to notice an itty bitty
    sausage

IS: In his itty bitty diorama

KR: WHAT

KR: YES

TM: Holy shit

TM: Like a teeny tiny one right??? Made to scale

KR: FIFTEEN TINY SAUSAGES IN HIS TINY LIL
    BEDROOM

TM: Someone loop in Mika!!!!!!!!!

KR: am literally walking to their room right now lol

KR: OH

KR: WAIT nvm

KR: they left this morning

KR: last-minute trip to Cornell

KR: to see jaaaaaaaaaaade 😙

TM: Is it finally happening????? 🤯

KR: UMMMM HOLD UP

KR: SPEAKING OF GRAND GESTURES

KR: TESSA WHY TF ARE YOU IN PENN YAN

KR: WHAT DID I MISS

KR: ARE YOU TWO GIRLFRIENDS?????

62

I almost drop my phone. "I—um."

Tessa lets out a nervous laugh. "Right."

The rain's finally stopped, but we're still in her car. Which is still parked by the griddle. Because, it turns out, alternating between kissing and texting is a wholesome and well-balanced way to spend thirty minutes. In fact, I'm pretty sure I could have rounded out the whole hour like this, if it weren't for a particular text from Kayla. Asking a particular question.

In all caps.

Which, incidentally, is exactly how the question appears in my brain.

WELL, TESSA, ARE WE?? ARE WE TWO GIRL-FRIENDS??????

"Like, we don't have to decide that. Obviously." I nod, staring straight through the windshield.

"Right! Totally not. Maybe we just . . . let it play out?"

"Yeah! That sounds—that's great!"

"Okay, great," she concludes, pressing her hand to my cheek. Then she kisses me with such tender focus, it makes my brain go blurry.

It's another ten minutes before I talk myself out of Tessa's car and into my own. But before I even turn the ignition on—

"Imogen, wait!" Tessa calls through her lowered passenger window. She gestures for me to lower my window too. "Hey. I want to see you again."

"Me too." I break into a smile.

She shoots me a thumbs-up. "Okay! cool. See you soon, then."

"Definitely."

I reach for the keys.

"Okay, just clarifying, though—I don't mean it in a cool-yeah-I'll-be-in-touch way," she adds. "More like in a what-are-you-up-to-next-weekend kind of way. Or midweek. Anytime." She laughs, a little breathlessly. "Is that too much? We don't have to say midweek. I'm shutting up."

"Midweek's good."

"Or tomorrow."

"Even better." I laugh.

"Okay, wait, one more thing! Just putting it out there that I do enjoy a good prom, if that were to arise."

"Noted."

"I'd be a really good date. Wouldn't blink in the pictures. Highly doubt I'd forget the corsage. Very devoted in general."

415

She nods solemnly. "In related news, I'm known to be an excellent girlfriend."

"Is that so?"

"Big-time. Just as a general FYI, of course. Anyway! Like we said. No need to decide right now. Let's just see what we want—"

"I want to be your girlfriend." It leaps off my tongue before I can stop it. "Okay?"

"Wait—" Her mouth slips open. "Really?"

"If you—"

"Are you kidding?" She springs out of the driver's seat and around the front of her car, closing the distance between us with one last bounce of a step. "Underlined, bold, giant-font yes."

I laugh through my open window. "Wow, you sound pretty sure about that."

"Tattoo it on my face."

"I can't wait for the part where you kiss me," I say.

And it's true: I can't wait.

I can't wait, so I don't.

ACKNOWLEDGMENTS

I've been thinking a lot about the idea of community. Or *communities*, plural. For me, the word holds a good deal of messy complexity—its nuances are hard to pin down. What does it mean to belong to a community, or several? Who sets the boundaries? Is a community always a tangible group? Can it be a feeling, a vibe?

No idea. I just know I could never have written this book without mine.

Here are a few of the people I mean:

My editor, Donna Bray, and my agent, Holly Root—who both immediately understood why this book mattered to me, carved out the space for me to write it, and helped me find all the sweet parts.

My beautiful/brilliant/iconic/amazing teams at Balzer + Bray, HarperCollins, Root Literary, UTA, and my international publishers, including: Paige Pagan, Taylan Salvati, Katie Boni, Patty Rosati, Sabrina Abballe, Shannon Cox, Shona McCarthy, Maya Myers, Almeda Beynon, Lisa Lester Kelly, Lana Barnes, Alessandra Balzer, Alyssa Maltese, Heather Baror-Shapiro, Mary Pender-Coplan, Laura Pawlak, Tom Bonnick, Rachel Horowitz, Sam White, Sarah Lough, Sarah Alice Rabbit, and Leonel Teti.

Chris Kwon and Leni Kauffman, for this absolute dream of a cover.

Kelly Quindlen, Ashley Woodfolk, Emery Lee, and Carlos Silva, for being the world's smartest, most thoughtful early readers.

Julie Waters for helping me crack this story open.

Jennifer Dugan, for Shop Talk and lots of beautiful adventures upstate.

Jeri Green, who's seen me through all of it.

Sophie Gonzales, who kind of saved me.

Gillian Morshedi, whose essay changed the whole game.

The absurdly talented Caitlin Kinnunen, for giving Imogen her voice.

Jewell Parker-Rhodes, Lilliam Rivera, Joe Bruchac, and Meghan Goel, who are the best thing to ever happen to my Mondays.

Alex Andrasik, Katie Smith, and the rest of my upstate New York literary family.

Gabe Dunn, who showed up with courage, compassion, and sincerity for one of the hardest, most important conversations I've ever had.

The friends who helped me keep my head above the discourse: Jasmine Warga, Mackenzi Lee, Aisha Saeed, David Arnold, Adam Silvera, Angie Thomas, Jacob Demlow, Rod Pulido, Rose Brock, Jaime Semensohn, Matthew Eppard, Katy-Lynn Cook, Kate Goud, Brandie Rendon, Anderson Rothwell, Amy Austin, Dahlia Adler, Lauren Starks, Louise Willingham, Heidi Schulz, Jaime Hensel, Tom-Erik Fure, Sam Rowntree, Diane Blumenfeld, Steven Salvatore, Rachael Allen, Julie Mottl, Mason Deaver, Emily Townsend, Julian Winters, Lindsay Keiller, Adib Khorram, Emily Carpenter, Manda Turetsky, Chris Negron, George Weinstein, Sarah Beth Brown, Becky Kilimnik, Adante Watts, Nic DiPrima, Jason June, Mark O'Brien, Nic Stone, JC Lillis, Cale Dietrich, Zabé Ellor, Cindy Otis, Leah Johnson,

Kimberly Ito, Kat Ramsburg, Jamie Pacton, Casey McQuiston, Savy Leiser, RK Gold, Eline Berkhout. And SO MANY OTHERS. I'm so lucky to know you.

The many, many incredible librarians, booksellers, influencers, and all the rest of you bookworms. You make this job so much brighter.

My family: Eileen Thomas, Jim and Candy Goldstein, Caroline, Mike, and Max Reitzes, Sam Goldstein, Leigh Shapiro, Gini, Curt, Jim, Cyris, and Lulu Albertalli, Brittany Girardi, Gail McLaurin, Lois and Don Reitzes, Linda Albertalli, and all my Thomases, Bells, Wechslers, Levines, and Bermans.

Quincy—you are so loved and so missed.

Teddy and Willow, who were as persistently and noisily helpful as always.

And Brian, Owen, and Henry. Obviously, obviously, obviously.